THE DAY OF THE
JACK
RUSSELL

By Bateman

Cycle of Violence
Empire State
Maid of the Mist
Wild About Harry
Mohammed Maguire
Chapter and Verse
I Predict A Riot
Orpheus Rising

Mystery Man novels
Mystery Man
The Day of the Jack Russell

Martin Murphy novels
Murphy's Law
Murphy's Revenge

Dan Starkey novels
Divorcing Jack
Of Wee Sweetie Mice and Men
Turbulent Priests
Shooting Sean
The Horse with My Name
Driving Big Davie
Belfast Confidential

For Children
Reservoir Pups
Bring Me the Head of Oliver Plunkett
Titanic 2020
Titanic 2020: Cannibal City
The Seagulls Have Landed

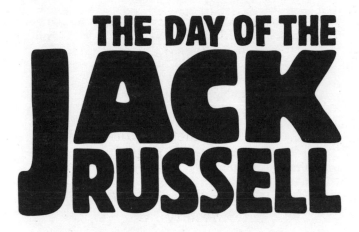

THE DAY OF THE JACK RUSSELL

BATEMAN

headline

First published in 2009 by
HEADLINE PUBLISHING GROUP

1

Cataloguing in Publication Data is available from the British Library

ISBN 9 780 7553 4676 9 (Hardback)
ISBN 9 780 7553 4677 6 (Trade paperback)

Typeset in Meridien by Palimpsest Book Production Limited,
Grangemouth, Stirlingshire

Printed in the UK by
CPI Mackays, Chatham ME5 8TD

Headline's policy is to use papers that are natural, renewable
and recyclable products and made from wood grown
in sustainable forests. The logging and manufacturing
processes are expected to conform to the environmental
regulations of the country of origin.

HEADLINE PUBLISHING GROUP
An Hachette UK Company
338 Euston Road
London NW1 3BH

www.headline.co.uk
www.hachette.co.uk

For Andrea, Matthew and Patch

1

It was the Tuesday before Christmas Day when *The Case of the Cock-Headed Man* walked into No Alibis, the finest mystery bookstore in all of, um, Belfast.

In some ways he was lucky to get me, because with business being so quiet I had resorted to letting my mother woman the till for that short part of the day when she could manage to keep off the booze, i.e. between the hours of nine and eleven twenty-nine in the morning. If he had walked in ten minutes earlier he would have walked straight out again, because while still undoubtedly sober, Mother is not one for suffering fools or anyone gladly and she's gotten ten times worse since her stroke. She has always been ugly and mean, but she used to restrict her glares and tempers and violence and venom and sarcasm to members of her immediate family, but since the stroke she has expanded her circle of viciousness to include distant cousins, vague acquaintances, most other members of the human race and several dogs. Mother is wired differently to you or me. A stroke usually affects just one side of the body, but she has lost the power in her right leg and left arm, making her appear lopsided from whatever angle you care to look at her, although most people don't, and stagger from side to side like the drunk she is when she tries to walk. It is funny to watch her. When she's drinking she now only has to consume half as much as before to get legless. And half of that again usually drools out of her mouth on to her blouse, because another side effect of the stroke is the loss of all feeling in her lower lip.

But as it happened, *The Case of the Cock-Headed Man* walked in just as Mother finished. In fact, he held the door open for her as she left. Since her stroke I've had the disabled ramp removed from outside the shop, so it takes her a while to manoeuvre her walking frame and calipered leg down the high step and on to the pavement. The man with the Sidney Sidesweep and goatee beard smiled and offered her his arm and said, 'Can I give you a hand, dear?'

Mother glared at him for the briefest moment before spitting out: 'Fuckaff!'

Her diction isn't great with her face the way it is. Before the stroke she looked like she'd been punched by Sonny Liston; now she sounds like it as well.

Mother's job – she tells her cronies that she's head of customer relations, which would actually be quite funny if she wasn't serious – is a sad reflection on the changing face of the book trade, wherein I cannot afford to hire good and proper help, but have to rely on friends and family and idiot students to fill in for those few hours when I need to concentrate on stock-taking, e-mails, stalking my ex-girlfriend and actually *reading*. I have to know what's out there. While I am not entirely convinced by the recent vogue for Scandinavian crime fiction – who's to say if it's the author who is a genius, or his translator? Also, it's difficult to care if a Norwegian gets murdered – my customers expect me to know the authors and to be able to help them navigate to their best work. You would expect a brain surgeon to be up to date on the latest operating procedures, and you would be shocked if a butcher served you up half a pound of gristle because he didn't know any better, yet you can walk into a major bookstore and ask if Hammett's *The Glass Key* is superior to *The Thin Man* and they'd look at you like you were on day release from a secure mental hospital, which, incidentally, is something I know all about. So I need a little time each day to keep up to date, and my best time for reading is in the mornings, when I'm not so groggy from the anti-psychotic medicine I order on-line from a Good Samaritan in Guadalajara, Mexico.

It was a *really* quiet time of year in No Alibis, and not just because customers were put off by Mother's fearsome visage glaring out of the window and daring them to enter. Although books continue to make fantastic gifts, people no longer have the time to browse at Christmas or to ask for guidance from an expert. They go to one of the big chains and push a trolley around, piling them high and buying them cheap, like beans, or pasta, or onions, or potatoes, or rice, or tinned peaches, or fig rolls, or Tuc biscuits, or midget gems. But books are not beans. It's not all about profit. It's about the book. You have to appreciate the effort that goes into the writing of a book. The love and sacrifice. The years of torment. The long and tortured journey from first inkling of idea to appearance on a shelf. Nobody ever cared that much about the genesis of a bean. Once they finally appear, so many fine books are ignored, remaindered and pulped because they fail to find a *me*. My place in society, my role in life, is to select the finest crime fiction, and then make sure that it connects with the right people, a thankless task, particularly as there are so few right people around. No shortage of the *wrong* people. One example of the wrong people – and I have learned that you *can* often judge a book by its cover – was the beardy man approaching the counter without even the pretence of looking for a book. Despite his polite offer of assistance to Mother and his refusal to react angrily to her abuse, something about him immediately put me on edge. Perhaps it was because he wore the kind of extravagant clothes that people buy to try to disguise the fact that they have no personality.

'Do you have internet access?' he asked brusquely.

'Yes thanks.'

'No, I mean, to show you something.'

'No thanks.'

He was a pedlar with a lazy attitude to direct selling. He was trying to hock his wares by showing me a sales video at *my* expense over the internet.

He smiled whitely. 'I understand you meddle in crime-solving.'

'No.'

'Oh. I was given to understand . . .'

'I don't meddle.'

Arrogance is no bad thing in crime-fighting, and God knows it's compulsory in the book trade. He wouldn't have known it, but I was quietly pleased by his presence in the shop. My reputation was clearly growing. Booksellers who use their expertise to solve baffling crimes are pretty thin on the ground. In fact, booksellers are pretty thin on the ground. Indeed, I am pretty thin on the ground, thanks to my diet, and allergies, and incurable diseases, and broken heart, and the economy. But people come to me because I am their last resort. Because the crimes against them are too difficult or trivial for the conventional forces of law and order to tackle or be bothered with. I glanced at my watch as if I had an appointment. When he didn't immediately volunteer anything, I snapped a pleasant 'Sorry, is there something else I can help you with?'

The smile remained fixed, like his teeth. 'You do know who I am?'

I shook my head. 'Nope.'

'You really don't recognise me?'

He had tiny incredulous eyes and the bags under them sagged with middle age, giving the lie to his Botoxed brow. His beard was, I'm sure, perfectly fine; except I'm allergic to beards. Food festers in them. Ticks and bugs and spiders breed in them. I hate beards. I hate people who wear beards. Even false ones. Like Santa. But now that I studied him, there was something *vaguely* familiar about him. I have made many enemies in my perilous work as a crime-fighter and bookseller, and I have to admit that despite his smile, my hand sought the comfort of my mallet, one of several weapons I have taken to keeping beneath the counter.

'Who are you, *exactly*?' I asked, taking care to keep my voice flat, so that he couldn't tell that I was now in a state of high alert. 'And what do you want?'

'You seriously don't recognise me? But you see me every day.'

I shook my head.

'Billy Randall?' He pulled his shoulders back, put his hands on his hips and gave his voice a mid-Atlantic twang. '*I'm Billy Randall   fly me?*'

He gave it a bit of a flourish and an American twang. He raised an eyebrow for added effect.

'Ah,' I said.

I *did* know him, after all. His head and shoulders, sixty feet wide, stared down at me from billboards in the south, east, north and west of this city of twenty-three stories. Billy Randall ran a low-cost, no frills airline and holiday company, Billy Randall Air, or BRA. It flew the great unwashed to cheap destinations, many of them in the Third World, most of them permanently braced for natural disaster or constantly teetering on the edge of civil war or desperately trying to recover from a crashed economy. People clamoured for his flights and holidays while at the same time despising his mugging arrogance, because quite often they were cheaper than taking a taxi and having a night out in their home city. He had a blazing self-confidence, pots full of chutzpah, and had made his millions *despite* not endearing himself to anyone. His *look at me*. The Northern Irish are quick to judge, and they dislike people who put their heads above the parapet unless they have a genuine talent, in which case they then worship them to death.

Billy Randall smiled beatifically.

'Billy Randall, of course,' I said, warmer now, because despite the fact that I had a growing urge to beat him with the mallet, he was rich, and I was poor, and if he was wanting to talk to me he clearly had a problem, and a fool and his money are soon parted. 'Sorry.'

'I wanted to show you something. On YouTube. Have you heard of YouTube?'

'I invented it.'

'You . . .'

'I can't talk about it. Litigation.'

He looked at me. He smiled. 'Well could I show you something? Go on to the site and just type in my name.'

I turned to my PC and slowly picked out the letters. I am a recovering myopic dyslexic. There was just the one entry on YouTube for Billy Randall. I clicked on it and saw his billboard poster in some busy and vaguely familiar-looking part of town, with traffic flowing past. We watched it silently for twenty seconds.

'What's the . . . ?'

'Wait.'

And then there was sniggering on the soundtrack as the camera followed a hooded youth carrying a set of ladders across the traffic. I say 'youth' because he was dressed in the teenage fashion; for all I saw of him he could have been an old man blessed with vigour.

'Go for it, Jimbo,' said an anonymous commentator.

The youth set the ladders against a gable wall, the tip of them just resting against the bottom of the billboard frame, and then he extended them, giving him what appeared to be an extra twelve feet or so and bringing him, as he climbed, level with Billy Randall's forehead.

I became aware that the gauche travel mogul on the other side of my counter was no longer looking at the screen. He couldn't bear to watch the youth take a can of spray paint from his hoody and begin to spray what slowly became an enormous cock and balls right in the middle of Billy Randall's gigantic forehead, although he couldn't help but listen as the accompanying giggle turned into a raucous cackle.

2

Like many provincial businessmen, Billy Randall had dreamt of transforming himself into an internationally recognised name, a Murdoch or a Branson or even a Heinz. He wanted his smug mug to be recognised in every corner of the globe, the Randall name to become synonymous with success and big bucks.

Beware of what you wish for.

Billy Randall was indeed becoming an international phenomenon, but for all the wrong reasons. Over a million people had viewed the video of the Cock-Headed Man. And the number of hits was growing with every hour that passed. People who had never heard of Billy Randall now knew him as the Cock-Headed Man. Billy Randall had gone viral, and he wasn't happy about it *at all*.

Still, every cloud has a silver lining.

'I've already tried the police; they're not interested.

I've had all manner of security companies ringing me up and promising me this or that, but none of them local, none of them who know these streets, none of them with your reputation.'

I was positively glowing.

'I told YouTube to take it down and they did; five minutes later it was back up again. It's spreading to other sites. It has even been on cable television. I'm getting abusive e-mails from all over the world. I want this stopped. I want them found. And I want them punished. I don't want people to think they can mess with Billy Randall and get away with it. They're destroying my business. People do not want to do business with someone they can't take seriously. People may not like me, they may be jealous of what I've achieved, but they also respect me for what I've done. I know that, they've told me that. I've worked for twenty years to get where I am, I employ over two hundred people right here in Belfast, not in some fricking call centre in Mumbai. I'm not going to have it all disappear because of a couple of hooligans. I'm not going to be disrespected, not me, not Billy Randall!'

There was sweat on his brow and fury in his eyes, and I liked him a little better for it. I don't trust people who smile too much, who are always interested in what you have to say, who are too touchy-feely, or even touchy-feely at all. I didn't for one moment think that Billy Randall had built his business by smiling all the time and being nice to people, I'm sure he shouted and raged like the best of us, but he had concocted an image and had to live up to it every time he stepped out of his front door. This flash of anger at least showed there was a relatively normal and flawed human being behind his inflated public persona.

'Okay,' I said, and managed not to smile as I added, 'but I'm not cheap.'

'Money isn't an issue. You can find them?'

'Oh yes,' I said.

'Okay. Find them, let me know where they live, I'll take it from there.'

I nodded, and then some more.

'What?' he asked.

'What will you do to them?'

'That's my concern.' And then he cracked his trademark smile. 'Nothing *illegal* – that's all I need! I'll think of something, something practical. A restraining order. Something.'

I was on the verge of reminding him of the old saying, that there was no such thing as bad publicity, of suggesting that he might parlay the massive exposure he was getting into something positive, if he could just embrace the joke instead of fighting it. It could help his image and improve his business at the same time. He would be known as a man who could take a joke, instead of being one. But then I thought it was all very well saying it; I wasn't the one who had to live with being known all over the world as the Cock-Headed Man, and also if No Alibis was going to survive the barren Christmas period, I was going to have to start earning money through some means other than bookselling, because for the moment, crime wasn't paying.

As Billy Randall left, Jeff arrived. Jeff continues to work for me on a part-time basis, as saving political prisoners for Amnesty International apparently doesn't pay very well. I have often thought that if Amnesty International paid its campaigners a commission they would achieve a lot more. They would also attract a better calibre of campaigner, because really, if you want to be taken seriously by despots, dictators and religious maniacs, you should at least ensure that your representatives look vaguely respectable and not like they've been dragged through a hedge backwards, and also that they are at least capable of conducting a reasonably intelligent conversation without falling back on punching the air and yelling out nonsensical slogans and making promises they can't keep. I'm still waiting for my free Nelson Mandela.

Jeff's eyes widened as Billy Randall passed by, and then he mouthed to me while pointing after him, 'Is that . . . ?'

I nodded and quickly ushered him into the shop and closed the door. 'He's hired me to solve a case,' I said.

'Us.'

'I'm sorry?'

'He's hired *us* to solve a case.'

'No, he's hired me. You assist me. I pay you. But he's hired me.'

'I thought we were a team.'

'No.'

'When Alison stormed out, you said I could replace her.'

Alison was the girl in the jewellery shop across the road. I'd given her my heart. And she had shoved it right back in my face. Although not before stealing my virginity. I had thought her to be warm, loving, thoughtful, caring and beautiful. Now I knew her to be cold, callous, calculating and ugly. I would never, ever forgive her. Her name is in my ledger. I have a big ledger. Once your name goes into it, it's impossible to remove. Even with Tippex.

'Nobody will ever replace her.'

'As your crime-fighting partner.'

'I don't need a crime-fighting partner.'

He snorted, and took off his jacket. This year's fashion for the young and politically aware student was a bottle-green combat jacket, ragged jeans and Lennon glasses. This year's fashion hadn't changed much in forty years. He stashed the jacket behind the counter and rolled up the sleeves of his cheesecloth shirt in what had become a regular charade by impli-cation that he was actually going to do some work.

'So what did the Dick-Headed Man want?'

'The Cock-Headed Man.'

'Dick,' said Jeff.

'Cock.'

'He's known all over as the Dick-Headed Man.'

'Cock.'

'Dick.'

'Cock.'

'Dick.'

'Cock.'

'Dick.'

'Cock.'

There was something oddly hypnotic about our exchange, and it might have gone on for ever if I had not broken the rhythm by suggesting that Jeff would shortly be out of a job if he didn't agree with me, at which point he conceded that in future we would refer to Billy Randall as the Cock-Headed Man, although not to his face.

I did not expect the solving of *The Case of the Cock-Headed Man* to present me with too many difficulties. I had been down a similar path before while investigating *The Case of the Fruit on the Flyover*, which also involved a graffiti artist making life miserable for those he chose to pick on. The main difference here was that the stakes were higher; it had gone global. It also seemed to me that it was too late to do anything about it. The video was out there and always would be; what Billy Randall wanted was retribution.

But that was no concern of mine. I was being paid handsomely to track down the culprits, that was all.

I watched the video through several more times. Simple observation led me to conclude that it had been shot at a billboard on the Annadale Embankment. I very quickly deduced that the actual graffiti artist,

Jimbo, was a tradesman. It was the ladders. Everyone has ladders, but usually they're only big enough to get you up to change a light bulb. These were fully extendable. They could take you right up the side of a large house and on to the roof. It seemed to me therefore that they were *professional* ladders. There was always the possibility that Jimbo and his accomplice might have borrowed them, but in re-examining the video, I noticed that Jimbo flicked the lever to allow the extension and then switched it back to secure it in its extended position without apparently looking down, suggesting an easy familiarity with their oper-ation, which again suggested that he might do this for a living. So he could be a roofer, a decorator, a satel-lite installer or perhaps a window-cleaner. And one who very probably lived in the area of the Annadale Embankment, because it seemed to me that they weren't going to take the trouble of driving or even carrying the ladders across town to carry out their attack. They were going to do it close to where they lived. First of all, because it was easier. Second, if as it seemed they were doing it for a laugh, then they would want their friends to see it – they weren't going to say, hey, we did this crazy thing, and then expect their friends to travel across town to see it. They'd want to do it right on their doorstep. The fact that they'd deliberately filmed their action and put it on something as international as YouTube didn't negate the idea that they lived locally. They wanted to be admired by their pals, but also, in this networking era, further afield. According to the site info, the video had been posted by someone with the moniker RonnyCrabs. I presumed this was the cameraman and Jimbo's partner in crime. Ronny was quite possibly his Christian name, Crabs perhaps his nickname. I was looking for Jimbo and RonnyCrabs. Forgive me tarring everyone with the same brush, but if they were painters or roofers or window-cleaners, then I was looking for a working-class area that abutted the Annadale Embankment. I'd barely been on the case for five minutes and I was already close to cracking it.

Easy money.

3

Jeff made himself scarce as soon as he saw Alison crossing the road to No Alibis. It was dark outside and I was on the point of closing up. If I'd been a trifle quicker I might have managed to bolt the door and pull the shutters down, but she was right in front of me before I could do anything other than open the door and allow her to enter. I gave her the look she deserved.

She looked around the inside of the shop as if she hadn't seen it before, then snapped: 'I've come to collect the money for my comics.'

'Good luck,' I said.

'You owe me money.'

'I haven't sold any. They clearly weren't very good.'

'That's not what you said before.'

'I was just being nice.'

'Well there's a first. So where are they?'

'I threw them out.'

'You threw them out?'

'I threw them out. You insisted on putting them in the window, even though I'm not a comics shop, and they turned yellow in the sun, so I threw them out.'

'You insisted on putting them in the window because you said they were fantastic.'

'I lied.'

'You're a miserable little shit.'

'So's your face.'

'That doesn't make sense.'

'Neither does your face.'

'You're a big baby.'

'So's your face.'

'Shut up.'

'Shut up your face.'

She laughed involuntarily. Then shook her head vigorously. 'I was laughing at you. You think you're so funny.'

'Not as funny as your face.'

'You used to love my face.'

I glared at her, then was thankful for the distraction of the door opening and a woman coming in with a small fat dog on a short lead. She wore a red knee-length coat with a fake fur collar. It had buttons like a duffle coat. It was undoubtedly expensive, but looked cheap. She said, without any introduction at all, 'You have to help me. Every night when I'm going to bed there's this man standing at the bottom of my front garden staring up at me.'

This, as it turned out, was *The Case of the Dog-Walking Man*, and I was grateful for the distraction of a potential client but also rigid with fear. I'm allergic to dogs. I sneeze and I sneeze. One only has to look me in the eye to set me off. I immediately held my nose. My eyes began to water. I gagged. Alison rolled her eyes.

'What on earth is wrong with you?' the woman asked.

I pointed at the dog, and then at the footpath.

The woman said, 'He goes where I go.'

I nodded, and pointed at the footpath again.

Her lip curled up, but she was in a bind; she needed my expert help. She turned wordlessly and escorted the rat creature outside and tied him up. He looked at me through the glass. He had mean eyes.

The woman came back in. It wasn't much relief. Even people who have been around dogs set me off. She should have gone home for a shower and a change of clothes. I sniffed up and rubbed at my eyes. I didn't like her, instinctively. I don't like most people, instinctively. There's a basic difference between clients and customers. Customers buy books because they want to read them. Clients put their smudgy fingers on books and bend the covers and crack the spines while they work up the courage to approach the counter and spill the details of the sordid little cases they want me to solve. This woman was also the second potential client in one day not to even bother with the formality of pretending to peruse the books.

Alison turned away, as if to study the shelves behind her, but not before I saw, or thought I saw, a tear on her cheek.

I nodded at the woman. 'This man?'

'Every night at the same time.'

I nodded. 'Would you like to join our Christmas Club?' I asked. 'It's not a prerequisite of me taking your case.'

Said in such a way that she could have no doubt that it *was* a prerequisite. This stopped her in her tracks. 'What are the benefits?'

Which stopped me in mine. The Christmas Club wasn't exactly constructed to benefit anyone but me, which might account for the slow uptake in membership. There weren't even enough members yet to call it a club. I shrugged and said rather vaguely, 'Money off?'

She studied me. 'Are you in charge here?'

Behind her, Alison snorted.

'I'm the owner.'

'You're the private eye?'

Behind her, Alison snorted.

'Yes. One hundred per cent success guaranteed.'

'That's impressive.'

Behind her . . .

I quickly asked, 'This man, what does he do?'

'He just looks. His hands are hidden by the hedge. *God knows* what he's doing. I just see his head and shoulders. He stares up at me, then he moves along the hedge a wee bit and looks up again. He goes the whole length of the hedge. I don't know what to do. I told the police but they say there's nothing they can do until he actually does something, which is like, yeah, useless. But when he looks up, I feel like I'm being molested.'

'Are you naked?'

'No, of course not.'

'Are your curtains not closed?'

'Yes.'

'But you peek out?'

'Sometimes.'

'And he's still there?'

'Usually.'

'He's looking directly at you.'

'Yes. I think so. I can't really see his eyes. It could be me he's looking at or just the house. But I don't like it. He gives me the creeps.'

'Well that's not right,' I said.

'Can you help me?'

'Yes, of course.' She was, I suppose, an attractive woman. Late thirties maybe, black hair, shoulder length, her eyes pale blue. 'It must be driving you mad. Pervert staring through your window like that.'

Alison had pretty much perfected the art of snorting, but it was less effective now. It just sounded odd.

'So what would you do, and how much would it cost?'

'Well don't worry about the money, I'll see you right.'

Alison . . .

'That's very kind of you.'

'No, not at all, I understand completely. It's very frustrating when nobody takes your concerns seriously. This is what we'll do. We'll put him under surveillance, get some shots of the guy in action. Then we'll track him down to his lair. We'll find out everything there is to know about him – if he has a family, what he does for a living, if he's doing this to anyone else, if he has a prison record, if he's on the sex offenders register. Maybe he's not a pervert at all; maybe he has it in for your family or bears a grudge; maybe he's just staking out the property late at night so that he can come back and rob it during the day. He could be up to anything. We could have a quick word, warn him off, most likely you'll never see him again. But that's not really getting to the root of the problem. And if he is planning something else, that might just drive him underground. What we need to do is observe, build up a profile, work out what he's really up to and then we'll decide the best course of action. There aren't many quick fixes in this business, I'm afraid, it's going to take time. But he will be dealt with.'

'Couldn't you just beat him up?'

Alison gave it a double snort.

'That's not what we do. But I can assure you, once we deal with him, he'll stay dealt with.'

I had no idea what that meant, but it sounded permanent.

'Alternatively . . .'

It was Alison, turning from the shelf with a book in her hand. It was *The Riddle of the Sands* by Erskine Childers, one of the first and certainly one of the greatest spy novels. The author later suffered the most severe literary criticism imaginable.

My potential client turned to her, a little surprised. I gave her a devastating look. But not so devastating that she noticed.

'Alternatively?' the potential client asked.

'Well I couldn't help but overhear. The man at your hedge . . .'

'Excuse me, but I believe I'm dealing with this?'

She ignored *me* completely.

'Don't mind him,' she said, smiling sweetly. 'We're very competitive over these cases, but we do work well together. So let me get this straight. This guy, he stands at your hedge. He looks up at you or the house. He moves along a little bit. He looks up again. Then he leaves.'

'Yes.'

'And this is every night.'

'Yes.'

'About the same time.'

'Yes, that's right. About eleven.'

Alison looked at me and shook her head. She smiled again at the potential client. 'Did you ever consider the possibility that this man might have a dog you can't see because of the hedge? And the dog stops for a sniff or a pee every few yards, and the man has no alternative but to stand there with him? That he's not

23

really looking up at your house, he's just waiting for the dog to finish his business?'

The woman in the red coat stared at Alison. Her mouth dropped open a little bit. 'Good God,' she said, 'I never even thought of that.' She looked at me, then back to Alison. 'You're good,' she said, 'you're *really* good. You're quite a team. That's exactly what he's been doing, and I've taken it the wrong way. I've told half the neighbourhood he's a perv. I'm going to have to sort that out. How much do I owe you?'

Alison shook her head. 'Nothing. It's on the house.'

'But . . .' I began. Alison raised an eyebrow. The woman looked confused. 'Would you like to buy a book?' I asked. It was only slightly less pathetic than shaking a tin at her, but it could mean the difference between three slices of curled-up cooked ham for Christmas dinner and a big fat factory-stuffed turkey. I waved an encouraging hand around the shelves.

The woman laughed. 'No, sorry, I don't read that shit.'

And then she was gone, out the door, and crouching down by her dog, clapping her hands and talking to him like he had a clue.

We both stared at the door.

'What a bitch,' said Alison.

'So's your face,' I said.

4

Against my better judgement, and tempted beyond reason by Alison's invitation to Starbucks, I found myself seated in said heaven less than an hour later, sipping a frappuccino – she paid – while attempting to maintain my frown. I have frown lines you could plant potatoes in, though since Alison's flight they had lain largely fallow. Life was good without her. I had my books. I had my business. I had my customer. And I had my mother. Three out of four ain't bad.

I like Starbucks not only because of the wonderful coffee and buns, but also because it is what it is. It does not offer insurance. There is no deal on mobile phones. It does not mix and match, but stays pure, like its coffee. I detest places that try to be all things to all men. In No Alibis you might on a very rare occasion be offered a cup of coffee, but you certainly won't come in and order one. You come in to buy a book. The clue is in the title: book*shop*. A further clue is in the sign above the till that says, *This is not a fucking library*. Certainly you can browse. Certainly you can read the back cover. But you will be discouraged from actually opening the book and reading. That is like attempting to have sex on a first date. You have to build a relationship with a book. You can't just plough in. You have to admire it first, you have to nuzzle it and pet it and slowly get to know it. You have to drive it home with that ecstatic sense of anticipation, but not rush it. You have to get rid of your problem children and narking wife and turn off the television and sit in a comfortable chair and then slowly draw it into the night air and carefully, carefully peel back its cover. You must read about the author, you must look at his back list, you must focus with extraordinary concentration on the very first paragraph, because you know, you know very soon if this is the one for you. Sometimes authors can be quite deceiving – you read that first paragraph, that first page, and think this writer has nothing to say for himself, there is no personality, there is no vim or vigour, no humour, and you want to give up. Sometimes you are completely right to do so. Other times, if you stick with it, the personality slowly begins to emerge, you realise that this author is no Flash Harry, because anyone can concoct an explosive opening paragraph, but sometimes there is nowhere to go after that. Books are like women. They can be hard on the outside, or they can be soft. They can be fat, they can be thin.

They can be funny, they can be serious. They can be utterly demented. There can be lots of sex, there can be no sex at all. Some books might tease you along with the promise of sex but ultimately chicken out. Trying to read more than one at a time can be dangerous. And when you're finished with a book, you can put it in a box in the attic.

I am, I suppose, like a literary dating agency. I match people up with the right books. People who have spent years trying to find *their* author, but are lost, or bitter, scarred by numerous unfortunate encounters, or spinstered off after one early disaster, come to me in desperation, one last attempt before they give up for good. They tell me what they need in a book, and a little bit about themselves. Quite often they inflate their own CVs to make them sound more interesting, better educated. They might *say* that they are looking for something literary, something laden with numerous broadsheet recommendations, something, God forbid, translated, but it is my job to see through these little acts of foolish bravado, to make them understand that what they think they should be reading is not necessarily what they need. Even within the ghetto we call crime, there have been numerous occasions when I've had a customer in the shop saying they want a James Ellroy when I can tell just by looking at them that they will be much happier with a Robert B. Parker. I'm a doctor of crime fiction, and what I'm giving them is a literary prescription. Take one Parker a week, madam, but beware, there is a very real danger of overdosing; under no circumstances attempt to read more than this without first consulting your bookseller.

'Hello. Earth to . . . ?'

'What?'

Alison shook her head. 'Well you haven't changed.'

'Neither's your face.'

'Will you stop that, it's stupid and it's juvenile.'

'So's your face.'

'Please.'

I shrugged. I sipped my frappuccino. In the preceding six weeks I had worked my way through the menu three times. One of the waitresses said to me, 'You again, you'll be getting shares in this place.' That was just a stupid thing to say. But I didn't tell her that. Sometimes I can hold my tongue. It comes with maturity.

'So how have you been?' Alison asked.

'Great.'

'Miss me?' I gave her my screwed-up-face look. 'Like a hole in the head, huh?'

I maintained a diplomatic silence. There was Christmas music playing in the background. There were damp footprints on the wooden floor. Stuffed shopping bags sat under tables.

'Did you really throw my comics out?'

'Yes.'

'How would you feel if I threw your favourite books out?'

'I wouldn't lend you my favourite books.'

'Well that's true. Even when we were going well.'

'Were we ever going well?'

She smiled. 'Cup half empty as ever.'

'Realist.'

'Pessimist.'

'So's your—'

'Please.'

I glared.

She said, 'This is stupid.'

I was very tempted.

'We *were* going well,' she said. I shrugged. 'We shouldn't throw this away. I'm *sorry*. There's only so many times I can say it.'

'It's not me you have to apologise to.'

'I tried. Your mother told me to, and I quote, fuck off. At least I think she did; it's hard to make out what she's saying.'

'Because you caused her to have a stroke.'

'I did not, that's just ridiculous.'

'She is partially paralysed because you insisted on charging into her room like a banshee.'

'That's simply not true.'

'You mean you didn't?'

'I just wanted to see if she was okay. I wanted to see if she existed.'

'Existed.'

'You know what I mean.'

'She went into shock. She had a stroke. She is permanently paralysed. She will never recover.'

'Yet you have her working in the shop.'

'You don't miss much. I'm trying to help her.'

'She's driving away your customer.'

She smiled. I did not. I had no idea what I was doing there, apart from enjoying the coffee. I had once admired her from afar, and then she had seduced me. She had taken my virtue, paralysed my mother, and was now coming back for more. She was a vampire, insatiable.

'Come on.'

She put her hand out across the table and took my own. I took it back. She sat back. She tutted. We sat in silence for a little while. The Christmas music was annoying.

She said, 'You have a new case.'

'Do I?'

She nodded. 'Billy Randall.'

'How do you know that?'

I knew how. She was a witch and had witch powers.

'Jeff told me.'

'What're you doing talking to him?'

'Why, have you told him not to?'

'Yes.'

'Why would you do that?'

'Because I don't like him doing what he's obviously just been doing. Talking about my business.'

'He can't help it. He loves me.'

'Don't flatter yourself. He loves anyone who shows any interest.'

'Billy Randall, the Dick-Headed Man.'

'Cock.'

'Dick.'

'Cock.'

She shook her head. 'Are you ever wrong?'

I raised an eyebrow. Sometimes it is better to stand your ground and show backbone even if you are wrong. Empires have been built upon it. In this case, of course, I was not wrong.

'It's not much of a case,' I said. 'It shouldn't take long.'

'Well that's good. Is he as obnoxious as he appears?'

'Pretty much.'

'You should get on well then. I looked it up on YouTube. Annadale Embankment, no?'

'Maybe. If it is, it's no concern of yours.'

'I was thinking of heading over that way myself.'

'It's none of your business.'

'I was thinking of tracking down Ronnycrabs and Jimbo and then giving the dickhead a call.'

'Why would you do that?'

'To show you I'm indispensable.'

'Nobody is indispensable.'

'Also I hear he's single.'

'You'd seduce a cock-headed man.'

'I usually do.'

'He'd see right through you.'

'You didn't.'

'Did I not?'

'No.'

'Right.'

'In fact, you're still in love with me.'

'Really.'

'Yep. You're just too pig-headed to admit it.'

'And you think I live in my own little world?'

'You do. And you are. Admit it and let's stop this craziness. We're made for each other. You know it, I know it. Who else would have you?'

'You're really winning me over.'

'At least we're talking.'

I stared at her. She was evil incarnate.

'I'm six weeks pregnant,' she said.

'So's your face.'

5

Next morning Jeff said, 'You appear distracted.'

I said, 'You appear not to be working.'

He rolled his eyes and returned to not working.

Jeff has it easy. Because I don't trust him to order books or keep track of the stock and because customers are few and far between, he has relatively little to do. I don't allow him to surf on the premises, or to have his friends in, or to use the landline or even his own mobile, so most of his time is taken up with staring into space and imagining unimaginable horrors being perpetrated on political prisoners in Third World countries. I had suggested that given his current employment with me he might be better off working in his spare time for an organisation like PEN, which specifically represents writers banged up abroad, rather than his current choice, Amnesty International, but he rejected that on the grounds that he couldn't summon much interest in the type of writer that PEN represents, and after due consideration I found myself in that rare situation, total agreement with him. There is an inescapable irony to the fact that while every nation on earth boasts its own crime fiction, no crime fiction writers are currently locked up. That is because they have a healthy respect for the law. Literary authors, who tend to think that the sun shines out of their ink holes, believe that they are above it. When they rattle on about this or that they think they are promoting freedom of speech, but what they're actually supporting is anarchy. They believe that just because they can string a few words together their views are more important or relevant than anyone else's. But mostly we won't support PEN authors because their books are usually shit. People would pay a lot more attention if John Grisham or James Patterson were locked up for criticising the state, although obviously, some would clamour for that even if they kept their traps shut.

Jeff was right. I was distracted.

I do not like being put on the spot. When Alison told me she was pregnant, and then assured me that she was serious, and then showed me the testing kit, I suggested that that proved nothing and that she was just trying to win me back by using fabricated evidence. What she really wanted was control of the shop and my money and my repu-tation and to make another murder attempt on my dear mother.

She burst into tears.

At that point I was veering towards believing her, because I'm a pretty good judge of character and also it was roughly six weeks since we'd had sex for the first and last time and I could do the maths, though that didn't rule out the possibility that she had also slept with her ex-husband or anyone else who asked. There was also the way she clung to me, and said she didn't know what to do, and please could I not harbour a grudge and really she hadn't meant to scare my mother so badly, and that she really did blame herself for her stroke, and given that Mother now had one largely useless arm and another that wasn't much better, how was she ever going to be able to hold the baby?

I told her not to worry about that, as the shock of learning that she was going to be a grandmother would probably kill her.

'Perhaps you want to tell her yourself, and finish off the job?' I asked.

This wasn't exactly what she wanted to hear. She snapped at me, I snapped back. We sat for a while. I ran my finger round the inside of the frappuccino and then sucked it. Alison said she felt ill. I said it was a little early for morning sickness. She told me to fuck off.

Outside, in the damp wind, we stood together but apart, her shop along a bit, mine on the other side of the road and down.

'So,' she said.

'So,' I said.

'Food for thought,' she said.

I nodded. 'I'll think then.'

'Don't think for too long.'

She nodded. She walked off. I returned to the shop. Because I'm a crime-fighter, I'm used to threats. And Alison had threatened me. It was subtle, but undeniable. *Don't think for too long*. What she had neglected to add was 'or'. Don't think for too long *or* I'll do something, like *get rid of it*. That was it. She had given me an ultimatum, but in a typically non-specific girlie way. She was telling me either I could get on board the team bus, or it was destined for the scrapyard. Or, if I didn't play ball, she was going to keep the ball and take it home and say it was her ball and she could do what she liked with it. She would have him adopted. Or she would deny me access. She would move somewhere else, like South Africa or Portstewart. She knew I couldn't travel outside of Belfast due to long-standing allergies to heat and dust and flies and grass and cows and beetles and corn and fruit and tin and wood and stuff. What might seem like an innocent relocation to a more pleasant environment would actually be a calculated act of torture. She was wicked to the core.

I didn't need a child. A baby. I am like Mr Chips, I have thousands of them already. My books are my children; I nurture them, I protect them, then I send them out into the world. They travel, they educate, they change things, they inspire, they offer an escape, hope, humour, a climax and, almost always, a solution. Occasionally they return to me, battered, worn, sometimes even parts of them are missing, but they are always welcomed home and soon restored to health, ready to face the world again and at only slightly reduced charge.

A baby.

I tried to make myself think of the good days with Alison. She *was* lovely. She was caring. She did look out for me and after me. She was funny and beautiful and didn't really have a bad bone in her body, which reassured me that if she really was pregnant, she would do nothing to harm the baby and that I had time to ponder our situation and come to the right decision. I had a bookshop to run and crimes to solve. Dames were one thing, babies another. You could count on the dislocated fingers of one hand the number of private eyes who had a mewling baby waiting at home. Babies weren't just distracting, they were dangerous; in this game, if you were even five per cent off your mark, you were a goner.

'Is there anything I can help you with?'

At first I thought Jeff was talking to a customer, which would have been funny in itself. But no, there he was, in the doorway of the stock room, looking confused, a little bit like a Labrador who knows something is up but hasn't quite got the intelligence to work out exactly what.

'Yes,' I said. 'You could move some of those boxes.'

He started to say something else, then nodded and went over to where I was indicating. He was, after all, just an employee.

6

I am nothing if not professional when it comes to work. *The Case of the Cock-Headed Man* was not going to solve itself. So I set my personal problems to one side and applied myself to identifying the perpetrators of the crimes, viral and otherwise, against Billy Randall.

I had already established that I was seeking two youngish tradesmen answering to the nicknames of Jimbo and Ronnycrabs, and that they either lived or worked, or quite possibly both, in the vicinity of the Annadale Embankment. I spent an hour on the phone calling as many decorators, roofers, TV aerial men and other outdoorsy types of manual labourer as I could track down in that general area in the Yellow Pages and then over the internet, but without success. It seemed to me that they were the types that did not advertise their services in the traditional media, but rather relied on handwritten notices in local shop windows or upon word of mouth. I was pretty sure they didn't pay tax and quite possibly they exploited old women with estimates that wildly exaggerated the amount of work required. It would be good to take them down.

Ordinarily I would next have reverted to my wide and varied database of customers, alerting them of my need to track these two delinquents down, but it was Christmas week, and not a good time to be asking anyone anything; also my polite e-mail enquiry would doubtless have remained unread, most probably because I had bombarded these very same customers with enticements to join my Christmas Club every day for the past eighteen weeks and they were quite probably suffering from No Alibis fatigue. They would discard my appeal as mere spam, which was what I would be eating for Christmas if I didn't get to the bottom of *The Case of the Cock-Headed Man* fairly quickly. My only choice, therefore, was to take to the road in the all-new, purpose-sprayed No Alibis van. My last, having recently been burned out, had been replaced by a larger, sleeker model with a sliding door and plenty of room for stock inside. Jeff had been instrumental in its selection and I had foolishly succumbed to his enthusiasm; fortunately I had come into a little money as a result of solving my last case, although I would probably have been wiser to invest it in National Savings. The No Alibis logo, with *Murder Is Our Business* in bloody red lettering below, did at first look impressive, and the vehicle did handle well. I was more or less comfortable driving it, though I took care to keep to my upper limit of 30 mph while I negotiated the speed bumps and other dangers one associates with the dark streets of Belfast. However, as soon as Jeff referred to it as 'the Mystery Machine', I began to have my doubts. These worsened when I was forced to drive my mother to a hospital appointment. She was claiming disability benefit because of her stroke but had to be assessed before they would hand over the money that might see us through the winter. Mother wanted to maximise the impression of her incapacity by using a wheelchair. Jeff suggested it would look much more effective if she arrived at the hospital in the No Alibis minivan and disembarked via a ramp. It was on our first practice run that Jeff referred to Mother as 'Ironside', and the nickname stuck in my head as surely as the tumours that will one day kill me. Mother, thereafter, began to regard the van as her own personal taxi, despite the fact that she had a perfectly good set of calipers and a Zimmer frame with which to traverse the city. Jeff, helpfully, worked out a way to bolt her wheelchair into the back of the van, and also adapted the seat belt so that no matter how hard I braked, there was no way of hurling Mother out of her chair and through the windscreen.

I drove carefully to Annadale Embankment and then along it until I came to the billboard featuring the now repaired or replaced image of Billy Randall. Although he was cock-free, there were now several holes in his head caused by stones, rocks or pebbles, bits of rubble, discarded beer tins, overripe fruit or mice in bottles. The Embankment itself is a busy thruway devoid of buildings, but there is a large area of public housing close by, leading on to the shops on the Ormeau Road, and it was here that I chose to park the van and begin my search for Jimbo and Ronnycrabs.

I stopped at the first newsagent's window I came to and read the handwritten cards displayed there – teachers offering extra tuition, a lost cat, an ironing service, oriental massage, and several advertising the services of general handymen, which was a category that Jimbo and Ronnycrabs might well have fallen into. I called these handymen and asked for and about Jimbo – I couldn't quite bring myself to enquire about Ronnycrabs – but without success. They may have known him, but were adhering to the general handyman's code of silence, their *omertà* (distinct from their usual *culpa lata*). I moved along then to the window of an Oxfam store, which featured a similar series of advertisements, and then a Save the Children. Each offered several possibilities, but led me nowhere. I stood and looked up and down an Ormeau Road thick with traffic and exhaust fumes, but framed above and at the sides by the twinkling of Christmas lights, and tried to figure out what to do next. Red-faced shoppers bustled anxiously along the footpaths in search of a late bargain: it was a low-rent area, largely devoid of franchise and multi-national outlets; what in America they'd call mom and pop stores, but which I preferred to think of as cheap and nasty. I wouldn't shop here if my life depended on it. There were dozens, perhaps hundreds of these little fly-by-night businesses and I could have spent weeks going from door to door asking questions, but it was cold, and I am susceptible to chills and flu. More than once have I lain at death's door because of the weakness of my immune system and exposure to poor people; it was important not to dawdle here amongst the underclasses. I don't like the smells of poverty: the damp, the stained, the abandoned, the threadbare, the stitched in time, the decaying, the turned, the mothball, the charity, the hopelessness, the malice, the fear, the hunger, the embalming fluid, the hatred, the bigotry, the fact that the Save the Children shop had a display of books in rather good condition but which still smelt like they'd been soaked in sweat and pressed face down into a manky carpet. It was Billy Randall territory and I didn't like it. I had to track down Jimbo and Ronnycrabs fast and *get out*.

It was getting close to lunchtime, which in my world means dipping back into the well of medication that keeps me in this mortal coil. I had sixteen pills to take, but such was my state of distraction vis-à-vis Alison that for the first time in years I had neglected to bring with me the bottle of Vitolink I always wash my medication down with, and so I was forced to return to the newsagent's shop to peruse their shelves of soft drinks. They did not, of course, have any bottles of Vitolink. It is only available via the internet, and is shipped to me in powdered form from Mexico. Three hundred health-giving vitamins and minerals are hand-crushed by pre-pubescent señoritas wielding flat rocks. The vetting process is so rigorous that the señoritas each have to pass a severe medical examination before they are allowed to crush the vitamins and minerals in case a disease or bug falls off them into the powder and contaminates it. The good people who invented Vitolink were so taken with my enthusiasm for their product that they asked if I would like to purchase the marketing rights for Northern Ireland. While flattered, I declined their offer. I'm a crime man through and through and I've no interest in mixing businesses; also, if people die of perfectly curable diseases through ignorance of Vitolink, it is no concern of mine.

I selected a bottle of Coke.

There was an elderly woman in the queue ahead of me. She said, '*Woman's Realm* for my Sadie.'

The newsagent, a rotund man with a dark quiff, knelt behind the counter and produced a copy of the magazine. As he handed it over and accepted the money he said, 'Give Sadie me best.'

The elderly woman shuffled off. I put the Coke on the counter and said, 'This, and *Painter and Decorator* for Jimbo.'

It was what you call a light-bulb moment, though for the moment it was flickering.

The newsagent's brow furrowed. 'What was that?'

'Nothing,' I said.

'You said *Painter and Decorator* for Jimbo.'

'Possibly. Is there a problem?'

'Jimbo asked you to pick up his *Painter and Decorator*?' I cleared my throat in a positive manner. 'Right then. *Painter and Decorator* it is.' He produced a copy of said magazine. It had a logo and a dull photo of a man with a paintbrush on the front. The name *Jimbo Collins* was handwritten in the top right-hand corner. 'Pound for the Coke and three fifty for the magazine,' said the newsagent. 'And not forgetting . . .' He knelt beneath the counter again. When he stood, with no little effort, he was holding a precariously towering column of similar magazines. He quickly set them down on the counter and just managed to stop them from toppling over. He peered out from behind them. 'Sixteen weeks he's been avoiding coming in here so he won't have to pay for this lot. So you can bloody shell out for them.'

'This is the same Jimbo Collins? Chlorine Gardens?' I'd parked there; it was just around the corner.

The newsagent steadied the column again before reaching out for a small hard-backed notebook. He quickly flicked through several handwritten pages. 'Chlorine . . . has he moved? I have Marston Court.'

'Aye, sorry, Marston Court,' I said. 'Number twelve.'

'Fifteen,' said the newsagent.

'Right,' I said.

I had played him like a banjo. And it only cost me fifty-five quid for the sixteen issues of *Painter and Decorator* Jimbo Collins had failed to pick up.

7

'Do you want a hand?'

I recognised the voice before I saw her, my view being obscured by the leaning tower of *Painter and Decorators*.

'I'm fine,' I said, and then staggered a few yards along the footpath until I reached a bin. I tipped the lot into it before turning to snarl at Alison. 'What're you doing here?'

'I'm on a case,' she said.

'No you're not.'

'I've been tracking down Ronnycrabs and Jimbo.'

'No you haven't. You've been following me and hoping to pick up crumbs. You're a sad, sorry individual.'

I started to walk towards the van. She fell into step beside me. She took my hand. I took it back.

'So you know where they live?' she asked.

'Yes.'

'Both of them?'

I grunted.

'Marston Court?' she asked.

I just kept walking.

'At least that's where Ronnycrabs is; I haven't been able to find Jimbo.'

I don't know if she saw my small, satisfied, yet triumphant smile. I had a whole orchestra of banjos at my disposal.

'As I understand it,' she said, 'your job is merely to verify where they live, so once you eyeball them, that's it tied up and the cheque's in the post.'

'If it's any of your business,' I said.

'Anything the father of my unborn child does is my business.'

'Don't start.'

'It's in our interest to see you do well, and to lend assistance where we can.'

'Christ.'

We walked in silence. Away from the main road our footsteps echoed on the damp pavement. There were Christmas lights in the windows of almost every house. It was not an area where anyone in their right mind would venture out carol-singing, but it was in the air.

'I'm going for my first scan next week.'

'Brain?'

'What?'

'Nothing.'

'I was wondering if you want to come.'

'No.'

'Why not?'

'No interest.'

'I know you're afraid of hospitals . . .'

'I'm not afraid of hospitals.'

'. . . or allergic to them, but I'm going private. It's a consultant's home I go to; he has an office in the grounds. The *grounds*. They earn a fortune, those guys. That's where I'm going. You could manage that. There won't be bugs. Or if there are, they'll be a better class of bug. Nothing to be scared of.'

'I'm not scared. I'm just not interested.'

'In your own son?'

'Says who?'

'And when I say son, I don't know if it's a boy or a girl. It could be either. Or both. Could be twins. Or some kind of amalgam.'

'Amalgam?'

'You read about it. Babies that are like a mix. It's to do with pollution or global warming or mobile phones. That would be something. Doesn't have to be like the Elephant Man, could just be webbed feet or a hump or something.'

If there had been traffic, I might have pushed her into it. It is funny how quickly you can go from loving someone to just plain hating them. And it's not even funny. It's tragic.

We were approaching the van. It looked shiny and new and inappropriate to its surroundings. Alison, who *must* have seen it before, parked as it was every day outside the shop, clapped her hands together.

'Isn't it lovely?! It reminds me—'

'Don't.'

'Don't what?'

'Tell me what it reminds you of.'

'What? Okay. The Mystery Machine!' She cackled like the witch she was and ran her hands along the paintwork. '*Murder Is Our Business*! It's so appropriate!' Then she said: 'What was that?'

'What was what?'

'That noise. A scraping and groaning . . .' She put her ear to the side panel. 'What have you got in there?'

'Nothing.'

'Yes you have, you've a dog, you've gotten yourself a guard dog, you big scaredy-ba.'

'I do not have a dog.'

'You big eejit, with me not there to protect you you've gotten yourself a pooch . . . Whoa! It sounds vicious! Let me see, go on, let me see.'

'Just mind your own business.'

'Och, come on, come on, come on, you know I'm going to keep at you till you show me.'

'I'm allergic to dogs, you know that.'

'What the hell is it, then? A Vietnamese pot-bellied pig?'

'Don't be ridiculous.'

'Come on, come on . . . whoa! It bloody whacked the side there! Man, dear, there's no half-measures with you, is there? But I'm telling you this, when the boy comes along, you'll have to get rid of it. I'm not taking any chances. You hear about these monster dogs eating children and . . .' Her eyes widened. 'I have it! I know you too well, mister – it's the Hound of the Baskervilles! What was that, like an Irish wolfhound? I can't remember, I read it yonks ago, but I don't really like Sherlock, too gay . . . but that's it, isn't it? You've gotten yourself a vicious big wolfhound and you won't show me it because you're scared of it yourself!'

It was cold and winter dark and I wanted to get home to No Alibis. I dug my fists into my pockets.

Alison raised an expectant eyebrow.

I just looked at her.

'Is it something really embarrassing? It's probably a Labradoodle.'

'Your face is a Labradoodle.'

'Open the door.'

'You can't order me what to do.'

'Yes I can, we're partners.'

'If we were partners we would have to agree mutually. And we're not, anyway.'

'We're partners for life, and you know it. And if I'm eating for two, I'm also voting for two, so you're outvoted. Open the frickin' door!'

'No.'

'I'll stay here until you do.'

'Feel free. But I'm driving off.'

I had the keys out and was moving around to the driver's side.

'You wouldn't leave a pregnant woman alone here in this neck of the woods, would you?'

'Watch me. Besides, I'm sure you didn't walk here. Where'd you leave your broom?'

'You're funny.'

'So's your face.'

'I'll only follow you to Marston Court.'

'Feel free.'

I got in behind the wheel and started the engine. Alison stood looking at me. I put the van into gear and pulled out. Her mouth opened slightly, as if she couldn't quite believe that I was actually driving off, but I had no qualms about it at all. When you're solving a crime you have to remain focused. I've always been focused.

But I have not yet invested in satnav.

I slid the divider across and glanced into the rear.

'Mother,' I said, 'have you any idea where Marston Court is?'

8

I'd been watching the house for about five minutes when I noticed in my side mirror that Alison had pulled in behind. She had lately been driving a red Volkswagen Beetle that was hard to miss. I knew it was her car because on nights when Mother's drunken rages get too much I sometimes walk out to her house and stand in the bushes in her front garden. I find it quite calming. I hate her, but still feel protective of her. I'm pretty good at blending in. The dark clothes and balaclava help. One night she opened the front door and guldered, 'I'm calling the police, you fucking nutter!' into the darkness, but I'm not convinced it was directed at me. It's an odd neighbourhood. Alison exchanged her old Mini for this Volkswagen the week after we split up, or nine days after she caused Mother to have a stroke. I think it was a way of assuaging her guilt. Really, for the guilt-assuaging to work, she should have bought my *mother* the Volkswagen rather than treat herself, though obviously she would then have had to have the steering wheel and gears and brakes adapted.

Alison made no attempt to get out of her car, though she knew that I could see her. Once in a while, and purely for my benefit, she gave the universal sign for wanking. It was an odd situation to be in. I was watching a house for signs of Jimbo and Ronnycrabs while Alison was watching me. For the first time in my life I was both stalker and stalkee.

The house in Marston Court was an end of terrace. The gable wall, which faced where I was parked, was completely covered in a mural commemorating and celebrating soldiers who had fought and died during the Battle of the Somme. Sometimes the art world is astonished when a seemingly worthless painting goes in for cleaning and the experts discover a work by an Old Master hidden beneath the first layer of paint, and something similar was true of this First World War scene, except it wasn't terrifically well hidden and was of no value. Thanks to the quality of the paint, or perhaps the degree of absorption of the brick-work, it was still possible to make out the original mural, which celebrated the Red Hand Commandos and their murderous exploits during the Troubles. It crossed my mind that Jimmy and Ronnycrabs, being painters and decorators, might have created either one or possibly both of these murals themselves, which in turn suggested that they might once have supported or even been members of a terrorist organisation. Since peace had broken out, terrorists of a Republican leaning had laid down their arms and embraced the political process; freedom fighters from the Loyalist side had pretty much held on to their guns and started (or more usually continued) to deal in coke. The only thing that had really changed was the geographical boundaries within or without which it was considered safe for them to deal. As borders had come down all across Europe, so they had across Northern Ireland. The peace dividend for Republicans was power-sharing; for Loyalists it was enlarging their market. I smiled happily. One glance at an historical mural and I had *defined* Jimbo and Ronnycrabs. Their pedigree, or lack of. I had been good at this crime-busting right from the start, but with experience, I was definitely getting better.

There was a tap on my window. Alison smiled in. I rolled it down and said, 'What?'

'I was thinking.'

'Always a bad—'

'You have a shop to run, and you could be here for hours.'

'Jeff's perfectly—'

'You think?'

'What's your point?'

'I'm off for the rest of the day; nothing to do but grow a baby. I could hang around here and wait for them to arrive and take their pictures, or if you want I can sketch them.'

'Sketch them. You think they're going to pose? Anyway, I've seen your stuff.'

'What's that supposed to mean?'

'Well, Billy Randall would want to be able to recognise them. If I showed him your version of them he'd think I was mental.'

'You are mental.'

'Or on drugs.'

'You are—'

'You know what I mean. Your stuff isn't exactly realistic. It's surreal.'

'You don't know your artistic arse from your artistic elbow; stick to what you know, Mystery Man. And anyway, I can *do* normal. I can do *any* style.'

I looked at her. She raised an eyebrow. I had a camera on the passenger seat. It had the appropriate lenses for long-range work. I missed my shop and I didn't fully trust Jeff. Was there any harm, really, in letting a pregnant woman hang around outside the home of two drug-dealing ex-terrorists trying to surreptitiously take their photographs? Hardly any. There was only a negligible chance of her being beaten up. Besides, she was volunteering not because she wanted to steal the case from me but because she was trying to win her way back into my affections so that I would look after her and her unborn child. Also I'm manually illiterate and usually I manage to screw up even foolproof cameras. And she was doing it for free. There was no downside.

But I wasn't just going to cave in.

'What if you break the camera?'

'I won't.'

'You promise to wear the strap?'

'Even though I'll be in my car, yes.'

'It's an expensive camera. If there's even a scratch on it, you'll have to buy me a new one.'

'Okay.'

'It means if they don't arrive until tonight, you'll have to stay until you get them.'

'That's not a problem.'

'What if you need to pee?'

'I'll hold on.'

'I thought if you're pregnant you have to pee all the time.'

'That's not till I'm all fat and horrible.'

I raised an eyebrow.

'You're funny,' she said.

'So's your face,' I said.

I stopped on the way home to let Mother out before continuing on to the shop. I checked the till to make sure Jeff wasn't stealing before letting him go. I sat in my chair and put my feet up on the counter and opened a Twix. I had decided, in the absence of customers, to treat myself to a leisurely reread of one of Ross MacDonald's non Lew Archer novels, *The Ferguson Affair*, but had barely gotten past page one when the door opened and Alison came in, beaming. It wasn't much more than forty-five minutes since I'd left her.

'Fed up or beaten up?' I asked.

'Ta-da!'

She placed the camera on the counter and pushed it across, with the digital screen facing me. I took my time placing the bookmark properly and then set the book, which was a long out-of-print Knopf edition, back under the desk. I sighed. I positioned the camera so that I had the best view of Alison's picture. It showed two young men in T-shirts and track bottoms, posing with their arms folded before the First World War mural.

'That's Jimbo,' said Alison, pointing at the one on her left, 'and that's—'

'I get it.'

'Real name Ronny Clegg. They were extremely co-operative.'

'Did you promise them sexual favours?'

'Yes.' I kept my eyes on the picture, though inside something churned. 'They arrived home just after you left. I knocked on the door and told them I was taking photographs for a book on Belfast's murals and could I take the one on the side of their house, and by the way did they happen to know who painted it? Couldn't have been more helpful. They invited me in, made me a cup of tea.'

She reached across and pushed a button. A different photo appeared, this time of them sitting on a sofa, with cups in their hands, grinning inanely. It was a wide-angle shot. The room looked cramped and cluttered. A Jack Russell dog stood off to one side, ears erect. My nose crinkled, ready to sneeze. There was a computer sitting on a desk to their right. 'Make yourself at home, why don't you?'

'I did. I liked them. They're into dope and comics.' Alison beamed.

'What?'

'They let me flick through their collection. And guess what?'

'What?'

'Guess.'

'Alison, I couldn't—'

'They had one of mine! They bought it here!'

'They . . .'

'They're customers of yours!'

'They . . .'

'What are the chances of that?!'

Given the narrow breadth of my customer base, pretty damn remote. However, I shrugged modestly.

'They bought one of *your* comics; it doesn't make them customers of *mine*. Your comics are hardly representative of what—'

'Oh boil your head. It made *my* day.'

'I'm happy for you. Thanks for your help.' I picked up the camera and placed it under the counter. 'Seeing as how you got so pally with them, did they happen to mention Billy Randall?'

'Yes, as a matter of fact, they brought it up themselves. I think they were trying to impress me.'

'You're easily impressed.'

She gave me a look. 'Aren't I just. They showed

me the YouTube video. They're very proud of it.'

'I suppose you cackled along and told them they were great.'

'Kind of. I asked them why they did it. They said, *because he was there*. As in . . .'

'Everest.'

Alison nodded.

I nodded.

We had a minute of silence while I waited for her to get to the point I knew she was getting to.

'You know, they're quite harmless.'

'They've made a worldwide laughing stock out of an innocent man.'

'They were just messing around.'

'Uhuh.'

'Doesn't it change things?'

'Doesn't what what?'

'The fact that they're customers.'

'God no.'

'You've got few enough; once word gets around that you've sold two of them out to the likes of Billy Randall, you're going to have none at all.'

I laughed.

That was obviously bollocks.

9

To get her off my back I told Alison that I would sleep on whether or not to sell her only two fans out to Billy Randall. Obviously, with my ailments, I don't sleep; they've yet to invent a pill that can knock me out. But that is neither here nor there. As soon as she left, I e-mailed Billy Randall the two posed photographs of Jimbo Collins and Ronny Clegg together with their address and a grossly inflated bill. I expected it would be dealt with by one of his secretaries, but within a few minutes a response came pinging back from the man himself.

Thanks, mate! I owe you!

Yes he did. And he wasn't my *mate*. He was using *mate* in a way I despised, adding it to his speech to try and connect with his working-class customers, because that's how they spoke. *Mate* on the end of everything. I wasn't sure what I resented more, the uninvited familiarity or the fact that he thought *I* was part of his constituency. I stared at the e-mail. I knew what Alison would have said. You're reading too much into it. He's just saying thank you. But what did she know? She worked in a jewellery store selling cheap bangles. He could have gotten away with saying mate to her. Except you don't say mate to a girl. Love? Dear? Sweetie? As I pondered this, and waited for the Twix to settle the bile in my stomach, an instant message popped on to my screen.

Working hard?

It was Alison.

I typed, *Yes*.

Then I switched the computer off and returned to *The Ferguson Affair*.

Within twenty minutes she was at the door, yipping and yollering that it was Christmas and it was snowing and I had to come out and play in it. A brief glance confirmed that it *was not* snow but sleet. Alison was bouncing up and down with excitement, breaking off only to gather up *stuff* and throw it at shoppers walking with their umbrellas up but at an angle to stop their red faces getting further stung by God's inclemency. They glared at her and she shouted Merry Christmas and some of them forced a smile but mostly they just kept walking. Her cheeks were flaming. She had her favourite woollen flying cap pulled down over her ears and loosely tied under her chin.

'I love Christmas!' she shouted.

'Technically it's not yet Christmas,' I said, but I don't think she heard. I remained behind the counter. 'Could you close the door?'

With the delicate state of my immune system it simply wasn't safe for me to be exposed to vagaries of temperature. If it was cold, I could cope; if it was hot, with the central heating on and a hot-water bottle at my back, as it had been, I was fine. But sending my body mixed signals like this, with one foot in the Amazon and the other in the Arctic, could only lead to confusion, breakdown and death from a bizarre mixture of heat stroke and hypothermia. Fortunately I have so few customers that this is not ordinarily a problem.

Eventually, after what seemed like an eternity, Alison came in and closed the door. She briefly rubbed her pink, damp, freezing hands together before suddenly turning the *Open* sign to *Closed*, and flicking the lock on the door. She spun around to face me, grinning defiantly.

I tried saying something, but I was so incandescent with rage that I only managed a weak splutter, like sugar in a moped's exhaust.

'Sit where you are and shut up, Mystery Man,' said Alison. 'I'm gonna make you an offer you can't refuse.'

She crossed to the counter.

'Whatever you're selling,' I finally managed, 'I'm not buying. Particularly if it's comics.'

'Shut up. This is going to be our baby's first Christmas. I think we should all spend it together.'

'I have other plans.'

'You and the vegetable.'

'Don't start me.'

'You're going to plonk her in a chair in front of the telly, stick a paper hat on her head, and spoon-feed her mash and gravy. And that will be the highlight.'

I just glared at her. Actually I wasn't intending to let Mother out of her room. I would sit by her bed and read *Psycho* aloud to her. And there wasn't anything she could do about it. At least, she hadn't yet.

Alison folded her arms on the counter. I leaned back in my chair.

'Have you even ordered a turkey?'

'You don't have to have—'

'This is my offer. You and . . .' She cleared her throat. 'You and your mother come to my place for Christmas. Lovely big meal. All the trimmings. Neither of you will have to lift a finger, not that you would or she can. It'll be my way of saying sorry to her. Have you told her about the baby?'

'What baby?'

'Well then Christmas will be a splendid opportunity. The best present ever. How will she feel about becoming a granny?'

'I can't see how it will improve her demeanour. She despises being a mother.'

'Look. Will you come?'

I loathe Christmas. I hate the greed, the panic, the hypocrisy, the myth, the red suit, the mewling children, the carols, the forced bonhomie, the shopping, the wrapping, the drinking, the overindulgence, the television, the weather, the inappropriate presents, God, Jesus, angels, twisty winky lights, toppling trees, artificial trees, real trees, tinsel, cards, postmen, stamps, doorbells, cards that say we tried to deliver, aftershave, socks, jumpers, book tokens, book tokens, book tokens, stuffing, sprouts, cranberry sauce, Christmas pudding, Christmas cake and Lord protect us from Baileys Irish Cream.

'Okay,' I said.

Her mouth dropped open, surprised by my sudden capitulation.

'Brilliant!'

I was a little surprised myself. It wasn't the baby. There was no wish to repair fences. Partly it was because I knew Mother would hate it. Mostly it was the free food.

Definitely not the baby.

I detest babies.

Alison was near overcome with excitement. She leaned across the counter to try and kiss me, but I stayed out of range. She wasn't fazed in the slightest. She clapped her hands together. 'I'll tell Brian to bring a couple of extra chairs!'

10

I need not go into the detail of what happened at Alison's home for waifs and strays on Christmas Day, suffice to say that Mother played up, while Brian, Alison's ex, got very drunk and began to accuse me of somehow causing the severe beating that very nearly cost him his life while I was solving my previous case. This was clearly preposterous. I tried to explain to him that sometimes, when fighting crime, innocent civilians get hurt. He was merely what we refer to as collateral damage. This did not sit well with him and he called me names. He also flew into a temper when I denied eating the last roast potato and then went into a giant huff when Alison announced that she was pregnant. Mother, being drunk and unconscious, seemed to take the news well. Later, having succumbed to a glass of wine myself, even though I was well aware of the effect it would have on me, what with my massive intake of prescribed and imported medication, I approached Brian in the dark corner of the living room where he'd hidden himself and put my arm around him and gave him a squeeze and told him it wasn't true. A light of renewed hope suddenly appeared in his eyes. 'You mean she isn't pregnant?'

I shook my head sadly. 'No, I didn't eat the last roastie.'

He chased me into the garden. He pounded my head repeatedly into the sleet-covered grass while Alison tried to pull him off. Mother, waking in a temper, rattled her walking stick against the window frame and screamed, 'Kill him! Kill him!'

So it was a relief to reopen the shop on Boxing Day.

That lasted for all of about thirty seconds.

I had rather hoped that with No Alibis being closed on the Sunday, and then also the next day, Christmas Day, there would have been a queue of customers snaking away down Botanic Avenue, all anxious to convert their book tokens into quality crime fiction hand-picked by an expert, but there was nobody waiting at all.

I raised the shutters, unlocked the many and various locks and combinations, and had just entered the shop and switched on the computer when the front door opened behind me and I glanced hopefully around, only to see a familiar figure step through the breach. Although he has been a regular in the shop, and bought numerous books, some of them quite valuable, I have never quite been able to either relax in his company or regard him as a proper customer. It seemed to me that there was always an unspoken and ulterior motive to his visits, that since I had once bettered him, he now felt he had to keep a professional eye on me. Or perhaps he wanted me to teach him a thing or two about crime-busting.

I said, 'Hello, Detective Inspector, merry Christmas, et cetera, et cetera.' He was wearing his usual charcoal suit and black moustache. 'Did you have a good one?'

DI Robinson patted his stomach. 'This'll see me through to spring.'

It had just gone nine. He was lucky he hadn't gotten Mother, but I'd decided to give her the morning off. It was Christmas, and her idea of goodwill to all men did not extend to all men, or any.

'Hoping to pick up some cheap bargains in your post-Christmas sale.'

Cheap, bargains and sale – three words not bandied about lightly in No Alibis. Nevertheless I smiled indulgently. I nodded around the shelves. 'See if there's anything you fancy, I'll see what I can do.'

But instead, he moved closer to the counter, and my spider-sense began to tingle.

'So did you have a good Christmas?' he asked.

'Quiet.'

'Home with Mother?'

'Alison's.'

'Ah. That's back on, is it?'

'Did you hear it was off?'

'Word on the street. She's a lovely little lady.'

I had never considered that he might have an interest in Alison. Just because I didn't want her, it didn't mean I would allow anyone else to have her. I surreptitiously checked his wedding finger. No ring.

'She has her moments,' I said. 'We're having a baby.'

'Really? Congratulations are in order.'

I nodded. He nodded. They didn't seem to be forthcoming.

'So that's where you were Christmas Day.' He picked up my copy of *The Ferguson Affair* – which, frustratingly, I'd left in the shop over Christmas – and briefly studied the plot summary on the back cover. 'You still doing some of this?' he asked.

'Reading?'

'Investigating.'

I took the book from him. 'If you're not intending to buy, *don't touch*! Fingerprints reduce the value.' I forced a laugh. He forced one back. 'Investigating? Now and again. Why?'

'Oh, no reason. Still doing your creative writing class on a Saturday?'

'It's finished for this year, starts again in the spring.'

'With Brendan Coyle?'

'Possibly. Why, were you . . . ?'

'Well, they say write about what you know. Thought I might give it a bash. The old crime novel, don't you know? Poacher turned gamekeeper. Or the other way around. What do you think?'

There was something quite alarming about the thought of DI Robinson writing a crime novel. It would have lots of plot but little character. Still, it hadn't stopped Christie. 'Yes. Ahm. Absolutely. Do you think it'll be one of those open-ended ones, where the mystery never quite gets solved?'

His brow furrowed. 'Why do you ask?'

'Writing about what you know.'

He seemed to look at me for a *long* time. And only then did he smile, and presently the smile became a soft chuckle, which gradually morphed into a laugh. 'You, you're quick, aren't you? Very good. Open-ended. So, anyway, you were at Alison's all day Christmas Day? And at night?'

'There . . . too . . .' It was an abrupt return to his original line of questioning, and worrying. 'Why?'

'You didn't tune in to the news or anything?'

'Just the Queen.'

DI Robinson nodded. 'We've been holding a friend of yours down at the station.'

I snorted involuntarily. The very *notion* of friends. 'Oh yeah?' I decided to maintain the charade. I liked the idea of friends, but not the reality.

'Name of Billy Randall.'

He couldn't help but see my surprised look. 'He's no friend of mine.'

'But you do know him?'

'Professionally, yes.'

'He buys books from you?'

'No, he hired me to track some people down.'

'Track them down. What are you now, a bounty-hunter?'

'No, just their addresses.'

'And you did that?'

'Yes.'

He nodded. He took a BlackBerry out of his inside pocket. He spent four minutes trying to find something on it. When he eventually looked up he said, 'This would be James Collins and Ronald Clegg?'

'Sounds like them.'

'Anything you want to tell me?'

'About what?'

'Anything.'

'Nothing I can think of.'

'You met them. You were in their house.'

'Nope.'

'You're sure about that?'

'Positive.'

'Yet your van was spotted right outside. It's a distinctive van.'

'Yes. Well. Like I say, I was trying to track them down.'

'But you never met them.'

'No.'

'And you still maintain you never went inside their house.'

'No, I didn't. What's all this about?'

'Why don't *you* tell me what it's all about?'

'That's just stupid.'

'Do you think murder is stupid?'

'Murder.'

'Murder.'

'Murder murder?'

'Murder murder.'

'Billy Randall?'

'Billy Randall.'

'I thought maybe it was some kind of scam – time-share, or something.'

'It may be yet.'

'He's murdered . . . ?'

DI Robinson glanced at his BlackBerry again. The page he was looking at had disappeared.

'Jimbo Collins and Ronny Clegg,' I said, helpfully.

'He didn't necessarily murder them, though they have been murdered. He's what we call a person of interest. He's in custody. Between you and me, we think he may have hired someone to take them out.'

'Seriously. God.'

'Someone like you.'

I smiled, and waited for him to. But he did not.

'Get away to fuck,' I said.

He remained stony-faced. 'He hired you.'

'To find those guys.'

'You were spotted outside their house.'

'Outside.'

'You sent him an e-mail saying the job was done.'

'It was done, I found them.'

'And you charged him two thousand pounds.'

'That's what I charge.'

'To find two guys who're in the Yellow Pages.'

'They aren't in the Yellow Pages.'

'Yes they are. Jim and Ronny, Painters and Decorators.'

'Not in mine.'

It was behind me, on a shelf under the sign that read *This is not a fucking library.*

'That,' said DI Robinson, his head tilted sideways to read the spine of the directory, 'is eight years out of date.'

'So's your face.'

He blinked at me. 'Excuse me?'

'I'm sorry, but this is ridiculous.'

'Two thousand pounds is a ridiculously large amount to find out a couple of addresses. But it's probably just about enough to hire a low-rent hit man. The market around these parts has crashed, there's a lot of un-employed killers out there. And it's a world you seem quite comfortable in.'

That was it, then. He was bitter at my success, and now that an opportunity had come along, he was determined to have his revenge.

We stared at each other.

Then I thought, no, that's stupid; I helped solve the case, but he had the satisfaction of arresting the killers and putting them away. He wasn't serious. He was winding me up.

I studied him for a telltale sign: a glint in his eye, the slight widening of his firmly set lips, a subtle rise of an eyebrow; but he was good, as good as a cop should be. But I knew.

'You nearly had me there. This is the plot of the novel you want to write. You're funny. Okay. Fine. Got me, got me good.'

Nothing.

Nothing at all.

Just a steely look, and: 'We believe Billy Randall is at the very least an accessory to murder. The problem, my friend, is that we can find nothing to link him to the actual murder scene. Which is more than we can say about you, and your DNA.'

'That's impossible,' I said.

'So's your face,' said Detective Inspector Robinson.

11

He didn't arrest me.

That's not how he works.

He puts information or misinformation out there and then watches and listens and sees how you deal with it, what you do once he's gone, who you talk to, who you phone or e-mail, if you empty your bank account and head for the airport. And he did have my DNA on record. But there was no possibility that he'd found a match in Jimbo and Ronny's house unless he'd planted it there himself.

Or unless Alison had.

I sat and thought about that for a while. Was she so bitter and twisted over my lack of interest in her baby that she would actually seek to implicate me in a murder? She was, after all, evil to the core, and a practising witch. I drummed my fingers on the counter. One night, while we were still together, we sat in her apartment and watched a DVD. She'd given me carte blanche to choose one and I'd rented *Presumed Innocent*, the Harrison Ford movie based on Scott Trurow's book. It is one of those few adaptations that not only does an acclaimed book justice, but actually improves upon it. It's about a bitter wife murdering her husband's mistress and then framing him for it. Could I have been the unwitting architect of my own demise? Had Alison scooped up a handful of my DNA and hurled it around Jimbo and Ronny's house before cold-bloodedly murdering them?

I needed more information. I surfed on to the *Belfast Telegraph*'s website. The headline read: *Christmas Horror*. There were photographs of Jimbo and Ronny, arms around each other, cans of Harp beer in hand, at a party. They looked several years younger than in the pictures of them I'd forwarded to Billy Randall. There was no mention of Billy Randall, and, crucially, no reference to me or the No Alibis van or Alison. It said the murder scene was a bloodbath. They had been beaten with a blunt instrument.

I mixed up a pint of Vitolink. It was important to keep my levels high. I took my antipsychotic pills, and my bipolar pills, and my fibromyalgia pills. My antihistamines. My blood pressure pills. My cholesterol pills. My antidepressants. My hormones. Taken together, they would keep me going until lunchtime, when I would have to take my full list of medications. Alison has never really appreciated the fact that any one of my ailments could kill me at any time. She believes that I am something of a hypochondriac. She is wrong about most things. If my doctor was not prevented from doing so by the Hippocratic oath, he could tell her a thing or two about the condition of my bowels and liver and heart and blood and veins and head. He could tell her that I am just one of those people who has to live with life-threatening illness. He could tell her that he once prescribed me a placebo, which I turned out to be allergic to. Alison had no need to plant my DNA at a murder scene if she wanted revenge; she had no need to do *anything*. I was a dead man walking, or limping, already. I probably wouldn't see New Year's. I once asked my doctor straight out how long I had left, and he said, 'How long is a piece of string?'

I rest my case.

The clue is in *piece*.

If he was meaning longevity, he would have said how long is a *ball* of string.

A piece of string is what a cat plays with.

I am also allergic to cats.

DI Robinson had accused me of being a low-rent hit man and then had the nerve to ask for a discount on a signed copy of Dave Goodis' *Dark Passage* before he left. I refused the discount, but did knock thirty pence off because there was a slight tear in the cover.

Low-rent?

There was nothing low-rent about me.

Many's the time Alison had said the very opposite, complimenting me by saying I was high-maintenance.

If I was any kind of a hit man, I was an expensive one, cool, calm and efficient.

I shouldn't have said that last bit out loud, which I tend to do when I'm alone.

Walls have ears, and, sometimes, listening devices.

I spent an hour sweeping for bugs and dust mites. Thinking, thinking all the time. Dark thoughts. I hated being accused of things I hadn't done. Why did everyone pick on me? I just tried to help people, but it almost always backfired. Why couldn't they leave me alone? I should close down the detective business. And the store. I should go home and look after Mother and never go out except for milk. I stopped brushing, chilled by a sudden thought. The medication I was on occasionally caused blackouts. I don't mean fainting, but periods where I just couldn't remember what I'd done. What if I really had killed Jimbo and Ronnycrabs? What if I'd forgotten to take my anti-psychotic medicine and become . . . psychotic? What if I'd gone round there late at night and beaten them to a pulp with my mallet? Maybe I was just being paranoid. Maybe I'd forgotten to take my antiparanoid medicine. Sometimes it is difficult to keep track. I take something to help me with that. I checked my pulse. It was racing. I took a couple of settlers. I made up another pint of Vitolink. It was barely lunchtime but it was almost black outside. There was hail. My doctor says I'm the first patient he's had with Seasonal

Affective Disorder who gets depressed by all four seasons. He says his nurse calls me Frankie Valli.

Breathe.

Breathe deeply.

Relax.

I tried yoga once, but got tendonitis.

Breathe.

Across the road, Alison's jewellery store had reopened with a sale and was busy with customers. I knew she was there, but with the rain-streaked windows on both our shops it was difficult to get a proper look at her. However, I was pretty certain she was keeping an eye on me and nervously wondering why the police hadn't dragged me away yet.

The phone rang.

'Shows how much I know,' a male voice said.

'I'm sorry?'

'I was just saying to the plod here, shows how much I know. I said to myself, I've got one phone call; who am I gonna call? My lawyer, my wife, my mistress, my children, my accountant?'

'I'm sorry, but who is this?'

'And turns out I didn't say it to myself, but I said it out loud, sometimes I do that, and the plod says that that's not true, that you're only allowed one call, it's not the dark ages, you can have as many calls as you want as long as you're not, like, ordering pizza or anything.'

'I . . .'

'So you're not top of my list, I called my wife, I called my lawyer and now I'm calling you. Third isn't too bad, bronze medal.'

'Is it about a book?'

'No. It's me. Billy Randall. You heard what—'

'Billy?' My knees felt weak. They *are* weak, generally, I have a problem with my cruciate ligaments. Weak*er*. 'Yes . . . yes . . . I heard . . .'

'So we should have a chat.'

'Yes. No. It's not really any of my—'

'They're letting me out of here. We should go for a coffee.'

'Yes. No. I'm kind of busy. If you send me an e-mail, I'm sure—'

'There's a Starbucks across the road from you; say I see you there at three?'

'I . . .'

'Looking forward to it. I could just murder a frappuccino. Or you could do it for me.'

He laughed suddenly, then abruptly hung up.

I stood with the receiver in my hand, and my shirt stuck to my back.

I stared at the phone.

Billy Randall, having not yet settled his bill, was still theoretically my client. He and I were implicated in a double murder. He wanted to meet in my favourite coffee house. I didn't like it, I didn't like it one bit. I didn't know what to do. I needed help. Advice. Another settler. I drained the Vitolink. There was nobody I could phone. Not DI Robinson, not Alison;

the way my luck was running, even the Samaritans would rat me out. Nobody I could trust. Nobody I could lean on. Not one human being in the entire civilised world I could reach out to.

Then Jeff arrived.

12

'Fucking hell,' said Jeff, 'fucking hell.'

'Helpful,' I said.

'And *did you*, like, blank out and beat them to death with your mallet?'

'No!'

'Because the odd time you have blanked out in here you haven't remembered what you've done.'

'And did I kill anyone? You, for instance?'

'Not exactly, no.'

'Not exactly? What did I do?'

'You rearranged the bookshelves.'

'I rearranged the bookshelves.'

'Yes. But the point is, you didn't remember, then flew into a temper and accused me of doing it.'

As I recalled, they were rearranged out of sequence, i.e. they were normally alphabetical but someone had rearranged them into different categories of crime fiction – serial killers, cosies, pulp, golden age, etc. It's an impractical way of displaying books; there are too many that belong in several categories. Yet Jeff was convinced I had done it.

. Which was worrying.

The Strange Case of Dr Jekyll and Mr Hyde would have been infinitely less interesting if Dr Jekyll had merely reclassified his medical texts rather than hacked people to death, but I would have settled for that. The important thing, I suppose, was that while there *might* be evidence that I blanked out from time to time, there was absolutely none that it ever led to violence.

Jeff reached under the counter and took out my mallet and meat cleaver and jackknife and claw hammer. I asked him what he was doing. He said he was checking for bloodstains and brain matter. I took them off him and replaced them, although checked myself as I did so.

'What,' I asked, 'am I going to do about Billy Randall?'

'Wear a wire.'

'Wear a wire.'

'In case he says something, not so much to incriminate himself, but something that might get you off the hook.'

'But what if I say something that incriminates *me*?'

'But you say you haven't done anything.'

'But I could say something that might be read in a different way to what I mean. Sometimes I—'

'Slabber. Okay. But *we'll* have the tape. We can just edit it out or lose it.'

'Not if *he's* wearing the wire.'

'Aha.'

'If they think he's involved in these murders, then they've released him pretty damn quick. Maybe they've done a plea bargain with him, if he can get me to admit the murders on tape.'

'That makes sense. God, you'll be trying to get him to admit something and he'll be trying to get you. It'll be like a game of chess. Two criminal masterminds trying to outwit each other.' He blinked at me. 'Not that you're a criminal mastermind.'

'Okay. But where on earth would I get a wire? I need a tape recorder or a dictaphone.'

'Use your mobile, there's bound to be a recorder on it.'

I checked. It was old, but there was.

'But what if as soon as I go in, he frisks me and finds the phone and sees that it's recording.'

'Keep it in your pants.'

'He'll be thinking the same, and be wearing his in his.'

'You could, like, spill a drink over him. Short it out.'

'Or you could go in first, hide it in the toilets. Then I let him frisk me, go to the toilet, pick up the phone, come back in.'

'He'll only frisk you again. Everyone knows that one. Maybe it's out of your hands anyway. If Robinson thinks you're both involved, then he's already tapping your phone, so he knows about the meet. He'll have the whole place wired, or someone at the next table.'

'Not if you're at the next table.'

'Me?'

'You sit there with a coffee, you take your mobile phone out, you pretend to be playing a game, but actually you're recording what we're saying.'

'That might work. See, we're a great team.'

I let that one pass.

I looked at the clock. I would have to remember to take my medication at the right time and in the right order. It wouldn't do to doze off or be hyper during the meet. I had to be focused, alert, my radar working perfectly. I needed to speak clearly and succinctly rather than mumble and drool. I had to tell Billy that I knew nothing about the murders and didn't want to be involved in his case in any way. Our brief business relationship was over. I'd completed my task and he needed to settle his account and leave me in peace.

Ten minutes before three, Alison arrived. I said, 'I can't talk to you now.'

'Course you can,' she said. She looked at Jeff. 'Jeff, could you give us a minute?'

Jeff looked to me.

'He's fine where he is. We're closing up for a little while.'

She looked from me to Jeff and back. 'You never close up for a little while.'

'Well we are. We have something to do.'

Her eyes narrowed. 'Did I see DI Robinson over earlier?'

'Possibly.'

'When I say "did I see", what I actually mean is, I saw him clear as day.'

'So.'

'Bit of a shock.'

'What is?'

'Jimbo and Ronnycrabs. Looks like I might have been the last person to see them alive.'

She was such a *player*. Of course she was the last person to see them. She killed them.

'He says my DNA is all over the living room.' She shook her head. 'The nerve of the man. Of course it is! I just visited them! He thinks it's still the good old bad old days, first fingerprint you find, you put them away for thirty years; trouble is, nobody else thinks that way, not the solicitors, not the judges, nobody but him. Didn't he find yours too?'

'Possibly.'

'He tried that on me too, like he was Sherlock Holmes or something, trying to get me to rat you out. How come, he says, if you're the only one who entered the house, how come your partner in crime . . . and he really said *that* . . . left his DNA there as well? And he gave me one of those looks like . . . *ta-da!* And it took me about ten seconds to work it out. I'm new to this game, but I'll get better. I'm sure you had it in, like, three.'

I nodded.

'Once I said it,' she continued, 'that fairly shut him up. You should have seen his face drop. I think it's quite sweet that my comics had your DNA on them. You must have been missing me and licked them.'

Jeff snorted. 'It's the price stickers. Instead of paying for new ones, he's using this job lot he's had for years. Most of the stickiness is gone out of them, so he licks them down.'

'It means I can afford idiots like you, Jeff.'

Jeff made a face. Alison laughed. She was still a witch, but maybe she hadn't tried to incriminate me. Or she had, in a different way, and I just hadn't found out about it yet.

I had to remain on my guard.

'Anyway, now he's off your back, I've something to show you.' Alison pulled her handbag round from behind her and began to search through it. 'It's just . . . here . . .'

'It'll have to wait.'

I was already at the door.

'Jeff,' I said, 'lock up and follow me over. We're late already.'

As I hurried out, I caught, out of the corner of my eye, the briefest glimpse of what Alison was removing from her bag. A small black and white photograph with a blurry image on it.

A scan.

Or, as I preferred to think of it, entrapment.

13

Billy Randall had chosen a seat at the window upstairs in Starbucks, a part of heaven I rarely venture into because of my vertigo. It gave him a perfect view of Botanic Avenue and No Alibis. It was fortunate indeed that I'd left the shop ahead of Jeff, otherwise Billy would have seen us together and our carefully thought-out plan to tape the coming exchange would have been spoiled. As it was, he was not quite alone either. A bodyguard sat at the next table. He didn't have a badge or anything, but there was no mistaking him. Cropped hair, steroids, black suit, earpiece and watching me like a hawk. Billy himself was wearing a crumpled black suit. No tie. His shirt was pink. He was unshaven yet smelt of Calvin Klein aftershave. I recognised it because one day I spent eight hours at the corner pharmacy familiarising myself with all the different brands they had on sale and now it had paid off in spades. I heard the pharmacist committed suicide a while back. Business can be tough.

Billy Randall didn't stand, but he did offer me his hand. I hesitated. I don't like shaking hands at the best of times, but I didn't want to get off on the wrong foot. His fingers were damp and pudgy and I squeezed them with the enthusiasm of a vegetarian being forced to massage half a pound of pork sausages. There was a vague outline of a tattoo running across his knuckles: 'LOVE', it said. I glanced at his other hand. Those knuckles bore the legend: 'HAT'. His little finger was missing. I couldn't help but stare at it. Or not at it. At the space. The stump. And wonder what had happened. I wasn't sure if it qualified him as disabled, or if it would have stopped him becoming a professional tennis player, or golfer, or mountain climber, but it certainly would have put a family of five finger puppets into mourning.

'This is some fucking fuck-up, isn't it?' said Billy.

'Yes,' I said.

'Here, I got you an espresso.'

He pushed a cup and saucer across the table. I thanked him and tried not to look at it. It would interfere with my Starbucks schedule if I even inhaled. I'd have go back to the start of the menu. As I sat opposite him, I quietly moved it to one side.

'Mr Randall . . .' I began, but he immediately cut in.

'Some Christmas that was, taken away from my wife and family in the dead of night. My youngest thought she could hear Santa Claus moving around downstairs, but it was the fucking Murder Squad. Took the door off its hinges. Still, I'm insured.'

He laughed. The bodyguard laughed. I laughed too, because sometimes toadying helps. Billy continued laughing, right up to the point where he stopped abruptly and snapped out: 'So what're we going to do?'

'We?'

'Sure, we. Aren't we in this together?'

'Well, technically . . .'

'Someone's trying to stitch us up. And technically I'm still employing you.'

'Well actually . . .'

'Well actually I haven't paid you, so you're still being employed by me, and it's up to me if I change the parameters. You should check your employment law.' He suddenly clicked his fingers at me. 'What's that old saying . . . about the piper . . . ?'

'The . . . piper . . . ?'

'The piper . . .' He clicked them again. 'The piper . . .'

'Peter Piper pilked . . . ?'

'No.'

'Peter Piper picked a pelk . . .'

'No.'

'Peter Piper picked a peck of peckled . . .'

'No.'

'Peter Piper picked a peck of pickled peppers . . .'

'No . . .'

'Peter Piper picked a peck of pickled peppers. Did Peter Piper pick a peck of pickled peppers? If Peter

Piper picked a peck of pickled peppers, where's the peck of pickled peppers Peter Piper—'

'Will you just . . . shut the fuck . . . *up*?!' Billy Randall was staring at me: 'Christ!' He lowered his voice as two new customers sat down at the table immediately behind me. I caught their reflection in the window. It was Jeff. And Alison. Also I heard Jeff whisper loudly, 'Which one is the record button?' Billy Randall leaned a little closer. 'What I mean about the piper is, he who pays the piper calls the tune, *capiche*?'

'Technically, it's *capisce* . . .'

'Just . . .'

'It's important to . . .'

'Listen to . . .'

'Because misunderstand—'

'QUIET. Listen to me. I am a very rich man. Rich men have enemies. I am being implicated in a double murder. I am innocent. And as the police are doing the implicating, I can't run to them for help. I need you to find out who is really responsible for these murders. I need you to bring them to justice. That is what you do, right?'

I looked at him. He was right. It was what I did.

I had sworn never again to get involved in cases that were in any way dangerous, that even hinted at murder or violence. I would concentrate exclusively on safe little puzzles, almost like animated crosswords, where ultimately it didn't matter if you solved them, but you got a nice little glow if you did. Something to while away a winter's evening with one hand while mopping up your mother's drool with the other. But here I was, within six weeks of that declaration, once again implicated in murder, and yet again through absolutely no fault of my own. Alison had hurled me into the maelstrom last time by insisting on breaking into the mysteriously shuttered detective agency next door and discovering the dead body of its owner; this time I had merely tried to track down a couple of vandals. Now I was going to have to find my own way out of it. If Billy Randall wanted to maintain the charade of me being his employee then that was fine with me, but I would be working to my own agenda.

'I said, that is what you do, right?'

'What?'

'I said . . . Do you by any chance have a short attention span?'

'I was thinking about the case.'

'Oh – I like that. You've got tunnel vision. I'm a bit like that with my business. You know, I think we're quite alike.'

Behind me, Alison snorted.

'I think,' he continued, 'that once we set our mind to solving a problem, we don't let anything stop us, we're super-focused. That's how I built my business, and I'll be damned if I'm going to let anyone take me down, and that's what this is about: someone wants in, and the only way they think they can do that is by framing me for this, because they know they can't beat me at business, I've got it all sewn up. So what do you say, are we a team?'

He held out his pork fingers to me.

I squeezed them again.

'Sucker,' said Alison, and we both turned to her. She made an elaborate show of tickling Jeff. 'I *am not* a sucker,' she giggled, 'you're the sucker!' Jeff squirmed away as she attacked him again.

Billy Randall shook his head. 'Young love, eh?'

14

Before I started the interrogation, I told him I'd need him to be completely honest, to answer each and every question without asking why, to show patience and courtesy, and most importantly, in order to get me back on track, he had to get me a caramel macchiato. He agreed to these conditions, except for a variation on the last, by which I mean he sent his bodyguard down to get it. Nobody tried to assassinate him while he was gone.

I said, 'So these guys, did you kill them?'

'No, don't be daft.'

'But the police think you did. What did they say?'

'They? *Him*. A DI Robinson. My solicitor says he's a law unto himself. He says the other detectives have a nickname for him. They call him Mr Marple. He's like a pernickety old woman. He said that when he entered there was blood everywhere, looked like a real slaughterhouse, but one thing that caught his eye was the computer, still switched on, with YouTube on the screen and paused on a video of my billboard being defaced. He said it didn't take a genius to work out that the victims were responsible for the graffiti. I mean, Christ, that was enough to haul me in? If there'd been a video of Kylie Minogue on the screen, would they have lifted her?' Billy shook his head. 'I should be so lucky.'

'And that's why they arrested you?'

Billy looked down at his coffee and added quietly, 'Well, that and the fact that I did go round and visit them.'

'Okay. Right. When was this? And why?'

'The morning after you sent me their address. See, most people in my position, they'd call the lawyers in, threaten them with this or that. I'm not like that. Don't get me wrong, I'm not an easy touch or anything, but I prefer to see if we can work something out. Charm them, you know what I mean? So we went round . . .'

'We?'

'Me and Charlie Hawk here.' He nodded across at his bodyguard. Charlie winked. 'I don't go anywhere without Charlie.'

'You came to see me without him.'

'He was waiting outside. Stopping your customers. You'll note that nobody else entered the whole time I was there.'

I let that one pass. 'But you went to see these guys

with your security guard. Might that not have been perceived as threatening?'

'No. He's very polite and friendly. More like a chauffeur or personal assistant. Which he is.'

Charlie gave me the thumbs-up. He still looked like a thug.

'So what'd they do when they saw who it was?'

'Surprised. People generally are, when they meet me in the flesh. But not unduly disturbed. They invited me in.'

'Charlie too?'

'Yes. But I suggested he wait outside.'

'Having established the threat.'

'Of course not.'

'And what was it like inside?'

'Jumbled. Run-down. I suppose, like a student house. They sat me down, got me a cup of tea. And then, bold as brass, they asked what they could do for me.'

'Lose your temper?'

'No. *No*. I just wanted them to know that we were coming from the same place, you know what I mean? Same roots. I pulled myself up by my bootstraps, but I grew up on the streets just like they did. I am a common man, and I work for the common man. I asked them why they were attacking one of their own, why they felt the need to put a cock on my head and film it and make me a laughing stock all over the world.'

'And what did they say?'

'Because I was there. Like—'

'Everest.'

'Yes. Exactly. No apology, no vendetta, no anything. I said to them, so you just did it for badness, and they said no, for a laugh. I said, do you not care if people get hurt? And they said, what people? I said, me, my wife, my children, my business. And they said all they did was draw a cock on my head and again I asked them why, and they said, 'cos you're a dickhead. They started laughing, and they wouldn't stop. I think they were on drugs.'

'So you got angry.'

'No. Not at all.'

'So you called Charlie in.'

'I didn't do anything.'

'You just took it on the chin.'

'What could I do? I said I hoped they would have been more co-operative and they'd given me no choice but to call my legal people in. They just kept laughing.'

'And then what?'

'Then nothing. They were rolling around the place. I thanked them for their time and I let myself out.'

'And Charlie went back later and beat them to death.'

'Not that I'm aware. Charlie?'

'Not me, boss.'

Billy looked at me. 'See?'

I said to Charlie: 'Has DI Robinson spoken to you too?'

'Marple? Sure.' Charlie shrugged. 'Seemed perfectly happy.'

Billy Randall talked some more about how important he was, how he didn't believe in violence, how he came up with the idea of using his own face on the billboards after vacationing in America, how he loved being able to shake things up in the travel industry, how his children had burst into tears the first time they'd seen the cock-headed man, how his office kept getting calls from newspapers and television stations wanting to do stories on the cock-headed man . . .

'Are you even listening?' Billy asked.

'Yes, of course.'

'You've got a kind of far-away look in your eyes.'

Alison snorted.

'Just thinking.'

'Well, that's good. Because you need to get the thinking cap on and get this sorted as soon as you can. Whoever set me up, damn sure they're going to find some way to exploit it, and sooner rather than later. The court of perception is not a kind one, sunshine. If it gets as far as the internet that I've been questioned about this, it'll be the end of me. I want this sorted. Twenty-four hours a day if you have to, *capiche*?'

'*Capisce.*'

He squinted at me. 'You're an odd one, aren't you? But I kind of like that. Here.' He reached into his jacket and withdrew a manila envelope. He flicked it against his fingers, then laid it flat on the table and pushed it across to me. 'First instalment.'

I looked at it.

'From here on in, sunshine,' said Billy, leaning forward, 'we're partners.'

'From here on in, sunshine, we're partners,' Alison mimicked, trying to hug me while letting loose with a witchy cackle. I recoiled. She stood awkwardly for a moment before backing into a chair and sitting. Jeff pulled up another chair. I had made them wait to join me until Billy Randall and Charlie had climbed into a Jag parked opposite and driven away.

As Alison sat, she nodded down at the envelope. 'Well?'

'No.'

'Look at it. Open it.'

'Go on,' said Jeff, 'open it.'

'If I open it, it'll be like . . .'

'Being paid to do a job,' said Alison.

'Open it,' said Jeff.

'Open it, go on, look at it, it's so thick.' Alison wrinkled her nose coquettishly. 'I like it thick.'

'So do I,' said Jeff.

We both looked at him. He seemed impervious.

'I *can't*. Look, last time we agreed a fee, I did the work, I invoiced him. But a brown envelope stuffed with cash, that's just . . . under the counter, shady. He can't just buy me . . .'

'He can buy *me*,' said Alison. She snatched the envelope up before I could stop her. Jeff leaned over eagerly. Alison sat back, holding it as far away from either of us as she could, before peeking inside. Her eyes widened. 'Holy shit!' she said. 'This is going to buy baby a lot of fucking bootees!'

Jeff started laughing, and then stopped. He looked at her, and then at me, and then at her. You could hear the cogs labouring. He started to say something. Then stopped. Alison turned the envelope so I could see. There was certainly a thick wodge of notes.

'Blood money,' I said.

'Blood money – would you ever get off your high horse? *Blood money.*'

'If he turns out to be the killer, and I accepted money from him, how's that going to look in a court of law?'

'*If.* Didn't he say he didn't do it? Isn't he only trying to prove his innocence? Aren't you just doing a job? Do you think a frickin' lawyer defending someone is going to refuse to be paid even though he bloody surely knows if his client is guilty or not? Jesus, man, make hay while the sun shines.'

It was a poor choice of words, given that she knew how badly I suffer from hay fever. I said firmly: 'Put the money down.'

'Down?'

'On the table. Nobody touches it until we know more about the case.'

'I like the *we*,' said Alison.

'I like the *we* too,' said Jeff.

'We're like *The Avengers*,' said Alison.

'Or *The Champions*,' said Jeff.

'Slip of the tongue,' I said. 'Now put . . . the money . . . *down* . . .'

'You look all serious,' said Alison.

'I am all serious.'

'I think I like you like that.'

'Just put it down.'

Alison replaced it on the table. She raised an eyebrow at Jeff. I took the napkin that had come with the caramel macchiato and used it to lift the envelope and place it in my jacket pocket. I nodded to myself, satisfied, then looked at Alison, who was brushing a crisp new twenty-pound note across her fingers.

Jeff giggled. 'How'd you do that?'

'Nimble fingers. Comes from working with jewellery. Also, my dad was a professional pickpocket.'

'Was he?'

'Nah, don't be daft.' She held it out to me. I went to take it. She pulled it away. 'Team?'

I sighed. She held it out again. I grabbed for it. She whisked it away and transferred it to her other hand.

'Team?'

Jeff yanked it away from her and passed it to me.

'*Thanks* for that,' Alison whined.

'Thanks for telling me you were pregnant,' said Jeff.

'It's not *yours*,' said Alison.

'How do you know?' asked Jeff.

Alison made a face.

I had to admit, if only to myself, that there was something vaguely comforting about the three of us sitting there in Starbucks. I loathed Alison because she was trying to blackmail me and also because of

how she tickled Jeff when she knew how pathologic-
ally jealous I was; and I despised Jeff, really just for
being Jeff. But there, in heaven, and about to order
something fresh in my eternal menu quest, it was all
surprisingly . . . nice. Yes, I felt a little feverish; of
course my tinnitus continued to resound like a permanent air-raid warning in a neighbouring town, and of
course the aches of rheumatoid arthritis continued to
plague me, but there was a definite feeling of excitement coming upon me, which could only partially be
put down to my growing addiction to caffeine. Despite
my preference for soft cases that offered no threat,
there was a tiny part of me that loved the challenge
of taking on something meatier, and *The Case of the
Cock-Headed Man* had certainly developed into that. I
wanted to solve it. Alison had already proved how my
DNA had come to be in the victims' house, which was
really my only connection to the actual murders, and
there had been no indication that I was in any danger
at all. The only person in danger *here* was Billy Randall,
and really that was more of a threat to his business
than to his actual person. So what was there to lose?
I had my team assembled, I had my customers on
standby, I had the internet, I had Starbucks and this
time around I had virtually unlimited supplies of
Vitolink.

Suddenly I was all fired up. Damn it, I *was* going
to solve this!

And blood money be damned!

I held up the twenty Alison had removed from the

envelope and which Jeff and I had both touched: impregnated with all of our fingerprints and DNA, it was now a symbol of our unity. We would become Avengers! We would become Champions! And together, though led by me, we would track down the killers of Jimbo Carson and Ronny Clegg!

'Jeff,' I cried, reaching the note out to him, 'go down and get three mint mocha chip frappuccinos!'

He looked truly startled. He stood, hesitantly took the twenty from my grasp, then began to nervously back away, convinced he was being set up.

'Christ,' said Alison, 'you're living on the edge a bit.'

'Jeff!'

He froze at the top of the stairs and turned slowly. 'What?'

'Get a receipt.'

15

'Okay,' Alison said, 'before we start, I think it's important that we have some ground rules, like not interr—'

'Just let me interrupt for a moment,' I said, 'because
while yes I agree that we should have ground rules,
I think it's important that it comes from me the fact
that I think we should have ground rules, rather
than you saying that you think we should have
ground rules. Because much as I like the idea of us
being a team, in reality that doesn't work. You need
someone to be in charge, and I'm the one with the
track record in investigating, I'm the expert, I'm
the one getting paid, and at the end of the day I'm the
one who'll carry the can if it all goes wrong, so I
think we should agree that I'm in charge and that
I get to say that I think it's important that we have
ground rules.'

'You just want a couple of gofers,' Alison said sullenly.

'No, I want you to be my assistant. And Jeff to be the gofer.'

'Cheers,' said Jeff.

'I don't mind being your assistant,' said Alison, 'if you listen to me, if you take me seriously, if you don't dismiss everything I say, if you're not sarcastic, if you don't belittle me.'

'Absolutely. Now be a good girl and pop down and get me another mint mocha.'

'And one for me too,' added Jeff.

'You're funny.' And before I could say anything, she immediately followed it with, '*So's your face.*' She shook her head. 'This isn't going to work.'

'It'll be fine,' I said, 'as long as we agree on the ground rules, and I think you just hit the nail on the head, or lots of nails on the head, or their heads. We listen, we're not sarcastic, we don't belittle.'

'Unless,' said Jeff, 'it's, like, really, *really* stupid.'

Silence descended.

Alison raised an eyebrow. Jeff yawned.

'Well,' said Alison, '*lead.*'

So I did.

For the moment, and until the facts suggested otherwise, I was going with the theory that Billy Randall was not physically responsible for the murders. He liked to depict himself as the nice guy going round to charm Jimbo and Ronny, and then, when he got nowhere, politely excusing himself. But the first time I'd met him, in the shop, he'd been spitting marbles, and even in general conversation he was quite combustible. So he had a temper on him, and definitely a big ego, but these defects didn't make him a killer. And just because Charlie looked like one, it didn't mean he was either. But I needed to find out more about both of them, because even though they might be innocent of the murders, it seemed to me that there had to be some kind of a link, that Billy's paranoia about his business rivals might not be completely without foundation. It also just seemed too pat, too simple, to say that Jimbo and Ronny had targeted Billy just *because he was there*. I understood that young people liked taking the piss out of 'the man', that the YouTube generation loved these kinds of viral annihilations, but in a World Wide Web sense, Billy Randall was very small fry indeed. A campaign against McDonald's, something that would have resonance from Istanbul to Quebec, I could understand. Picking on a small fish like Billy Randall once might be understandable, but to take it to such a huge audience, to keep reposting the video every time it was taken down, felt like more than just a practical joke. Billy Randall had crossed them in some way and they were out for revenge. *Or*, there was no previous connection and they had hatched this scheme to extort money from him; they had calculated that Billy Randall's fortune was intrinsically tied to his image, and that he might pay up to protect it. Perhaps the cock-headed publicity had grown much more quickly than they had imagined and they were now themselves powerless to stop it. Another possibility was that Billy Randall was a red herring. Both Billy and Alison had mentioned that Jimbo and Ronny were into dope; that meant dealers. Or they were dealers themselves. In that part of the city the drugs trade was usually controlled by paramilitary gangs. And the painted-over mural on the gable end of the house suggested at the very least sympathy for or a connection to such paramilitaries. So inter-gang strife. Unpaid debts. A drug deal gone wrong. Or, more mundanely, they worked as painters and decorators – could their day job have brought them into contact with their future killers? Had they discovered something that somebody didn't want them to know? Was there an argument over a bill that got out of hand, a dispute over a pastel shade or a second coat?

Alison said, 'Are you finished?'

'What?' I blinked at her. 'Did I say all that out loud?'

'*Duh*. Yes.'

I glanced at Jeff. He was struggling to keep his eyes open.

'Sorry,' I said, 'I was . . .'

'No, I agree with everything you say,' said Alison. 'But we still don't actually know anything. It's all ifs and—'

'Conjecture.'

'So we need to find out. Not sit on our arses.'

'But it's what I do.'

'Yes, I know that. You're like a cross between Stephen Hawking and Ironside.'

'Thanks.'

'I mean it kindly.'

We both looked at Jeff. He was now snoring gently.

Alison took my hand. 'We have to get on better, for the sake of Rory.'

I laughed and tried to take my hand back. She held firm. She has a good grip, although I do have arthritic joints and wasting muscles.

'Okay,' she said, letting go. 'Plenty of time for that. Let's concentrate on the case. An action plan. We need to find out more about Ronny and Jimbo. We should go to their funerals. It's a well-known fact that murderers usually turn up at their victims' funerals; it's a kind of compulsion, isn't it?'

'In bad movies, yes.'

'Is this the way it's going to be: you shoot down every idea I have and yet expect us to champion your own?'

'No. Not necessarily. Likewise, I don't see why I should have to support every bad idea you have just to give the impression that I'm being impartial and unselfish. Besides, if we were to go to the funerals, Marple is going to be there, and if he sees us, that will only reinforce his conviction that we're somehow involved.'

'Well that's his worry, surely? We're trying to crack this case ourselves.' Alison smiled slyly. 'If you didn't like that one, you're going to *hate* this one.'

I sighed. 'What.'

'We need to take a look at the murder scene. Their house.'

'No.'

'No?'

'No.'

'Just no, not even a why?'

'No, Alison, because last time we got into all kinds of trouble.'

'And it helped us solve the case.'

'Last time we just about got away with it because it was right next door to us, there *was* an odd smell, and that was a quasi-legitimate reason to go hoking about. *This* would be burglary *and* contaminating a crime scene. And it's in a dodgy part of town. It's all kinds of things.'

'Makes going to the funeral seem a lot more appealing, eh?'

'No.'

'Look, I was there before. They worked out of their home, so all the paperwork relating to their business is going to be there. Think how much fun you can have going through that looking for clues. You'll be in your element.'

'No.'

'One or the other.'

'Neither.'

'So it's your way or the highway.'

'No. Yes, in this case. And also, I am not calling any child of mine Rory.'

It was out, when I meant it to stay in. Of *course* she realised the importance of it immediately. She smiled.

'You saw what I did there,' I said.

'You acknowledged that it's your child.'

'It was a slip of the tongue.'

She was still beaming. 'Do you want to see the scan?'

'No. If you insist.'

She removed the scan from her handbag and held it out to me. Just as I was about to grasp it, she yanked it away.

'Cemetery or house?'

'Neither. Don't be childish.'

'Okay.'

She held it out. Then pulled it away just as I touched it.

'Choose one.'

'No.'

'Choose one or the other.'

'I said no.'

She showed me the scan, but facing away from me. 'Do you not want to hold your son? Rory.'

'Just give me the scan.'

She sighed. 'Spoilsport.' She held it out again. Then whipped it away. 'Cemetery *and* house, both of them. Now I'm playing hardball.' She teased me with it again.

'I will jump on you and pin you down,' I warned.

'In your condition? You'd break.'

'I have one good thrust left in me.'

'Nope, I think I had that one. So what's it gonna be?'

She taunted me with it, but this time as I made a grab and she jerked away, Jeff's arm suddenly shot up and he ripped it out of her hand. 'Jesus!' he snapped. 'Will you two give over? You're like two kids! Here – does this help?'

He tore the scan in half.

Then again.

And again.

It was only small to start with.

He threw confetti *made out of my child* into the air and let it rain down over us. 'Happy now?'

We both just stared at him. For about five seconds.

'You . . .' I said.

'You . . .' said Alison.

'You . . .' I said.

'You . . .' said Alison, and then burst into tears.

I took her hand and glared at Jeff. 'You've just . . . torn up . . . the first scan . . . the only scan . . . of our baby . . . you stupid . . . stupid . . . *shit.*'

'Oh,' said Jeff.

'You're sacked,' I said.

'Now fuck off,' said Alison.

It was a rare instance of unity in our relationship.

It couldn't possibly last.

16

Jimbo and Ronny's bodies having not yet been released to their respective families for burial meant that for the moment breaking into their house was the only one of Alison's suggestions that I could reluctantly go along with. It was the only way I could think of getting her to stop crying. She appreciated the gesture, and also the fact that I now had to organise the January sale at No Alibis without Jeff to assist me. I told her I wasn't aware that I was having a January sale and she said I was now. She had ideas for the business, she said. There could easily have been a fight, with slaps and screams, at that point, but I thought it better to let snivelling dogs lie.

Which meant that that very night, with the Mystery Machine being adjudged too stand-outish, we drove back to Marston Court in Alison's Beetle. It wasn't exactly blendy-inny either, but at least it didn't have

Murder Is Our Business etched on the side. If it had been up to Billy Randall, he would probably have corrupted my slogan to *Murder Is Our Business, So It Is, Mate* to better connect with his people.

We parked around the corner from the crime scene and sat in darkness. The street lights were broken. Typical. I don't mind the dark, it's a great equaliser. But here at Marston, there was something quite oppressive about it. Perhaps it was the images of dead soldiers staring down at us from the gable wall, or the fact that they were hiding something more sinister, both within and without. It was the area too. In the old days Mother, even if she could hardly afford to eat, would have spent half the day on her hands and knees polishing her front step; around here they expected the Government to polish their steps for them. Poverty these days was not being able to afford all of the premium channels.

'You're very cynical and such a snob,' Alison said.

'Did I say that out loud?'

'Of course. Sometimes you need an editing facility.'

'So does your face.'

'Please don't start.'

'I'm just saying. It used to be that religion was the opiate of the masses. Now it appears to be Sky.'

She sighed.

'In my day,' I continued, 'watching the Christmas lights wink on and off was about all the entertainment we could afford. And they were next door's lights.'

'Not *your day*. Your house. Your weird house with your lunatic mother and mysterious father. Still, at least you emerged unscathed.'

She was, obviously, trying to wind me up, and she was good at it, but I was too nervous to take the bait, although admittedly, it's sometimes difficult to tell the difference between nerves and my irritable bowel syndrome.

It was a little after ten p.m. For a while there had been a gang of teenagers on the opposite corner, but they dispersed without dragging us from our car and taking it for a joyride. Then Rottweilers and boxers got walked by asexual figures in puffa coats and hoods. There was an interesting contradiction here as well, in that each time one of the animals stopped to do its business, their owners very responsibly produced plastic bags to pick up the poo. But of the four we observed, two of them merely walked a little further along, checked to see if anyone was watching, then chucked the plastic bag either into the closest garden or thrust it into a hedge.

Alison was quite outraged by this, and would have been out of the car remonstrating with them about their lack of public responsibility if we hadn't been about to commit burglary on a slaughterhouse.

There was no 'right' time for doing it, or right method. We would try and gain access from the rear. Three things were in our favour. It wasn't the sort of area where *any* houses had burglar alarms, the lack of functioning street lights and the fact that locals were quite used to the sound of breaking glass.

'A snob *and* patronising,' said Alison.

There was no crime-scene tape. The experts had done their work and left. The house was in complete darkness as we approached. We moved along the gable wall and into an alley. A brittle-looking wooden fence hid the back yard from prying eyes, but the door in it wasn't locked. We slipped inside and closed it behind us. We crossed damp and cracked concrete flags. I pulled the sleeve of my jumper down over my hand, and tried the back door.

'Optimist,' said Alison.

It was locked. She opened her bag and took out a hammer.

'Christ,' I said.

'What?'

'That's what's called going equipped for theft. They could arrest us *now*. Without the hammer we can just say we're lost or curious.'

'Uhuh,' she said.

She lined the flat end of the hammer up against a small square of glass parallel to the door handle and gave it the gentlest tap. I could tell by the slight cracking sound that she'd broken the pane, but it did not shatter or fall. She was able to gently prise the glass on two sides of an invisible crack apart, and then remove both from their frame.

'You've done this before,' I observed.

Alison shook her head. 'I am practised,' she said,

'at peeling eggs. It's the same principle. The less violence the better.'

I put my covered hand through the gap and felt for the lock; a moment later we slipped into the kitchen.

We were a good team, I had always thought that.

Alison switched on the kitchen light.

'Shouldn't we just use a torch or . . .'

'Nope.'

She opened the kitchen door and entered the living room. Seeing that the curtains were already drawn, she switched on the main light.

'Isn't . . .'

'If it looks like we're sneaking around, we'll be rumbled; this way it looks like we're supposed to be here. People will think we're police.'

'But the police won't think we're police.'

'Pessimist.'

There was a very strong smell of disinfectant. It reminded me of a hospital. I am allergic to hospitals. I began to gag. Alison gave me a disdainful look and started hoking round. From what we knew of the murders, I had expected there to be bloodstains everywhere, perhaps chalk outlines and dusting powder for fingerprints, but the room appeared much as it had in Alison's photograph – cluttered, a little untidy, but pretty much as if someone had gone to bed without tidying up, rather than the scene of a savage double murder. It was a relief. Blood makes me faint, as do severely cold temperatures, rotting fruit, tulips and injustice.

Alison tutted as she moved to the corner of the room. There was a desk with a leather swivel chair and beside it a small filing cabinet. The top of the desk was notable for being clear but for a dust-free rectangle in its centre.

'Is your master plan in tatters because they've taken the computer?' I asked.

'Shut up.' She reached for the top drawer of the filing cabinet. She pulled it open. It was empty.

'Is there a plan B?' I asked.

'You're the big private detective, what's your frickin' plan?'

'Well,' I said.

'Thought not,' said Alison.

'Well, actually. I'm comparing what I already knew from your photo with what I find here. Apart obviously from the absence of Jimmy and Ronny and the computer.'

As she joined me, I moved off to the kitchen.

'So?' she called after me. 'I don't see any difference. And what're you looking for in there and has it anything to do with what you think is missing in here? Mystery Man, are you listening to me?'

I came back into the doorway. 'I haven't sneezed.'

'What?'

'What am I allergic to?'

'*Everything.*'

'When we were out the back, there was no smell of pee. Usually there is. Damp weather like we have tonight usually makes it more pungent.'

'What are you . . . ?'

'And then in the kitchen, no bowl on the floor, that's fair enough, a neighbour might be looking after him, but you'd expect there to be some food in the cupboards. Do you see what I'm driving at?'

Alison gave me a look. 'The Jack Russell?'

'Yes, the Jack Russell. I'm allergic to dogs, you know that.'

Alison folded her arms. 'Oh this will be good, I'm sure. Wait, let me try and second-guess you. The Jack Russell being a witness to the murders is now on the run scared for his life. We have to bring him in so he can identify the murderer by barking once for yes that's him and twice for he looks a bit like that but not quite, maybe try him with a beard. Or maybe Marple has him banged up in some canine Guantanamo Bay; maybe he's being denied a doggy lawyer; maybe the late lamented Jeff ought to start a campaign to get him released.'

'Finished?'

'Yes. Okay. So how does the bloody dog being missing contribute to our understanding of the case?'

I shrugged. 'I was only pointing out a *difference*. I don't see that it contributes anything to the solving of the case.'

'Right. Brilliant. Do you not think we'd be better spending our time . . .' She sighed. 'You are *so* annoying. And FYI, Mystery Man, the Jack Russell is dead.'

'How do . . . ?'

'He is no more. He is an ex-Jack Russell.'

Her eyebrow rose ever so slightly and a glint appeared in her eye. She was challenging me. For those few moments the murders no longer mattered. How Alison, with her inferior intellect and intimate knowledge only of bangles and comics, could have deduced the fact of the dog's demise based on one photograph and our current location defied logic. I quickly reviewed the evidence and immediately concluded that I had, almost literally, been barking up the wrong tree. Forensics officers had hoovered up every single doggy hair, which is why I hadn't sneezed. Yet there was no dog bowl in the kitchen, no dog food in the cupboards. Outside, there was no smell of dog pee. The only evidence for the existence of the Jack Russell was its photograph. It therefore seemed obvious that I had misread the photograph. The sign of a good detective is one who isn't afraid to re-examine the evidence and change his mind.

'The dog was already dead,' I said. Alison looked disappointed, but not, I think, surprised. 'That was a photograph of a stuffed Jack Russell.'

'Correctimundo.' They bought it at a car boot sale just for a laugh. Everything about them was a laugh, right up to the point where they got bludgeoned to death.'

'Okay. Dead dog. Let's file that under irrelevant. Can we go now?'

'Go? Man, dear, I've hardly started.'

And she was serious. I had to admire her commitment, though I didn't share it. I didn't like being in this house of the dead, in a dangerous neighbourhood where they would beat you to a pulp first and probably not ask questions later. My stomach cramped suddenly and I winced.

'I think I need to . . .' I thumbed upstairs.

'Just like a burglar. You do that. I'll concentrate on evidence-gathering.'

Although it wasn't in itself sarcastic, there was a sarcastic way about her that wasn't attractive. She was understandably in love with me, but that would wane, given time and experience. If the child proved to be mine – and I had every intention of seeking scientific confirmation – and presuming that the courts would sympathise with her, then I would have to find a way of getting it away from her. No Alibis was not neccssarily tied to Belfast; there were cities all over the world that were lacking a mystery bookshop. It would be just a question of finding the right one. It should enjoy a temperate climate, it would not be prone to revolution, its inhabitants would speak English as a first language, and it must not have an extradition agreement with the United Kingdom, which probably ruled out Douglas, Isle of Man. I was thinking about other possible locations as I sat on the dead men's toilet upstairs, looking down at a set of bathroom scales where their dead men's feet had once rested, with their dead men's dressing gowns hanging on the door, and their dead men's toothbrushes in a paste-encrusted glass by the sink but level with my eyes, and I was humming 'The Battle Hymn of the Republic' quite loudly to cover up the sounds. But the end of it coincided with hearing the pad of footsteps on the wooden floor of the landing outside, and immediately I regretted not closing the door fully and locking it. It is something I never do at home and rarely do when using the facilities in other locations because of my claustrophobia, but there and then I did not wish Alison to see me in such repose; it would be many years into our unworkable marriage before she would be allowed to see *that*.

My first thought as the steps grew closer was: *Whatever she's found, no piece of evidence is this important*, and I was already crying, 'Please don't . . . !' as the door was flung open.

My second thought was: *You're not Alison*.

A woman stood there.

A woman in a floral dressing gown.

A woman in a floral dressing gown and at least nine months pregnant, with sleep hair and bleary eyes, looking stunned, and horrified, and screaming: 'What the hell are you doing?!'

And I said the only thing that came to mind.

'A poo.'

17

I hate showdowns and confrontations and loud arguments; I am of the school that sees nothing wrong with throwing the quilt back over your head and waiting for a problem to go away. Burying one's head in the sand *works* for me, and look, here I am, a survivor. Other people will *sort it out*. Suffice to say I overcame my shyness and claustrophobia sufficiently to slam the door shut in the madwoman's face, and had the wherewithal to lock it and return to my throne and stretch across to turn the taps of both the sink and the bath on full and then clamp my hands over my ears to further drown out the screaming from without while I recommenced humming 'The Battle Hymn of the Republic'. Alison would deal with it. She is like that, reliable, a team player; she was in love with me, the father of her child; she wouldn't bolt out of the back door at the first sign of trouble, the way I would. She would rise to the occasion, instantly concoct a story believable enough to calm the woman down, take her downstairs, make her a cup of tea, and from the state of her, probably deliver her baby as well. All the while the woman would be blubbering and ranting that there's a nutter having a shit in my toilet, and Alison's lovely calming voice would be saying if he's going to have a shit, that's probably the best place for him to have it, and soon they'd be laughing and all would be well with the world.

I gave it twenty minutes. I switched off the taps and cautiously ventured out. There were voices downstairs. I sat on the stairs halfway down and tried to make out what they were saying. I couldn't. I tapped on the door at the bottom of the stairs and said, 'Is it all right to come in?'

Alison said, 'Yes.'

Alison and the pregnant woman were sitting on the sofa. They both looked like they'd been crying. The woman looked at me warily. I thought it better if I didn't attempt an explanation or an apology.

Alison said, 'This is my partner in solving crime.'

I nodded. There was no point in taking issue with *that*, yet. The woman said, 'I'm sorry, so I am, I didn't mean to walk in on you like that.'

See? Wait long enough, and they almost always apologise to *you*.

'That's okay,' I said.

'Pat's Jimbo's girlfriend,' said Alison. 'She's heartbroken. She's due any time.'

'I live across the way, so I do. I miss him so much, I wanted to sleep in his bed, so I did. I had a key, but I couldn't sleep, so I took some sleeping pills, too many, out like a light until . . . well, I thought youse were finished with your investigatin' . . .'

'We never sleep,' I said.

Alison rolled her eyes. 'You woke her up with your clumpin' around, you big eejit. Pat's been telling me all about Jimbo and Ronny, and wait till you hear. Go on, tell him.'

'Well I told it all to your mates, so I did, but youse always want to hear it again.'

'Wait till you hear,' said Alison.

'Him and Ronny had this house for years, they were best mates, so they were, but we were gonna get married after this one was born.'

'Wait till you hear,' said Alison.

I said, 'Alison, without interruptions, please.'

'Okay. But wait till you hear.'

'I'm sorry,' I said, 'she's new. Please continue.'

She did. At length. I will spare you all the highways and byways, the roundabouts and the trunk roads and the dead ends and the no entries and the U-turns. She rattled on with her *so I do*s and *so he did*s peppering every sentence until I stopped hearing them at all; they became like dark matter between the relevant words, there but inaudible. She seemed like a good, down-to-earth woman, made miserable by the death of a loved one, but apt, in the way of traumatised widows and mothers, to view the departed through rose-tinted glasses.

Jimbo was her childhood sweetheart, Ronny part of the gang they all hung around in. They were into football and music and spent too much time messing at school to go into anything but the trades. They were good at their painting and decorating, but had their fingers in several pies, nothing too shady, Jack the lads really, anything for a laugh. Yes, they smoked a bit of dope. Were they dealers? Scumbags who'd sell crack to kids through the school fence? Course not. They were good drug-dealers, only supplying their mates. Were they paramilitaries or in with them? Only in the sense that everyone round here was, you had to be. But they never hurt anyone. And since peace broke out, all that has stopped, hasn't it? So why do you think somebody killed them? Don't know. Any enemies? Well . . .

'Wait'll you hear,' Alison said.

'I don't know about enemies,' said Pat. She had been twisting a damp piece of kitchen roll between her fingers and now it was starting to disintegrate, bits of it becoming attached to her dressing gown, other sodden fragments falling into the sofa and carpet where if they weren't sorted they would dry and become part of the fabric, but at the same time never quite belong, like Romanians. The compulsive cleaner in me wanted to get down on my hands and knees and clean it up, but the sadist in me wanted to force her to do it.

'I'm sorry?' said Pat.

'You're sorry . . . ?'

'You said *chains*,' said Alison.

'Sorry. Yes. The chain of evidence. Getting ahead of myself. Enemies, you were saying?'

'Not enemies. Just. What with the baby. And Christmas. We didn't have much money, and what we have we were trying to save for the little one, so we were. So we'd agreed, so we had, that we weren't going to buy each other presents. They said I was due after Christmas, so they did, and that would be the biggest present, wouldn't it? But Christmas Day Jimbo knocks on my door and he has a present for me all wrapped up. And I was furious because we'd said no presents, so we had. But he said it was only a little one and he brings it in and it's big, like, but I hadn't a clue and then I took the wrapping off and I didn't really know what to say. You know the way you maybe buy your girlfriend or maybe your baby like a cuddly toy? Well Jimbo'd gone and bought me this stuffed dog, but not like a softy one you'd buy in the toy shop; it was like . . . like you'd see in . . . like a museum or something. You know, *properly* stuffed. A real animal with its bits hoovered out and . . . *stuffed*. It was one of them . . .'

'Jack Russells,' said Alison. 'But wait'll you hear . . .'

'Well, I mean, like, I wasn't exactly, y'know, thrilled.'

'So . . . ?' I asked, not exactly thrilled myself.

Alison nodded encouragement to Pat. Pat dropped some more bits of kitchen roll on the carpet.

'So it happens, to Jimbo. And Ronny. And I'm in bits, and I don't get on great with my family anyway, and I didn't like that Jack Russell one bit, but since it happened, you know, like, it was the last thing Jimbo gave me, the last thing he touched, and so I was hugging it and kissing it and it slept in the bed with me . . .'

'A comfort,' I said.

'Yeah, and then I was back and forth to the police station; they wanted statements, and photos of Jimbo, and I had to do like a press conference appealing for information and all that, so I did. But I come back home yesterday and someone's gone and broken into my house, and they messed it up pretty awful and one of them – not that I know there was more than one – one of them did . . . well, he did . . . a dump on my bed . . .'

I held my hands up in mock innocence, but she was too busy tearing the remains of her kitchen roll to shreds to notice.

'That's why when I saw you . . . but that wasn't the worst. When they didn't find nothing valuable, what did they do, just for badness, they took my dog, they took my Jack.'

'They took her Jack,' said Alison.

'They took her Jack,' I repeated.

We walked away, pleased with our night's work.

As we got back into the Beetle Alison said, 'Well?'

'Well what?'

'Aren't you going to thank me?'

'For what?'

'Saving your arse. Literally.'

'I expected nothing less.'

Alison started the engine. And sighed. 'That's a compliment that isn't one. She came wailin' down those stairs like a banshee while you sat up there doing God knows what. I had to calm her down.'

'Okay. Much appreciated. What'd you do, slap her?'

'Yeah, right, that would have helped. In case you didn't notice, we did have something in common?'

'You and her?'

'No, me and the man in the moon. *Yes*, me and her.'

'What?'

'Take a wild guess?'

'Talk too much?'

'No.'

'Annoying? Untidy? Sarcastic? Self-obsessed? Overdramatic?' And then I had it. 'Pregnant?'

'The penny drops. Yes, *pregnant*, dummy. It was the only thing I could think of. We got talking about our babies. We compared scans.'

'You . . . ?'

'Uhuh.'

'But Jeff . . .'

'I had two.'

'You . . .'

'You're *so* easy, Mystery Man.'

18

I had always known Alison was devious – really it goes with the territory, being a woman, I mean; it's always been completely clear to me why they didn't call it *The One Face of Eve* – but I hadn't realised she would sink *so* low as to use the image of my son-to-be as a bargaining chip. Not only had she lied to me and misled me, forcing me to cross into a working-class area of the city in semi-darkness, she had also caused me to sack my right-hand idiot. Jeff had been wilfully stupid in tearing up the scan, but the fact that there was another copy somewhat lessened both the dreadfulness of it and the sincerity of Alison's anguished reaction. She lacked scruples. She was mean.

I fumed all the way home. She parked outside my house and switched off the engine. I reached for the door handle.

'So it's like that, is it?' she snapped. 'Oh get over yourself, would you? It was important to the case.'

'You got Jeff sacked.'

'Then phone him in the morning and tell him it was a misunderstanding, and he was still an arse tearing it up. You should thank me for using my initiative.'

'Thank you for using your initiative.'

'You're so fucking perfect, aren't you?'

I studied the cars thereabouts. There were no personalised number plates in view, which was a pity, because I felt the need. I had my nail for the scoring of cars with personalised number plates in my pocket. I had taken to carrying it with me on a more regular basis recently, instead of taking it out on special occasions. Despite their scarcity in this area, the general problem of expensive personalised number plates seemed to be growing, even though the world was spiralling ever more deeply into recession. It was a conundrum. My book sales were also immune to the recession. They were as low as ever.

She put a hand on my leg. 'Aren't you going to invite me in?'

'No.'

'You could rip my clothes off and ravage me. Or we could make toast. Whatever turns you on.'

'No.'

'So you're just going to huff.' I gave her a look. She took her hand back. 'You'd cut off your nose to spite your face, wouldn't you? When you could *have* me.

Look at me. I'm gorgeous. But I won't be for long.
Once the twins start getting bigger.'

I would not rise to the bait. Either physically or
mentally. I had a case to think through, new evidence
to evaluate. I got out. I closed the door behind me,
then crouched down and indicated for her to open
the window, but she just glowered, started the engine
and roared off.

I have been around detective fiction all of my life, and
there is very little of substance that I have not read. I
have also read most of the insubstantial, and plenty of
barely literate garbage that has no stantial at all.
Irrespective of the quality, however, people, including
the police themselves, quite often make the mistake of
thinking that there is a huge gap between fiction and
fact, but I have discovered many parallels and coinci-
dences and learned much about the realities of life and
crime through mystery fiction. Modern policing's
reliance on science, I have found, is often at the expense
of old-fashioned detective work. So much emphasis is
put on the likes of DNA that what we traditionally refer
to as 'clues' are often missed out. For example, I was
quite certain that DI Robinson didn't have a clue about
the missing Jack Russell. Of course, it could still mean
nothing. But it could just as easily mean *something*. With
a remote possibility of *everything*.

I phoned Alison at midnight. My loins were stirring, plus I had decided to forgive her. But she wouldn't
come over, and embarked instead on a revenge huff.

I knew it wasn't *that* serious because she didn't hang up. I think perhaps her loins were stirring as well but she was too up herself to give in to my temptations. So to dampen our mutual ardour I turned to the case.

'We probably shouldn't get too excited about it,' I said. 'It's a classic mistake in detective fiction – they become fixated on the McGuffin even though everyone plus their aunt knows it's a McGuffin. It's a lazy way to write, but sometimes the McGuffin's all you have. Get rid of the McGuffin and the whole bloody thing falls apart.' There was silence from the other end. 'Alison?'

'What.'

'You've gone quiet again.'

'What's a McGuffin?'

'Oh. Sorry.' I had forgotten. Her field of expertise was bangles. 'It's just like a thing that seems like it's really important, but ultimately isn't that important.'

'Like you.'

'Ho. Like, you know, in *The Maltese Falcon* where it's all about finding and holding on to this bird statue that you think must be dead important but isn't; it's just an excuse to go chasing about and to exchange some smart dialogue. Or like the top-secret plans in *The Thirty-Nine Steps*. Or the letters of transit in *Casablanca*. The government secrets in *North By Northwest*. The stamps in *Charade*. The case with glowing contents in *Kiss Me Deadly*. The—'

'I get the picture, Brainiac. Except, of course, this is real life.'

'All that means, Alison, is that we can't fast forward to find out if our McGuffin has any relevance to the murders. But at this moment in time it's all we have.'

'It *is* all we have. Okay, Sherlock, just to make sure we're on the same wavelength, which is, frankly, scary, we're thinking Jimbo gave Pat the Jack Russell not because he was all romantic, but because he wanted it out of the house, but not so far away that he couldn't get hold of it if he needed to? Right? So it's a stuffed animal, what's so important about it? Is it a favourite pet that they stole for a laugh? Or is it stuffed with something valuable? They were into drugs, weren't they? What about a Jack Russell stuffed with cocaine? We had a Jack Russell once, they're fucking manic, I wouldn't like to see one on cocaine.'

'Concentrate.'

'Right. The burglars at Pat's house. We have to presume there is no intrinsic value to a stuffed JR, so either they were specifically looking for it or they took it for badness. They're frustrated, nervous, probably drunk, they wreck the joint, one takes a dump on the bed, the other takes the JR and they either take it home with them or toss it over a hedge somewhere. *Or* they forced the whereabouts of the JR out of Jimbo or Ronny before they killed them, and then just waited their chance to nip in and get it, causing a mess to make it look like they were common or garden burglars. So far so good?'

'Not bad. But if you're leaning towards them going there with a purpose . . .'

'I am.'

'. . . and these are bad guys, murderers, and they very probably have criminal records so they'll have been careful not to have left fingerprints . . .'

'Agreed.'

'. . . then why would they leave a poo in the middle of Pat's bed?'

'Well maybe it's a warning. Like don't the Mafia . . . ?'

'Dead fish, or horses' heads. Yes. Untraceable. But you can trace a poo back to . . .'

'The pooer.'

'Unless . . .'

'They brought it with them. It's somebody else's poo.'

'They've covered their backsides.'

'If it was anyone with a criminal record, you could still trace it back to them, make a connection.'

'They would have thought of that. It has to be a random poo or a poo without a record. An innocent poo.'

'It's an awful lot of trouble to go to.'

'Which underlines how important the JR must be.'

'Or brings us back to them just being nervous burglars.' Alison sighed. 'She got rid of the poo. She wasn't to know it might have been vital evidence. You can't blame her. You don't want a strange poo hanging about your house. And certainly not on your bed. She burned the lot.'

The cogs turned.

Eventually I said, 'We've been thinking about para-militaries and drug-dealers because it's that neck of the woods, but let's not forget how we got into this.'

'Billy Randall.'

'Exactly. He employed me to find Jimbo and Ronny, and as soon as I do, they wind up dead. Simple doesn't make it wrong.'

'He has an alibi. It'll be good, or the best money can buy, otherwise they wouldn't have let him go.'

'But it might fall apart if we could establish a connection to the JR. What if Jimbo and Ronnycrabs, as part of their misguided campaign against him, stole his JR without realising what it meant to him or contained. Then when he saw your photos, with the JR in one of them, that's when he blew a gasket and decided to have them killed. Except when he or his hired hammer went there, the JR was gone.'

'I like it,' said Alison. 'The proof, of course, would be to find that the JR was back in his possession.'

I was about to agree with this when I caught myself on. 'No, Alison.'

'No what?'

'You know what.'

'I'm not a mind-reader.'

'Repeat after me.'

'What?'

'Just repeat after me.'

'Christ. Repeat after me.'

'We are not . . .'

'We are not . . .'

'Breaking into . . .'

'Breaking . . . Oh now I get you.'

'Say it.'

'I never say what I don't mean. Except in matters of romance and sex.'

'Just say it. We are not breaking into Billy Randall's house.'

'We are not breaking into Billy Randall's house.'

'I swear on the life of my unborn son.'

'No. That's just sick.'

'I want you to swear. You've already turned him into a burglar by default.'

'I have *not*, he just went along for the ride.'

'You corrupted a minor, and you're not doing it again. Agreed?'

Alison sighed. '*Okay*. Agreed. Absolutely. We will definitely not break into Billy Randall's. Absolutely defin-tootly.'

'Alison.'

'What?'

'I mean it.'

'Okay. Point made.'

We were both quiet then. At least until: 'I don't suppose . . .'

'No,' she said. 'You had your chance.'

She hung up.

19

Even before he had fully exited Starbucks, I'd already made my mind up about Billy Randall's minder. He had an aura of suppressed anger and violence. His eyes darted about like a paranoid, but there was also an innate cockiness to him, an ego based on steroid muscle and vanity. It didn't make him a murderer, but it would make you think twice about pushing his buttons. He had gone to Jimbo and Ronnycrabs' home with Billy Randall and there had been a falling-out. Perhaps he'd gone back later and killed them before removing the Jack Russell. It was a hunch based on nothing much, but he was certainly someone I needed to know more about.

His full name was Charles Hawk, Charlie Hawk to his friends, though who knew if he had any. You don't really need them. I've gotten by for years without them. Friends stab you in the back, sometimes literally.

Mother never allowed friends around to the house. She said they would steal and break things. Her friends were different, of course. They would sit in the front room and drink sherry until they were legless. And then *they* would steal and break things. I asked one time what the difference was between my friends and hers and she slapped me and locked me in the cupboard. Pretty soon I was too big for the cupboard. Fortunately, she had a wardrobe.

I used my contacts in the police and found out that Charlie Hawk had a record for assault and demanding money with menaces. Actually, that's a lie. I have no contacts in the police – a few nodding acquaintances, but nobody I could phone up and ask sensitive information of. I relied on my old friend Chief Inspector Google. The *Belfast Telegraph* had carried a court case. The judge had called him 'nothing more than a thug', which in his line of work probably wasn't a bad review. The report also told me where he lived, the street, though not the house number. There probably wasn't anything to be gained by watching him, but seeing as how I never sleep and I had nothing better to do, I thought I would at least see if I could pinpoint his actual house, just for future reference.

I drove up in the wee smalls. It was damp and cold and I had my gloves on and a pompom hat. I drove as I always drive, slow, methodical and always mindful of the Highway Code. To me amber is red, and not just because of my colour blindness. I found his street, a long terrace close to the City Hospital, and parked and opened a Twix and sipped from a flask of Vitolink and began to try to work out if I could guess which house was his purely by deduction. But I had been parked for barely two minutes, and was still getting my bearings, when I jumped at a rat-a-tat on my window and there was Charlie, glaring in, his slap cheeks blazing.

'What're you doing? Are you watching me? Are you watching my house? What the hell are you playing at? Wind the window down.'

'No.'

'What?'

'No!'

He was clearly a mentalist.

'Wind the window down! I have a wife and children in there, and you're watching my house! Think I don't see you, I know you're watching me, you in your murder van. Open the window!'

'No!'

'What?'

It wasn't a very practical way of having a conversation, even a threatening one, especially as he seemed to be a little deaf. I wound it down a fraction.

'I'm not watching your house. I just pulled in to make a call and eat a Twix.'

'Balls! This is my house, my street, what are the chances of that? You're watching me when you should be finding out who killed those boys.'

'No, really.'

'Balls! You're watching me. You're watching the

wrong man. I have a wife and children who can vouch for me. Even my neighbours. I was having a barbecue when they were killed . . .'

'It was Christmas!'

'Exactly! Everyone is sick of it. I have a barbecue every Christmas. Most of them got food poisoning, so they will remember.'

'Okay. If you say so.'

'Which means you're on a hiding to nothing, watching me day and night.'

'I wasn't, I just happened—'

'Shut your fucking face! If I ever, ever see you in this street again, I will break you up into little pieces. Do you hear me? Break you up.'

He aimed a kick at the van. Later I would find that he had stove it in, even though I saw in the mirror that he was wearing slippers. I wasn't sure if steroids could make your feet tougher, or maybe it was just the muscles that powered them. I started up and drove off. He continued to yell after me as upstairs lights winked on all along the terrace.

20

In the morning I knocked another fifty pee off one of the sale books I was advertising in the window, but when it failed to produce an immediate stampede I retired to my place behind the counter and went surfing. When that failed to yield the desired results I turned to the Yellow Pages and found listings for three local taxidermists. I phoned the second one, because I didn't like the pattern of letters in the first one's name, and asked him why he didn't have a website.

'Because I choose not to,' the man replied gruffly. His business was called William Gunn and Son, but I didn't know if I was speaking to the boss or the son of. 'What can I do for you?'

'There are very few businesses that don't have them these days,' I said, 'very few.'

'Really?'

I don't like sarcasm, and have no patience for impatience.

'Just saying,' I said, 'because I prefer to suss someone out via their website before I actually make contact. It's much easier, no awkwardness, no pressure. If I were you, I'd get yourself a website. It's good for business.'

'Uhuh? Well thanks for sharing that with me. Do you design websites by any chance?'

'No, I'm a private detective.'

'Well you must be a crappy one if you've time to phone me up and give me a hard time for not having a website. Now fuck off.'

He hung up.

I had meant no criticism, but sometimes people take my well-meaning observations the wrong way. I debated whether to phone him back, but being allergic to confrontation I opted to phone the third of our taxidermists, a Michael Streeth. He was much friendlier and actually quite excited to be talking to a real live private detective. We got on well enough for me to ask why he didn't have a website either and also to mention my brief conversation with William Gunn.

Michael – for we were on first-name terms, although I'd told him I was called Mario, after Mario Puzo; his *The Godfather* happened to be sitting on the counter, and I have a bookselling business and its reputation to protect – laughed at the mention of Mr Gunn and described him as a cantankerous old shit. He explained that local taxidermists had taken their websites down because they were continually being bombarded with abusive e-mails and occasionally viruses by animal rights groups. 'The phone's okay,' he said, 'because it's not quite as anonymous; calls can be traced, and anyway, they're not so brave when it comes to actually talking one on one. Gunny has had it worse than me; his place got its windows put in a couple of times, so yeah, he's nervous, and touchy, although I think he was a shit to start with.'

I had asked Michael some general questions about taxidermy before pressing ahead with the real reason for my call. Had he at any time – because it was impossible to know how long the animal had been dead – stuffed a Jack Russell terrier for Billy Randall?

Michael let out an exasperated groan. 'Please, before you go any further with this, and particularly because I know this will lead back to Willy Gunn, don't ever, ever make the mistake of saying to him what you just said to me. We *do not* stuff animals. We remove the skin, preserve it, then arrange it around a model of the original body. It's not about stuffing, it's about anatomy. A good taxidermist is a sculptor, an artist and a naturalist, all rolled into one. And Willy Gunn is the best in the business. If this Jack Russell you're looking for was done in this country, then Willy's your man. I don't touch pets – their owners get too emotional. I do mostly wildlife that's been accidentally killed or animals that have been legally hunted. It's all well regulated these days – though there are a few rogues out there offering cheap deals for shit work. Most of them don't know their arse from their elbow, which is unfortunate, from an anatomical point of view.'

It was also unfortunate that he wasn't the man I needed to talk to, because he seemed like a decent sort, and we got on well, which for me doesn't happen very often.

'I'd call Willy for you,' Michael said, 'but I had a fall-out with him myself last year. He's fine, really – just tread easy with the stuffing.'

Michael also ruled out the first name on my list of local taxidermists. I was still working off my out-of-date Yellow Pages, due to a dispute I had with the company, which I need not go into now but which involved them *ripping me off*. Seems Scott Parker had retired two years previously and gone off to live in Spain.

I told Alison of my predicament over lunch in the hope that she'd volunteer to call Willy Gunn on my behalf, but she said no, we should go and see him. She said she was an artist but entirely self-taught and her anatomy was useless and it might be instructive to go and see him at work.

'We could kill two birds with one stone,' she said.

'That's not funny,' I said.

I argued with her that all we needed was a couple of questions answered, but she wasn't having it. She said that if we hadn't actually gone out to Jimbo's house, but stayed at home like I wanted, we wouldn't have found out about the burglary at Pat's, and hadn't my sneaky visit to Charlie Hawk paid dividends?

'He damaged my car.'

'You heard his alibi.'

'He vaguely alluded to a Christmas barbecue; it's hardly an alibi.'

'He must have thought it was.' I sighed. 'So we're going to go wild in the country, are we?'

'No,' I said.

I don't like the country, with its potholes and cows of winter. I don't like animals alive, and no better dead. I fear fleas and ticks and bluetongue, mange and maggots and rabies. I detest wildlife, farm animals and pets. I once knelt on a gerbil. The roads weren't straight. There was black ice. It was a nightmare, especially in Alison's suspension-free little Beetle.

'This is a complete waste of time,' I said, 'and please keep both hands on the steering wheel.' She took the other one off. For badness. 'Please remember, there are three of us in this car.'

She laughed and rubbed her belly and said little Rory was in her corner and I was forced to leave it or there would have been a shouting match, which would have meant her taking her eyes off the road, which was all I needed. So I sat on my hands and applied the imaginary brake and kept my mouth closed while we drove out to William Gunn's address on the outskirts of Hillsborough. It was only twenty minutes from the city, but that was nineteen more than I preferred. His workshop was a variation of what people of my parents' generation would have called a Nissen hut. Its curved roof was rusted and moss strewn.

149

Jagged plants grew up the walls and hung down over the entrance and I had to be careful not to get stabbed by thorns and blinded by twigs. Alison opened the door and a bell jangled. We stood on one side of a counter and looked at a dead squirrel. The squirrel was holding a small card in its paws that read: *Please do not ask for credit, as refusal often offends.*

'What kind of credit could a squirrel give, anyway?' Alison asked.

'Nuts,' I said.

An elderly man appeared from behind a small curtain, rubbing his hands on a towel. He looked annoyed. 'Yes? I'm just closing.'

Mother could have taught him a thing or two about customer relations. I held my tongue. Alison stepped in. She can be very good when she puts her mind to it. She apologised for calling without making an appointment, she'd heard wonderful things about his work, we have a pet dog who's on his last legs, and forgive me if this is being morbid, we'd really like to have him preserved, do you do pets, is it possible to see your workshop and examples of any other dogs you might have done, how much does it cost, we'll pay whatever it takes.

That changed his tune pretty quick. Couldn't be more pleasant. Please, come this way.

William Gunn led us – slowly, I might add, for he appeared both fragile and arthritic – through the curtain and into the workshop beyond. Long wooden tables were festooned with bottles of chemicals, animal skins were pinned out to dry. There were half-built skeletons and a fox that looked as if the merest spark of electricity might bring it snarling back to life. There were stag heads with antlers mounted on the wall. In one corner there were rats kitted out in little suits and seated around a picnic table. One was wearing sunglasses. It was meant to be cute but just looked odd. The whole place stank of death and formaldehyde and blood and fur and guts and pain. I hated it. I had only recently been researching concentration camps, and this reminded me of the photographs of the hideous experiments crazy scientists had performed with Hitler's blessing. It was Auschwitz for squirrels. The whole time we were there I was on the verge of throwing up. I was allergic to virtually everything in the room. At any moment my head might swell up even further.

Gunn, though, almost purred with pride. He showed us examples of his work and Alison *oohed* and *aahed* over them while giving me *yuck* looks when he wasn't looking. I wanted out. We needed to get to the point. I asked him if there were any creatures he couldn't stuff.

William Gunn's head snapped towards me. 'We do . . . not . . . *stuff*. I am a member of the Guild of Taxidermists, a founder member. I have been performing taxidermy for fifty years. It requires the skills of a surgeon, the artistic eye of a great master and the manual dexterity of a craftsman. Please, please, *never* refer to it as . . . stuffing.'

'Understood,' I said. I nodded around the workshop.

'And very impressive, all this. But are there, like, any creatures that can't be . . . you know, done?'

His eyes held steady on me. 'No. Over the years, I've pretty much done them all.'

'Have you ever,' I asked, 'stuffed a whale?'

'Do not say *stuffed*.'

'I'm sorry, my mistake. Could you do a whale?'

'Do you have a whale you need me to do?'

'No, of course not. I wouldn't have anywhere to put it. But theoretically?'

'Never mind him,' said Alison. 'He's only out for the day.'

He softened a little. 'No . . . no. It is a good question. Theoretically, yes, I could do a whale, but I would need a whole team working with me. The size. The problem would be the skin – taxidermy really only works well where the creature has either fur or feathers. If there is only skin, it discolours. It does not look . . . well.'

'Could you stuff a human?' I asked.

'Please! Do not refer . . .' He stopped and sighed. 'It is a losing battle,' he said wearily. 'Seventy-five years of expertise between me and my da, yet it is always stuff this or stuff that.' His eyes flitted back to me and he pointed. 'You. Your voice is . . . familiar.'

I just looked at him.

'That's because he's as common as muck,' said Alison. She laughed. After a moment he laughed too, but his eyes held steady on me until Alison expertly drew his attention back. She said, 'I'm sorry, we're just heartbroken about our wee dog; we've had him for fifteen years, he's part of the family. We thought it would be nice to have a reminder of him.'

She looked about to cry. Gunn surprised her, and me, by taking her hand and patting it. 'Don't you worry,' he said gently, 'you'll have a fine reminder of him. Please, what type of a dog is he?'

'A Jack Russell,' said Alison.

'Ah, lovely,' said Gunn.

'I was thinking, if you've done Jack Russells before, maybe I could see one? Just, half of me really wants it, but the other thinks it would be a bit . . . you know . . . strange having him around . . . you know . . . dead 'n' all, do you know what I mean?'

Gunn nodded. 'I fully understand. Absolutely. Now, I've done quite a few dogs recently, but no Jack Russells. If you just hold on a minute, I'll see if my dad remembers doing one. See, I was off on holiday for a few weeks in July, so he might have and just not mentioned it.'

'That would be great, if it's not too much trouble?'

'Not a bit of it.'

Gunn gave me another sharp look before producing a mobile phone and moving towards the far end of the workshop.

'His dad?' I whispered. '*He's* about ninety, how old's the da?'

Alison shrugged. Then she punched me on one of my brittle arm bones. 'Quit it with the stuffing crap, okay? We're trying to get some answers.'

I made a face.

She made one back.

We were quite a team.

Gunn closed his phone then crossed to a tall green filing cabinet and pulled open a drawer. He rifled through it for half a minute before finding what he was looking for. 'I was right,' he said. 'Dad did do one in the summer. And we always take pictures of our work.'

He had three photographs in his hand, which he passed to Alison one at a time. She passed them on to me. They showed a Jack Russell. It was difficult to tell if he was alive or dead, but that was as much to do with the quality of the photographs as the quality of the work.

'They're . . . a bit distant?' Alison ventured.

Gunn looked at them himself. 'You're right. It's Dad. As a taxidermist, even at his age, he's a genius. Not so much a photographer.'

'Well . . .'

Alison glanced at me, but made sure that Gunn saw it. Realising that he might be about to see business walk out the door, he moved quickly. 'I'll tell you what, if you really want to see how the last one worked out, I'm sure I could have a word with the owners, see if they mind you seeing the little fella.'

'Do you think?'

'Well, one can only ask. Give me a wee minute.'

Gunn produced his phone again and moved away. Alison winked at me. She was actually pretty good at this game. I had taught her well.

Gunn didn't look quite so chipper when he returned. 'Well, it might not be that simple after all. Seems they had a burglary just recently, and amongst other things they went and stole their Jack Russell.'

'God,' said Alison, 'why would anyone do that?'

Gunn shook his head sadly. 'I'm not even going to tell my dad, with his heart. They're like his children.'

His *stuffed* children. It was an odd way to earn a living. That and undertaking.

'The owners are *devastated*,' Gunn continued. 'I suppose that's what happens when you're a VIP – they target you, don't they?'

'A VIP?' Alison asked. 'Anyone really famous?'

'I'm afraid I can't say.'

But he said it in a way that you knew he could say, and would say, and probably did say on a regular basis. It was a way of promoting his business. He probably told everyone who arrived at his door, including the postman, about his celebrity clientele.

'Oh go on,' said Alison, 'who is it? And you know I'm bringing our wee man here anyway. I'm very impressed.'

'Well that would be good. And of course I'll tell you, but you have to promise to keep it under your hat.'

'Yes, of course!'

'All right. It's yer man—'

'Billy Randall,' I said.

Gunn looked annoyed at the interruption, but wasn't fazed by the name. 'Billy . . . ? Oh aye, holiday guy? No, not him. Whatever . . . ?'

'Ignore him,' said Alison. 'Who is it, go on?'

So he told us, and she responded like she was impressed, but when she looked at me her eyes were as wide as mine.

It was time to get out. We had a new and potentially dangerous complication to discuss. Alison promised to return as soon as our JR popped his clogs and Gunn took a note of our bullshit telephone number and escorted us to the door and waved at us as we crossed the car park.

It was a huge relief to get outside. I'm usually allergic to country air, but on this occasion I took my life in my hands and sucked it in. Alison stopped at the driver's door and began to rifle through her handbag for the keys. It was a big bag, and it was full of lady nonsense.

She looked across the top of the car at me and said, 'What's wrong?'

'Nothing.'

'I know that look.'

She was right. I had unfinished business. I turned back to the workshop.

'What're you . . . ?'

'Forgotten to ask something, only be a mo.'

I re-entered the reception area. I pushed through the curtain and saw that Gunn was leaning over a work bench examining the indistinct photographs of the Jack Russell with the aid of a magnifying glass.

'Excuse me,' I said.

He looked up, surprised, and then peeved. 'Yes?'

'You thought you recognised my voice?'

'I . . . ?'

'Get a website, you creepy old fucker.'

I slipped back through the curtain, grinning triumphantly.

It was an inconvenient time for Alison to lose her keys.

21

Alison was furious with me, and did not wish to discuss the breakthrough in the case, nor take into account the fact that I had engineered it by suggesting we contact the taxidermist in the first place. All she could focus on was the smaller picture, and the fact that an old man had threatened to bash her car in with the shaft of a brush.

I had dismissed his claim that I had verbally abused him as the ramblings of a senile old stuffer, yet despite the fact that she and I were lovers, and I was the father of her child, and she wanted to spend the rest of her life with me, and had her eyes on my shop, and thought of herself as my equal and partner in detection, Alison chose to believe him over me. I told her honestly that I had returned to the workshop merely to ask a question in relation to the case. She demanded to know what the question was. I was not prepared to tell her, as it was already clear that she was doubting my version of events. William Gunn had threatened to hit her car with the shaft of a brush only because the end of it had already come off when he hurled it at me while chasing me around the locked car. It is unseemly and undignified for an old man to puff around exerting so much energy over something he had clearly misheard. It was, however, a sure indication of his impaired mental state and it reminded me to treat with caution everything he had told us earlier.

When Alison finally located her keys, in her pocket, and we departed to the accompaniment of hurled abuse, I sat on my hands and relocated to another dimension while she shouted and raved. For some reason, my lack of response infuriated her even more. It was not a comfortable journey home, although a lot of that had to do with the fact that we were in the vicinity of grass and bushes and sheep that looked at me with evil intent.

It was too late for me to reopen No Alibis, but I had to go back there to pick up the van. As she parked outside Alison said, 'Grow up and stop huffing.'

'Then stop shouting at me.'

'You started it. Calling him a—'

'I didn't call him anything. He's barking. Why won't you believe me?'

'Experience.'

'I wouldn't lie to you.'

She held her gaze steady. I folded. Malfunctioning

tear ducts. Alison shook her head. 'I honestly don't think you're even aware of it. What question did you ask him?'

'If you must know, I asked him about the JR. You will have noticed that in both photographs the dog had a tail that curled back on itself.'

'Yes. So?'

'Well, when I was growing up, JRs never had tails. When they were born their tails were docked. But they decided it was unnecessarily cruel a while back and they brought in a law to prevent it. I wanted to ask Mr Gunn when that law was brought in; it's the sort of thing he would need to know and it would be helpful to us.'

'Why?'

'Because it gives us the age of the dog. He said the law was brought in three years ago, which means that the JR in the picture, if it's the same as ours, cannot be more than three years old.'

'And what difference does that make?'

'None. It's just information. It may be useful somewhere further down the line. Three-year-old dogs should not require stuffing. Maybe there's more to his death than meets the eye. I mean, would you want to be the man who ran down a Jack Russell belonging to the Chief Constable of Northern Ireland? They'd put speed cameras outside your house.'

'Fair point,' said Alison.

I am an accomplished liar. I had known the exact date of the enactment of the tail-docking law all along.

It's not an area of particular interest to me, but I do keep abreast of the latest developments in tail-docking. I have a lot of time to kill at night, what with not sleeping and Mother praying loudly if indistinctly.

'So, the Chief Constable,' said Alison.

'The Chief Constable.'

'That complicates things.'

'It complicates them mightily.'

'So what are we saying, that somehow Jimbo and Ronny got hold of the Chief Constable's dog, and in getting it back he either killed them or had them killed? That's just daft.'

'Yes it is. Of course it is.'

'But.'

'Stranger things.'

'Say they refused to hand it back, or they tried to blackmail him, and he just snapped and killed them.'

'Or God knows, in his line he comes across enough murderers, and he struck a deal.'

'It might not even be about the dog itself, but about the principle of the dog. Can you imagine if it got out that the Chief Constable was burgled? What would that do to the reputation of the police? It would be a disaster, it would be political.'

'So let's say he's prepared to kill over a Jack Russell, then we would have to assume that he will go to equally extreme measures to protect himself from further investigation. And you know what that means?'

'I do. You want to drop the case because you're allergic to violence.'

'Exactly.'

Alison smiled. 'You're right. We have a baby to think of. And let's face it, the Chief Constable of Northern Ireland is not going to murder two painters and decorators over a stuffed dog. People do get very attached to their pets, but that is just plain silly.'

'Yes it is, crazy.'

'We shouldn't think about it for a minute more.'

'Not even a moment.'

'I mean, even if the Chief Constable, the head of our police service, the man we trust to keep us safe at nights, did kill Jimbo and Ronny, and we expose him, it wouldn't just be one man; it would rock our Government and jeopardise our fragile peace, and more importantly, it would put us in incredible danger. So we wouldn't want to be doing that. Even if we knew something, it would be much safer just to sit on it, because really it's none of our business, and we have to look after number one first.'

'Absolutely,' I said. 'Whatever we know can just sit in our consciences.'

I looked at her for a long time. She looked back.

'Explain conscience again,' she asked.

I knew what she was doing. She wanted to follow the case to its logical conclusion. She didn't give a good God damn about our safety. She wanted to unravel the whole ball of string. But this wasn't string; we were dealing with Christmas lights. Once ravelled, all but impossible to un. We could spend weeks trying to disentangle them, and when we finally did, we'd get electrocuted. Alison was young and enthusiastic, and could not always see the bigger picture. She thought she could play me. She thought she could implant some kind of autosuggestion in my brain box. She had bonded with the abundantly pregnant Pat and now felt morally responsible for tracking down whoever had killed the father of her unborn child, while hardly realising that by doing so she was putting her own at risk.

I was not built for big, important cases. I did not care about the fate of nations or police or politics. I had had more than enough of murder in the past and had only agreed to flirt with it again because Marple had attempted to tie us in to the deaths of Jimbo and Ronny. But there was no evidence. Billy Randall had browbeaten me into continuing the investigation and tempted me with an envelope full of cash. It might not have been blood money, but my instinct to reject it was absolutely right. I should have been strong and handed it back to him. I should have been decisive and told him that his predicament was no concern of mine, that I'd done my job and was now retiring from detection to concentrate on selling books, which has more than enough excitement for someone with my blood pressure, and varicose veins, and cholesterol, and brittle bones, and psoriasis, and angina, and rickets, and tinnitus, and the malaria I caught from a single rogue mosquito on a visit to Belfast's Botanical Gardens.

I was about to be a father. I had an invalid mother.

I did not need to be mixed up in murder. Jimbo and Ronny were two drug-dealers and I really did not care who killed them.

Did.

Not.

Care.

After she drove off, I sat in the No Alibis van for twenty minutes. Three times I switched the engine on, and three times I switched it off. Then I got out of the car and went up the back alley and entered the shop from the rear. I took my seat behind the counter and began to look again at *The Case of the Cock-Headed Man*.

Damn her eyes!

Three a.m. The phone rang.

Alison said, 'I couldn't sleep. I rang your mobile and couldn't raise you. I rang your house. Your mother said you hadn't come home. I was worried.'

'You spoke to my mother?'

'It wasn't exactly a conversation.'

'What did she say?'

'She said, it's nearly three in the morning, how the fuck do I know where the dirty stop-out is?'

'Were you thinking I was with another woman?'

When she finished laughing, Alison said no. 'You're working on the case, aren't you?'

'Maybe.'

'I knew you would. You're a curious old Hector, aren't you?'

'I thought it would be worthwhile to spend a few hours of quiet contemplation reviewing the facts. It doesn't mean anything.'

'Well at least you're thinking about it. So?'

'We have a lot of don't knows and possibilities and maybes, but very few facts.'

'Oh.'

'But I did turn up a photograph of the Chief Constable and his Jack Russell.'

'How the hell did you manage that?'

'I have the combined wisdom of ten thousand fictional detectives whizzing about in my brain.'

'Let me rephrase the question. How the hell did you manage that?'

'I typed Chief Constable of Northern Ireland and Jack Russell into Google. Wilson McCabe was appointed just over a year ago. He did a lot of press when he first arrived, liked to project himself as the friendly neighbour-hood bobby, family man, all that fantasy crap. One of these was a photo shoot for *QIP* magazine . . .'

'*QI* . . . ?'

'*Quite Important People* – it was supposed to chron-icle the lives of the rich and famous here, but we don't have very many of them and those we do have are dead boring. People weren't the slightest bit inter-ested. It collapsed after three issues. But not before they persuaded Wilson McCabe to pose with his wife and two boys and their sweet little six-week-old Jack Russell pup. You can check them out yourself, they're all on-line.'

'And what does that do for us?'

'Well, the JR was just a pup, but I compared it with Jimbo's, and the markings are identical. Just smaller.'

'Okay. And what does that do for us?'

'Well, we know that the JR was taken from Pat's. If it turns up at the Chief Constable's house, there's your direct line. If it's at Billy Randall's, there's another.'

'And if it's at neither?'

'Well then we're scundered, it's the only thing we have. No stuffed JR, then we leave the police to investigate the murders themselves, which means that they might yet rope us back into them.'

'So we're going to find the pup?'

'I didn't say that.'

'Darling, you know you won't be able to sleep until you've worked out where it is.'

'Darling,' I responded, 'I haven't been able to sleep since 1976.'

22

Come four a.m., I realised I was being watched.

The shutters were down, but there are security cameras front and back that feed into my computer. I had them installed after being bushwhacked outside my own yard during my previous investigation. I also like to watch, and have spent many hours, watching. I have seen couples fornicate, drunks urinate and burglars speculate. Botanic Avenue is a commercial street, with cramped student housing running off it. There's a hotel a hundred yards down from No Alibis, but it doesn't have its own parking. There are bars and nightclubs and restaurants; a lot of people drive down, and then leave their cars overnight. What all this means is that there are generally few parking spaces available, day or night. But still, people come and go at all hours. There was nothing remarkable about the BMW parked opposite No Alibis and the man inside it, or the fact that the first time I noticed him, or the light from his mobile phone, was at two a.m., or that he was still there just before four. People wait for hours to sober up, or to be absolutely certain that there are no police around to catch them drink-driving. But at exactly four a.m. the BMW's lights came on, and it pulled out, and drove off, only for another BMW to immediately pull into the space and switch off, with the driver making no attempt to leave his vehicle. That did not suggest he had lucked into a convenient parking space; it suggested a change of shift.

Call me paranoid. Many people have, including several who know what they're talking about. Just as I am a glass-half-empty kind of a guy, I generally go for the guilty explanation rather than the innocent one. But the swapping of the BMWs might possibly just have been a weird coincidence if I had not noticed their number plates, as I tend to do, and saw that their registrations were but one digit apart, which suggested: fleet vehicles.

I phoned Jeff. He answered, eventually.

I said, 'Do you want your job back?'

'It's . . . four in the effing morning.'

'Just answer the question.'

'No.'

'No?'

'I've been offered one in the university bookshop. The hours are shorter and the pay is better.'

'Jeff. Don't be ridiculous. I need you here, now. We've forgiven you, even if you are an arse.'

'I'm ridiculous and an arse. You're winning me over one insult at a time.'

'Jeff, just get down here. I'm up to my neck in *The Case of the Cock-Headed Man*. It all seems to revolve around a stuffed Jack Russell that used to belong to the Chief Constable of the Police Service of Northern Ireland. He may be involved in a double murder. This case resonates at the very highest levels of power; it's a conspiracy. You love conspiracies. You love abuses of power. This is exactly like that shit you slabber on and on about in Amnesty International, but here it is, right on your doorstep. Or mine. Please, I'm in the shop, I'm alone and I'm scared to leave because I'm being watched. I need your help.'

'Like I said, I've been offered a job in the university bookshop and the hours are better and so is the pay.'

He hung up.

I rang him back. 'I can't match what they're offering, but whatever extra they're paying you they'll take it out of you in tax, you won't be gaining anything, plus you'll be contributing to Government coffers and I know that goes against the grain.' I had him there. 'And we can talk about the hours; they won't be a problem.'

'What about the coffee?'

'What about the coffee?'

'You keep sending me out to Starbucks for coffee, but you never buy me one. You make me use the instant.'

'I'm not buying you Starbucks coffee.'

'Okay,' he said, and hung up.

171

I rang him back and said, 'One a day, tops.'

'Okay,' he said. 'Plus—'

'I'm not negotiating.'

'I believe you are.'

'Look, I'm being watched, they could come for me at any time, and you're discussing fucking coffee! Please come and help me.'

'Bullshit. That place is done up like Fort Knox. You could withstand a nuclear strike. What's wrong with Alison?'

'Nothing. She's pregnant. I don't want to put her in harm's way.'

'But it's okay to put me in harm's way, and you'll still stiff me on the coffee?'

'Okay! Frick. If I get something from Starbucks, then you can have something from Starbucks.'

'From any part of the menu?'

'Yes!'

He said nothing. I could hear the cogs. Eventually he said, 'Okay, then.'

'Right. Christ. We have a deal?'

'I suppose. What do you want me to do?'

'I'm going to drive home shortly. If I'm right, whoever is watching me will follow. I'll try and shake him, but I want you to follow him, see where he goes.' Jeff was laughing. 'What's so funny?'

'Sorry. Just. The very notion of you shaking someone. You've never driven faster than twenty-five miles an hour in your life. He would have to be walking for you to shake him.'

'Will you just get down here?'

'One thing.'

'What?'

'I don't have a car. My mate has an ice-cream van, I can borrow that.'

'You . . .'

'Only winding you up. Give me ten minutes.'

'Make it five,' I said.

'I live ten minutes away. I can't make it five unless you rewrite the laws of physics.'

What I hate about the younger generation is that they always have an excuse. In my day people just *did*.

Right up to the point that he started following me, I couldn't be sure that I was right, though I usually was. As soon as I backed out of the alcove and turned right on Botanic, I picked him up in the mirror. The roads were almost completely empty of traffic at that time, so he knew to stay well back. But he was there.

And behind him, Jeff.

My first attempt to lose him consisted of approaching a junction, indicating to turn left, but actually turning right. When that failed, I drove through the next set of traffic lights on amber, knowing that they would be red by the time he reached them. And he stopped. But it was a straight road. And I have an almost physical mental block about speeding, so he was able to patiently wait for the lights to return to green and still catch me up within a minute. But I can be a wily old fox when I need to be. I might not have been able to outrun him, but I am a dab hand at confusion and embarrassment. I led him the full length of the Lisburn Road until I came to a suitably large roundabout, whose main tributary led on to the outer ring surrounding the city. For me it was like the edge of the world. There might as well have been a big sign saying, *Here Be Dragons*, instead of *Lisburn*. I moved on to this roundabout, checking in my mirror that he was also joining it, but then I *stayed* on it.

I went round, and I went round, and I went round. He went with me.

It would have been even more ridiculous if Jeff had also joined us, but I had planned sufficiently far ahead to call him and warn him to pull off short to await developments.

By the end of the third circuit, my tail knew for sure that I was fooling with him, rather than just dithering about which exit. Whether off his own bat, or having taken instruction, he cut off and back down the Lisburn Road. Jeff took off in pursuit.

I continued to drive around the roundabout. There was something quite relaxing about it. There were no surprises. I knew exactly where I was going, and where I had come from, and where I was going, and where I had come from. It was my kind of a journey. The grass was short, the traffic was light and there were several escape routes. I could have stayed there all night. Also, the easy, casual rhythm of it gave me time to think about who it was in the BMW.

The fact that I had only noticed him in the early

hours of the morning did not mean that he hadn't been with me for some time, but I am usually pretty well aware of my surroundings, and number plates, and would like to think I would have realised I was being watched or followed. It's a bit like a spider-sense, although obviously I suffer from arachnophobia. I was reasonably sure he hadn't been with us on our visit *to* William Gunn's workshop; being the nervous passenger that I am, I had kept an eagle eye on the road and would surely have noticed if we were being followed, particularly as we got lost a couple of times on the way there and had to do some backtracking along narrow country roads. But with Alison shouting on the way back I hadn't paid much attention to the traffic, so he could easily have picked us up there, which meant he could have been tipped off by William Gunn.

The roundabout was well lit, but the BMW hadn't gotten close enough for me to get even a rough impression of the man driving. It could have been Marple. It could have been Gunn himself. It could even have been the Chief Constable, or the killers he had employed to top Jimbo and Ronny. I did not doubt that I would find out. I have been collecting number plates and tracking down their owners all of my life, because I like to. Tracing my original watcher or his replacement would not be hard. In fact, it was made terrifically easy because Jeff, going against the habits of his short lifetime, turned out to be rather good at tracking his target.

He phoned rather breathlessly fifteen minutes after he left me.

'Just parking . . . He's . . . man, you're not going to believe this.'

I said, 'Hold on till I pull over, I'm starting to feel a little dizzy.'

It wasn't just the roundabout, it was the medication.

I took the first exit I came to and parked a hundred yards up. It had begun to rain quite heavily. It was dark still and cold. I liked it.

'Okay,' I said, 'shoot.'

'Do you want to know where I am?'

'Yes. Jeff. Obviously.'

'And you've agreed to the pay rise and the Starbucks and to cut my hours and not to shout at me.'

'I never agreed to a pay rise. And I'll shout if I damn well . . .'

'Well I think—'

'Just tell me where you are!'

'You see? That's *exactly*—'

'Jeff. Will you stop pissing around and tell me what—'

'Oh shit!'

'Jeff?'

'Shit shit shit shit shit!'

'Jeff . . . ?'

'They've spotted me, they're coming for me!'

'Jeff, I'm not falling for it . . .'

'Oh shit, oh shit, oh shit . . .'

'Will you just tell me where you are and quit—'

'Oh shit . . .'

'Uhuh. If *they* are really there, just drive away.'

'I can't! They've parked in front and be—'

I heard a sudden loud tapping, like metal on glass.

'Jeff?'

'What'll I say?!'

'Jeff . . .'

'They want me to open the window . . . there's four of them!'

'Jeff . . .'

'I'm not insured!' There were voices I could not make out. Then Jeff: 'Sorry, I think I'm lost, is this the way—'

He did not finish; his door opened; there were grunts; someone said, 'Now.' There was a brief rush of static on the phone, but the line remained open. Then footsteps. A car door slamming. Then breathing.

'*Jeff . . . ?*'

'Just remember one thing.'

It wasn't Jeff's voice. It was cold and hard and sterile.

'What?'

'Murder is *our* business.'

23

It was still some way short of dawn when I returned to No Alibis. I parked around the back and spent a harrowing few minutes opening the locks and punching in the codes before I reached the safety of what Jeff had more than once referred to as 'the bunker'.

Jeff!

Poor imbecile, seized by unknown forces, and perhaps even now floating face down in the Lagan or tied to a chair with his ear cut off. Still, an idiot for getting caught, and at the end of the day, he was only part-time help, not family. My first concern was my own safety, then Mother, then the baby, then the carrier. Better to lead them back here to the shop. There was no way of gauging how much 'they' knew or even if they were interested in knowing anything. They had taken Jeff because he had followed one of them, and if he had not been so keen on the chit-chat he might have told me what he'd discovered before he was seized. Now all I had to go on were the registrations of two BMWs and the few words of threat one of them had uttered to me on the phone.

I flipped on the computer and checked the security cameras. There was no sign of any watchers outside, front or back. Perhaps they thought their warning was enough.

Or was it a warning? It was down to semantics.

They had said: Murder is our business, with the emphasis on the *our*.

What did that mean exactly? That they murdered people for a living? Or that they dealt with murder, making them cops? Or were they just taking the piss out of the No Alibis slogan?

I phoned Mother. She slept as little as I did, but whereas I kept myself busy, she sat in a chair by her window, drinking, and watching. There was not a thing that happened on our street that she did not know about. She knew the comings and goings, the affairs, the fights, the huffs, the pets, the deliveries, the names of the trees. She had a critical word for everyone and everything, including the trees. She was a mean, vindictive old biddy, but she missed nothing.

I said, 'It's me, are you still up?'

'Yes, of course I'm still up, you stupid little shit.'

'Are you at the window?'

'I'm always at the window, at least when I'm not in your stupid little shop.'

'Mother, please, I need to know. Have you noticed anything unusual out in the street? Any strange cars parked there, anyone sitting inside any strange cars, anyone watching our house. Anything unusual at all.'

'Why? What have you done now? Do you owe people money? Are you in with drug-dealers now?'

'No, Mother, I—'

'I knew that shop would be a disaster, you're fucking hopeless, I don't know why I ever adopted you.'

'You didn't adopt me, Mother.'

'If I had I could have sent you back, you pathetic little shit.'

I waited. She wasn't like this *all* the time. It was like bleeding a radiator: once in a while you had to let the steam out, but you also needed to know exactly when to tighten the valve to stop the boiling water spraying out after it. If you caught it right, then whatever passed for normal service was resumed. I regularly had to tighten Mother's valve. After about a minute of silence she said, 'What sort of strange cars?'

'Any sort you don't see there regularly. Maybe a BMW.'

'There was one here earlier; it drove off.'

'How long was it there for? When did it drive off?'

'Been there since teatime, maybe drove off an hour ago.'

'You didn't happen to notice its number plate?'

'No, because I'm not a sad little shit like you.'

'Mother, there was someone in the car?'

'No, it drove itself, arsewipe.'

'I mean, when it was sitting there, there was someone inside, watching the house?'

'How do I know if he was watching the house?'

'But you know it was a he?'

'Yes, of course. He was wearing a suit, a shirt and tie. He got out and had a pee in Mrs Abernethy's bushes.'

'But he didn't come up to the house? He didn't try to speak to you?'

'I don't owe him money, I never owed anyone a penny in my life, it's you who brings shame on the family, you retarded little—'

I could say a lot of things about Mother, but at least I knew where I stood with her. At school football matches, she would shout encouragement to the other team. In those days I played sports, before the extent of my ailments became apparent. I cut the line and phoned someone who I at least knew wouldn't greet me with a torrent of abuse.

Alison said, 'What the . . . It's six in the . . . What is it, Brian?'

'It's me,' I said.

'Oh.'

'Sorry to wake you.'

'I was up half the night with morning sickness. I only just got over it. What's wrong? You hardly ever call me. When you do, you want something.'

'Listen to me, I'm not messing around. I want you to go to your window, tell me if you see anything unusual.'

'Like what, aliens?'

'Just look. Please.'

'Okay. Okay.' I heard the creak of the mattress on aged springs. 'All right. I see . . . dark. What am I looking for again?' She yawned.

'They've taken Jeff.'

'Who . . . what?'

'Jeff. They were outside the shop. I got Jeff to follow them. They've taken him, captured him, murdered him, I don't know! Christ, why do I always get myself in hot water? What do I know about detection? I like books. I love books. Books don't do anyone any harm, what the hell was I thinking . . .'

'Okay – just *calm down* . . . What about Jeff? Who're *they*?'

'I don't know!'

'But they have Jeff?'

'Yes.'

'Have you phoned the police?'

'It might *be* the police!'

'It can't be *all* the police.'

'Yes it can.'

And then I told her what they'd said, about murder is our business, and she agreed that that wasn't good, and that they may have followed us from William Gunn's, and that it made sense to take a really proper look out of her window. Then she said no, there didn't appear to be anyone watching the house, no BMWs in either direction, though of course that didn't include the one earlier.

'The one . . .'

'When I came home, this car stopped beside me and asked directions. It may have been a BMW; I'm a girl, what do I know?'

I started to go into some detail about chassis and manifolds and horsepower, but soon gave up. 'Directions? Where to?'

'University. She was miles off.'

'She?'

'Yeah. Nice woman.'

'And that was all?'

'Yes. No.'

'No?'

'Well I pointed which way to go and my bangle caught her attention and she said it was very pretty, where did I get it. And I said I worked part time in . . .' She trailed off then, and sighed. 'In retrospect, that may not have been a good idea.'

'Christ.'

'How was I to know? So they're watching both of us, they know where we live and work . . .'

'And they have Jeff. They may have killed him.'

'You only think that because they said murder is our business.'

'And because they've killed two already.'

'We don't know it was them.'

'Chances are.'

'It could have been, like, whatsername, who sang that song, whaddyacall it?'

'I'm sorry?'

'You know, the ironic one. Isn't it ironic? Sheryl Crow. Where she was saying everything was ironic, but actually, none of it was. She had a fundamental misunderstanding of the meaning of irony. Maybe they were being ironic? Murder is our business, when actually they're the good guys and they're only looking out for Jeff and he'll wander through your door in the morning wondering what all the fuss is about.'

'That's bollocks,' I said, and she agreed.

Normally I favour plans of inaction. I am not pro-active, I am inactive. I prefer sloth. I like books. My detections are about observation and deduction. It's all I have.

I opened up as normal at nine. I worked the computer with one hand and rested the other on the meat cleaver beneath the counter.

It was my father's.

He had an interest in cleaving meat.

Which was unusual, for a vegetarian.

Alison arrived. I did not like to put her in the way of danger, but I didn't see what difference it made; they already knew all about her. Alison, bless, came up with useless suggestions for what we might do. Our situation was not helped any by what I found out on-line about the registrations of the two BMWs I had observed outside the shop. They read as if they were normal, but in fact they were impossible; they were a series of numbers and letters that would not come into use for another three years.

Alison said, 'Perhaps they are from the future.'

She wondered sometimes why I did not think of her as an equal partner in the detection business when really it was plain for all to see.

'We can't just sit here and do nothing.'

'I'm not,' I said, the number plate breakthrough being clear, if unsettling, evidence of such.

'I mean, they have him, dead or alive; we have to tell someone. Won't his mother be looking for him?'

Ah, the concept of a mother who would look for one.

I wasn't aware that Jeff had any kind of a family. He was just someone who stacked books. God knows I was burdened with enough of my customers' troubles, but at least there was a remote prospect of squeezing some money out of them. I was *paying* Jeff, I didn't need to know anything at all about him. In fact I realised that I only knew one absolutely concrete fact about him, but it was the only one I needed.

'I know exactly who to call.'

'Uhuh?' She was rearranging books in the window in a frankly unconvincing attempt to persuade passing customers that the sale had been expanded.

'Amnesty International. He's wasted the best part of his adult life working for them; now it's payback time. If they can get excited over some blabbermouth in Africa whining about freedom of speech, just think what they can achieve here with one of their own! There'll be protest marches and hunger strikes and sit-ins; they'll cause so much trouble, they'll have to let him go.' I was quite excited by my plan. I even had the phone in my hand. I was just waiting for praise from Alison before I set the campaign in motion. But she was distracted. 'Alison, are you even . . . ?'

Then I saw what she saw, the BMW parked across the road, and the doors opening, and the suit coming towards us.

24

Instinct whispered *lock the door*, *dive for cover*, but I just stood there, stuck in a no-man's-land between being paralysed with fear and looking gormless. He came in, in his grey suit and black brogues, and short hair, and cursory nod, and began to look at the books. My hand recovered enough strength to curl around the handle of the meat cleaver beneath the counter. Sometimes, in the wee small hours, I have practised with it, fighting invisible enemies. But this was different. He wasn't imaginary. At least I didn't believe he was imaginary – with all the medication, you never can really tell. Hallucinations are rarely communal – unless the Virgin Mary is involved – so the fact that Alison was also watching him suggested that he was real enough.

I was about to say, 'Please don't kill us, we'll do anything you want,' when Alison butted in.

'Is there anything I can help you with, sir?' she asked as she clambered out of the window and moved around behind him to stand with me.

The man in grey selected a book, and turned to the counter. 'I'll take this,' he said. His accent was English, Home Counties.

My heart raced, my foot was drumming and God, my blood pressure. This was the man who had either kidnapped Jeff – or killed him. And here he was in my mystery bookstore, and here was I, defenceless apart from my meat cleaver and my girlfriend, who had once told me she could kill people with her feet, though I'd yet to see any evidence of it. He had chosen Horace McCoy's *They Shoot Horses, Don't They?*. I could have read a lot into the fact that it ended with a murder rather than started with one, but he had selected it way too fast to be making a deliberate point. Anyone who chooses a book that quickly either is a phoney or has been brainwashed by a crime-writing franchise.

'Six ninety-nine,' I said. My voice sounded as weak as my knees felt. Alison put a hand on my back and rubbed in a circular movement. She needed me to be strong. *I* needed me to be strong. God damn it, this was my shop, my living, and this was just a man in a suit. I had faced down greater foes before, including Mother.

Just . . . stand . . . up to him.

'Let's cut the bullshit,' he snapped. 'How much do you want for it?'

I cleared my throat. 'It's not in the sale, but six ninety will do.'

'I said cut the bullshit. You know what I'm talking about.'

'I'm not sure that I do.'

'We have your friend.'

'I don't have any friends.'

'You're pretty cool, considering.'

'Considering what?'

'That we have your friend.'

'You can keep him.'

'Don't try and play the tough guy.'

Alison snorted. We were a good team. I relaxed a smidgen. We were behind the counter, but it could have been a portcullis or a rampart or something, repelling boarders.

The grey man responded with a snarled: 'He told us everything.'

'He doesn't know everything.'

'So there is something to know?'

'There's always something to know,' I said.

'About the thing?'

'About what thing?'

'You know what I'm talking about.'

'I'm not sure that I do.'

'He broke like a twig.'

'You better not have hurt him,' Alison said.

The man in grey shook his head. 'You shouldn't have gotten involved in this, either of you. You don't know what you're dealing with. This isn't for amateurs.'

'Yet here you are,' I said, 'dealing with amateurs.'

'I'm not dealing, I'm giving you a chance.'

'No,' I said, 'we're giving you a chance.'

'Excuse me?'

'You want the thing, you better let Jeff go.'

'Jeff? He said his name was Marcus.'

'Was that before or after you broke him like a twig?' Alison asked.

'Let him go,' I said. 'He knows nothing about this or anything.'

'Then hand it over and that'll be the end of it.'

'A minute ago you were asking how much.'

'Sands shift.'

'Quicksand doesn't.'

'How much do you want?'

'How much do you have?'

'You're not making this easy on yourselves. We can go round and round, but at the end of the day you'll hand it over, because the alternative – you don't want to think about the alternative.'

'Maybe it's you that doesn't want to think about the alternative.'

Alison looked at me. And then at him. She shook her head. 'Jesus Christ, you're like two big kids.'

So much for being a great team.

'Alison, please keep out of this, I can—'

'No! God, we're getting nowhere! Let's all just be calm and talk about this and I'm sure we can work something out.' She put her hand out. 'I'm Alison. You are?'

'Greg.' They shook.

'Good. Let's do business. Who do you work for, Greg? Police?'

'No.'

'Billy Randall?'

'No.'

'Are you a paramilitary, or a gangster?'

'No.'

'Are you a painter and decorator?'

'No.'

'Alison,' I said, 'this could go on all day.'

'I can tell you that I work for the Government.'

'My auntie works for the Government,' said Alison. 'She sends out dole cheques.'

'I can't talk about what I do.'

'She's not supposed to either, but it doesn't stop her.'

He was thinking that Alison was the brains. I had to take hold of the reins again.

'Let's talk about the thing,' I said.

'No,' said Alison, 'let's not talk about the thing, or at least let's not talk about it until we're all agreed what the thing is, and who has it, and why anyone bloody wants it in the first place. All we want is Jeff back.' She turned slightly, and spoke directly to me: 'If he has him, then we just need to help him get what he wants and he'll hand Jeff over. It shouldn't be a problem.'

That got me spluttering. 'Yeah, right, we give him what he wants, next thing you know we've two neatly drilled holes in our foreheads and Jeff's face down in the Lagan, if he isn't already, and this guy has the thing and he's laughing all the way to wherever he's laughing all the way to.'

But she *would not* be spoken to.

'You are *so* fucking paranoid.'

Needless to say, she wasn't massaging my back any more. She turned back to the grey man.

'Listen, Greg,' she said, 'sorry about this – we're worried about Jeff. You just want the thing, right? I'm sure you're not going to harm Jeff, are you? Or us? I mean, that would be stupid, you working for the Government, and our cameras filming every second of this, streaming it all on to our website. Can you imagine, people all over the world tune in specifically to find out what's going on in a wee mystery bookshop in Belfast? Twenty-four hours a day! Even when we're closed! If you ask me, the half of them are fucking crackers, but at least in this case it's working in our favour. I mean, anything happens to us or Jeff, people will know it's you and whoever you work for.'

To give him credit, Greg's eyes did not even flicker or attempt to seek out the cameras, which was a good job.

Alison smiled sweetly. 'So, Greg of the Government, here's how I see it. You've been watching us for God knows what reason, but we spotted you and tried to follow you and then you turned the tables on us and picked up Jeff. All I can guess is it has something to do with the fact that we've been hired by Billy Randall to prove that he didn't kill those two painters in East Belfast. We're getting nowhere with it, but we must have ruffled some feathers to have you so interested. So, Greg, tell us, what's this thing you're talking about? Animal, vegetable or mineral?'

'I'm talking about a dog,' said Greg.

'A Jack Russell?'

'A stuffed dog.'

'A Jack Russell dog that belonged to the Chief Constable?'

'Yes, a stuffed dog that belonged to the Chief Constable.'

'A Jack Russell.'

'I would prefer to refer to it as the Chief Constable's stuffed dog. It is less breed-specific.'

'Is it *not* a Jack Russell?'

'There is some confusion in the breeding community as to exactly what constitutes a Jack Russell. If I refer to the thing as a Jack Russell, then somebody else who doesn't recognise it as such, well, there might be a misunderstanding. We might end up with the wrong dog. We prefer what we prefer. Either way, we want it back.'

'For the Chief Constable.'

'We want it back.'

'We don't have it,' said Alison.

'Then we don't have Jeff,' said Greg.

'You're forgetting the website,' said Alison.

'We can take it down.'

'You can take the feed down, sure, but a thousand copies will be back up in no time.'

'I didn't say the feed. We can take the internet down.'

'You can't just—'

'Don't underestimate what we can or cannot do.'

'We don't even know if you have Jeff.'

'Of course we have him.'

'Let me speak to him.'

'I'm afraid that won't be possible.'

'Then Patch won't be possible.'

'Patch?'

'Yep. We've become quite close. You let us speak to—'

'STOP.'

Surprisingly, it was me, not him. Both of them looked at me. There was no reason for Greg to know that I didn't have a backbone, but Alison had been aware of it for a long time, so she looked the more surprised. I would explain to her later about my epiphany, and then it would be as obvious to her as it suddenly was to me.

Greg's eyes burned into me. 'Stop?'

'Yes. Enough. Do you think you can . . . just . . . come in here and, and . . . threaten *us*? Well . . . you know what I think? I think . . . you've been talking out of your arse! Maybe you do work for the Government, maybe you are some kind of spook, but at the end of the day, you're *here*, trying to browbeat *us* into handing over your precious little stuffed dog, and that doesn't sound to me like you're in a very strong position, and it's not made any stronger by having your face plastered all over the internet. I mean, how dumb is that? If you ask me, you've lost Patch and now you're scrambling to get him back before someone important, i.e. not you, finds out. Eh? Eh? Is that not more like it? If I were you, *mate*, I'd make sure our Jeff turns up without a hair on his empty head out of place, and then maybe we'll talk turkey, *capisce*?' I pulled open a drawer, took out a business card and slapped it down on the counter. 'I've a case to solve and I don't need to be wasting time with the likes of you. So I'd have a wee think about it, and if you've anything to contribute, give us a bell, that's if you even have a job after this. But in the meantime, get the fuck out of my shop!'

It was a perfect ending to our confrontation. Alison's eyes fluttering up to me, impressed. I could have retired happy, there and then.

Unfortunately it wasn't *the* ending. Greg barely batted an eyelid.

'Very good,' he said, 'very *passionate*. But let me put you straight, arsehole. We've already been through this shitty little shop of yours, so I know you don't have any fucking cameras. We've been through your computer – you've got some weird shit on there. I could have come in with all guns blazing, but no, I thought I'd be nice, come in to speak to you, face to face. Your pal hasn't given us shit yet, but he will, and so will you pair. So if I were you I'd have a serious talk amongst yourselves and then give *me* a call.' He produced his own business card and slapped it face down on the counter. 'I'm going to give you twenty-three hours to

197

produce the dog. If you don't, I'll organise it so that all three of you go down for Jimbo and Ronnycrabs.' He nodded at Alison. 'Be sensible. I don't think prison would suit you, not in your condition.'

He raised an eyebrow, then turned and walked to the door.

As he went through it Alison yelled, 'Wanker!'

It wasn't quite Oscar Wilde, but it wasn't inaccurate either.

25

Righteous anger in a small burst is easy, particularly when there is no apparent physical risk. But if there is no positive outcome, then it is just a waste of emotion. On the other hand, sustained and focused anger, with an ultimate objective, is much more difficult to maintain and is definitely something one should aspire to. Obviously there was no point in me harbouring such aspirations. The spine I have is hopelessly buckled and incapable of supporting anything other than the brief flurry of bad temper I had just exhibited, or indeed any kind of organised sporting activity, like hockey, or soccer, or tennis, or golf, or netball, or rugby, or gymnastics, or baseball, or volleyball or dominoes.

Now that Greg was gone, I had to lean on the counter for support – as it clearly wasn't going to come from Alison. She was in no mood to fetch the portable defibrillator I keep in the kitchen cupboard, she being much too fired up by the spook's threat to think of anyone but herself and her suddenly best friend Jeff. I classify anyone who does not think of me first as selfish. She must have been aware that I was labouring for breath, but her self-centredness was so all-enveloping that she completely ignored my condition, choosing instead to focus on Greg's threat: she wanted to call the papers, the radio stations, and every other news outlet known to man, to expose him and his Government-sponsored blackmail. It was a typically female hysterical response, whereas if she'd taken the trouble to order me an ambulance and had me taken to hospital, I could, once I was satisfactorily hooked up to a life-support system, have calmly explained to her what she clearly failed to appreciate, that Greg had chosen his words carefully. We had *twenty-three* hours to come up with Patch, i.e. one short of a television series. He was making his point: don't even think about alerting the media.

I said it anyway, in between laboured breaths, and she immediately flared up: 'We have to! He's your friend!'

'Well actually he's—'

'And he works for you!'

'Well technically—'

'And he was doing you a favour when they seized him. You ordered him out of bed . . .'

'I didn't order—'

'And now he's languishing in some cell, for all we know hooded and waterboarded and his fingernails pulled out . . .' She burst into tears. It was probably the hormones, what with her being up the duff. 'We have to help him.'

I took her hand, despite the risk of infection, and patted it gently. 'Listen, sweetie, it's not like that any more. This is an Obama world. Torture and all that malarkey, it simply doesn't happen any more.'

She took her hand back. 'Christ, you just don't get it, do you?'

'I get it, I get it, I get it. Okay. I'm just trying to cheer you—'

'Well stop it.' She wiped at her eyes. 'You're actually serious, aren't you?'

'Always.'

'About Obama, and the torture . . . ?'

'Yes, of course.'

She sighed. 'Clowns to the left of me, eejits to the right, here I am . . .'

'If you feel you're stuck, you don't have to stay.'

'Will you focus? Our friend is being held by . . . by . . .'

'Spooks.'

'Spooks?'

'Spooks.'

'How do you know he's a—'

'Because while you were ranting and raving, I was putting his number plate into the system, and it's a Government car, and even Government cars have to be registered somewhere, and his is . . . here . . .'

I turned the computer monitor to show her. I had

a Google image of a recently built three-storey building in the middle of Holywood, five miles away from us.

'It's MI5's new regional headquarters; they opened it last year. If their regular base in London is attacked, they take over. Ten thousand square feet of spooki-ness, including a subterranean level, four hundred employees, and you can be sure they have the most hi-tech hi-techy stuff in the world, make an Xbox look like an abacus. When Greg said he'd been through the shop I didn't believe him, not with all the alarms and locks I have, but if he says he's been through the computer, that I'm more inclined to go with. I have firewalls on my firewalls, but their shit is bound to be better than my shit.'

'What sort of weird stuff *do* you have on there?'

'Just stuff.'

'Pervy stuff?'

'Define pervy.'

'On second thoughts, I don't want to know. Okay. You've worked your magic. I'm calmer now. Now what are we going to do about Jeff?'

'I had thought about recruiting a dozen former terrorists, training them into a cohesive unit and storming MI5 headquarters. We may not all get out alive.'

'Okay.'

'Alternatively, we do nothing. At the moment they think he knows *something* but is just holding out on them. If they really did use torture, they'd soon realise that he doesn't actually know anything, but they must be adhering to Obama because I know Jeff has a threshold for pain that is only marginally above my own. I've seen him cry over a paper cut. Never mind waterboarding; if they threatened to throw a glass of lukewarm milk over him, Jeff would give up his mother.'

'Okay. Fair point. That leaves us with the threat. Twenty-three hours to produce Patch or else. Or else what?'

'Well, if I'm right, and I usually am, and Greg's not in control of the situation, then he's going to be pretty desperate to sort this out, which makes him unpredictable. He could do anything. I don't mean we're necessarily going to end up face down in the Lagan with Jeff; it could be more subtle than that.'

'Like a couple of extra noughts added to your rates bill.'

'Well probably not as subtle as *that*. Maybe the best idea would just be to . . . you know, hide.'

'The emu approach to solving problems.'

'Ostrich.'

'Just conveniently forgetting that our chum is being held . . . Ostrich.'

'Yes.'

Alison shook her head. 'You're capable of so much more than this.'

'Capable, yes. But capability requires desire. Desire requires energy and application and courage.'

'You have all of those. Vast reserves of them. They just need to be tapped.'

'I assure you, you're wrong. I just want to be left alone to read my books and sell some.'

'You would give up on this?'

I nodded.

'And if I decide to continue, because I feel a connection to Pat, you would stand back and let me, even in my condition.'

'Your condition has nothing to do with me. You should have used protection.'

Her eyes narrowed. 'Stop it. I know what you're doing, you're just trying to wind me up, I know it's the nature of you, and I also know that you aren't really going to leave me to do this by myself.'

I looked at her.

She looked back.

She had me in a staring match again. My malfunctioning tear duct that causes me to blink in moments of stress did its work. I also have degenerative myopia. I've unsuccessfully applied three times for a cornea transplant.

Alison smiled as I blinked in defeat. I was transparent. It was a side effect of one of my medications. On a bright day with the sun at my back, you could see my liver.

'See? I know you better than you know yourself. It's not because of Jeff, it's most certainly not because of me, or our unborn, or justice; it's because it's a puzzle and you won't let it defeat you. And what makes it even more fascinating than normal is that there's a time limit, and you love having a challenge like that. Twenty-three hours to crack it. You will throw all the facts and clues and rumours and gossip up into the air and then you'll look for your crazy patterns as they land, and you *will* solve it. And the truth is that it will hardly scratch the surface of what you're actually capable of. You know that, don't you? You'll only use, what . . . ?'

'About seven per cent,' I said.

I have never been modest about my own abilities, and with good reason.

Alison clapped her hands together. 'Well, a seven per cent solution is good enough for me, Sherlock. Let's get to it.'

'Okay,' I said.

26

Alison was only partially right. She could never be completely right, because then she would be me. But it *was* a puzzle I needed to solve; it was a gnawer. If anything, it was even trickier than the Nazi case, which had eventually come down to numbers and patterns, my area of expertise; it was also *potentially* just as dangerous. *Potentially* because I was still in two minds about Greg's ultimatum. To stick to his deadline would be a challenge, but it also meant acknowledging that the threat was genuine, that there was a realistic chance of something dreadful happening to me if I failed to produce Patch at the specified time. Or, to a lesser extent, happening to Alison or Jeff. I wasn't entirely sure that such threats actually worked. Did anyone ever solve anything quicker because of the threat of extreme violence? How did it help you to think clearly about anything other than impending death? I can see how from a dramatic point of view a threat helps – because having the bad guy saying we'd really quite like it if you could solve this puzzle as soon as you possibly can probably doesn't put many bums on seats – but in reality, holding the Sword of Damocles over one's head is likely to jumble one's thinking rather than focus it. The fact was that there was no way of substantiating how realistic Greg's threat was; therefore I would ignore it. But I would embrace the time limit in the same way that a chess player accepts that he must sometimes complete his move within a specified number of minutes, or a contestant on *Countdown* must assemble a word from his randomly selected vowels and consonants before an annoying jingle tells him that his time is up. I had to accept that it was one of the rules of the game, and treat it as such: a game.

'Are we focused?' Alison asked.

'I am.'

'Because you've been staring into space while humming that annoying jingle from *Countdown* for five minutes, while all the while Jeff's life hangs in the balance and the clock is ticking.'

Sometimes you just have to let things go. I glanced at my watch. 'I'm good,' I said.

'Okay then, get stuck in. I'll pop over at lunchtime to see how you're doing.'

She moved to the door.

'You're working?'

'Of course I'm working. Bills to pay, cheap diamonds to sell.'

'But Jeff . . .'

'How're you supposed to solve anything with me staring down your neck? Go toss your clues. You need to do it by yourself and you need to do it somewhere where you know you aren't going to be disturbed.'

We nodded around the interior of No Alibis.

There was nothing to say.

She had plagued me for so long about being my sidekick, about being included, that to suddenly turn round and say she was leaving me to it was quite a surprise. A welcome one, I supposed, because it showed that she at last realised how I worked best – alone – but also disconcerting because it was so uncharacteristic. Perhaps the focus of *her* attention was moving away from solving crime to impending motherhood. Working in the jeweller's and actually earning money was akin to gathering the materials she would need for nest-building. Or she was planning to run away with my baby and needed the money. Or she was back to oneupmanship, intent on solving the—

'Focus,' said Alison.

I gave her the thumbs-up.

She exited No Alibis.

She crossed the road and entered the jeweller's.

I watched her front door for twenty-seven minutes in case she tried to escape.

Focus.

From the Latin, *focus*.

Focus, a point towards which light rays are made to converge.

Focus, an earthquake's underground point of origin.

Focus, a jazz album by Stan Getz.

Focus, the part of a sentence that contributes the most important information.

Focus, a novel by Arthur Miller.

Focus, a US Navy air-to-surface missile.

Just fucking *focus*.

I was thinking about the time line and the crime line, and decided to go back to the very beginning, because it all surely started with the death of the dog we now knew as Patch. The manner of his death might seem irrelevant, but I have always believed that until you know everything you possibly can about a case, you cannot properly sift through the facts to find the relevant. It's like looking for a Hallowe'en sixpence in a single bowl of apple pie and custard, when there are five other bowls it might equally be hidden in. To be absolutely certain, you have to go back to the original pie dish, before the portions are served up, and search not just through the sweet stewed apples and soft pastry, but the hard crust that gets left at the edge; indeed, you have to be sure that the sixpence has actually been placed in the pie in the first place and is not just a lie designed to test your honesty and patience, that in fact you haven't been set up and caught in the act, which results in you being locked in a dark cupboard with the corpses of trapped mice and not allowed out for three days.

It seemed clear to me that Patch had come to a sticky end, which had set the whole stuffed dog thing into motion. He wasn't much more than a pup, and surely too young to die from natural causes. More likely the exuberant little critter had charged out into the road and been knocked down. Working on the principle that where there's an accident there's an insurance claim, I decided to call Billy Randall. He sold cheap travel insurance deals with his holidays. He was connected. Insurance companies are like that. They conspire against you.

Despite the fact that he'd given me a number that he said was his direct line, I still had to work my way through a dozen different options courtesy of his automated answering service. Eventually I was put through to him.

He said, 'Have you never heard of the Data Protection Act?'

'Yes,' I said.

'Good. As long as you've heard of it. Then we can agree it's a lot of bollocks. Has this something to do with our case or are you pulling a scam?'

'Don't know yet.'

'No matter. Give me those dates again.'

I gave him the September before last, when Patch had made his first and only appearance in *QIP* magazine as a six-week-old pup, and last July, when he had been stuffed by the senior Gunn while his son was on

holiday. Datewise it was fairly vague, but it was con-
siderably narrowed down by what I presumed was the
location: the Comber Road in Hillsborough, where
Wilson McCabe had moved to on his appointment as
Chief Constable of Northern Ireland. Of course I didn't
tell Billy Randall he lived there.

'Okay, leave it with me.'

'As soon as possible,' I said.

'Keen.'

While I waited for him to call back, I brought up
my website and issued, first of all, an apology to my
small and annoying database of occasionally loyal
customers for the computer glitch that had caused
them to be bombarded with increasingly desperate
pleas to join my Christmas Club, and then followed
that with a different kind of appeal. What they lack
in spending power they make up for in diversity. Spread
out across the city, there was a reasonable chance that
at least one of them would spot Greg's BMW as he
drove it to and from Holywood each day. I thought it
better not to mention MI5. I was looking for his home
address or other locations he might frequent. This
would serve two purposes – first, if we were fairly sure
that Greg and his buds were rogue agents working
without high-up approval, then they had to be holding
Jeff somewhere apart from their headquarters. Second,
if Greg really did have access to my computer, then
he would soon know that I was on his tail as much
as he was on mine, and while that might not exactly
terrify him, it might give him pause for thought.

Billy Randall got back to me within half an hour. He said, 'Sure you don't want to tell me what this is all about?'

'Yes.'

'Is that you do or you don't?'

'Just tell me what you found out.'

'Keen *and* efficient. You're some pup. Just like the late and no doubt lamented pup in this case – the policy-holder made a claim against the Police Service of Northern Ireland for damage to his vehicle as a result of his hitting an unleashed dog, front driver's side panel, and a personal injury claim for whiplash.'

'And did they pay out?'

'No – the policy-holder withdrew his claim.'

'Why would he do that?'

'Probably accepted cash to settle it. Or, it being the police, perhaps he didn't want them turning the tables and investigating him. I know, you're shocked, but it happens.'

The policy-holder was a Michael Gordon; he lived on Windsor Avenue, he was twenty-seven years old. I was intrigued by the fact that this Michael Gordon had chosen not to pursue his claim. Ours is a litigious society.

'And what sort of a car was he driving?'

It was back to not knowing what was or wasn't relevant.

'Focus.'

'I am. But what sort of a car was he driving?'

'Very good, you're very quick. A Ford Focus.'

I laughed, and he said what, and I said nothing, and he said no, what, and I said, no, nothing.

'How's it going with our other thing?'

'It's going well.'

'Anything you can tell me?'

'Not at this time.'

'Do you need any more money?'

'No, I have more than enough.'

He laughed, and I said what, and he said nothing, and I said no, what, and he said, no, nothing.

He wanted to ask more, but I made my excuses and hung up. I liked the fact that he hadn't connected the dead dog to our case. He *could* have been laying a double bluff, but it didn't feel like it; I'm pretty good at reading people, although better at books.

I called the sandwich shop down the street and had them deliver a lunch. When it arrived, I checked it for glass and poison. Then I ate it. It was yum. I called Mother to check that she wasn't dead. I served a customer who for once had no ulterior motive beyond buying a book. After a grim start, it was turning into quite a good day.

I called Alison to tell her how well I was doing.

She said, 'See what you can do when you try?'

It made me feel like I was eight years old, but in a good way, like it was praise from an imaginary mother. When I really was eight years old my actual mother took me to our local swimming pool, inflated my armbands, slipped them on to my feet and said, 'This is what it feels like to drown,' before pushing me in.

But then Alison went and spoiled it by adding, 'And . . . ? What did Michael Gordon say when you called him?'

'I haven't called him.'

'Well call him *now*. Remember last time you imparted any kind of information to Billy Randall? Jimbo and Ronnycrabs were executed very soon afterwards.'

'But *he* was telling *me* about the driver . . .'

'Yes, but only because *you* asked *him* to find it out. Now that he knows, what if there is a connection, what if . . . ? Jesus, man, you're not trusting him now, are you? Don't you think—'

But I had hung up. She had a reasonably good and valid point. If Michael Gordon had any light to shed on *The Case of the Cock-Headed Man*, it would indeed be better to speak to him now in case there was some remote possibility that that light might be extinguished.

And there could have been a multitude of reasons why he wasn't answering his phone.

27

'We are a good team, aren't we? What with me being a cup half full and you being a cup half empty and cracked and leaking over your tractor trunks, we're made for each other.'

She was chirpy and not at all concerned about the dangers that came with blatantly walking along a Lisburn Road busy with traffic or the fact that we might be walking into a trap. Geographically, on a map, the Windsor Park we were heading for appears to be only around the corner from No Alibis, but actually physically walking it, it was at least a mile, and I wasn't happy. I'm not designed for hiking: extended motion causes my calipers to bite into my leg skin. Also, exhaust fumes set off my asthma. More pertinently, we were going to call on Michael Gordon to see why he wasn't answering his phone, and according to Alison, that meant that he was dead, murdered by Billy Randall or someone who was able to monitor Billy Randall's calls, and that meant getting ourselves into another dangerous situation, one from which we would have no easy means of escaping because we were bloody walking because Alison thought it would be good for us and for our unborn. I had tried running, once, and it wasn't for me. She also thought it would be better for the environment. I failed to see how my body decomposing on the sidewalk would be good for anything.

'Are we there yet?' I asked for the third time.

'Nearly.'

I had been phoning Michael Gordon right up to the point where I locked the shop up for the night, and then twice on my mobile as we walked, but still no response. There was nothing suspicious about it at all, I argued, we were only concerned because of the life we led: mystery books and murder. Lots of people didn't answer their phone. He didn't have to be in trouble; he could just as easily be at work, or at the laundry, or grocery shopping, or at the cinema, or buying pot plants, or discussing politics over a coffee in a fashionable café, or . . .

'Murdered,' Alison said.

'I'm cold.'

'Not as cold as him.'

'This is ridiculous.'

'I bet you all the money in the world that there's something up.'

'That's ridiculous. You don't have all the money in the world.'

'You don't know that.'

'Yes I do. It's impossible. It's so childish.'

'You're just scared of losing.'

'I'm not scared of losing. It's just stupid. Besides, we shouldn't be betting when there's a man's life at stake.'

'See, I've won already. You think he's in trouble.'

'I didn't say that.'

'You bloody did.'

'Just . . . shush.'

'Don't shush me, hypocrite.'

'I'm—'

She stopped me by kissing me.

It's an effective way to shush me.

There, in the middle of the footpath, with going-home traffic all around us, potentially hundreds of people who could see that I had a girlfriend.

Michael Gordon's home was a crumbly-looking semi. There were lights on. Alison said that didn't mean anything. His last dying move might have been to switch them on. The front-room curtains were closed, although what appeared to be a forgotten string of Christmas lights continued to wink on and off.

Alison approached the door.

I held back.

She said, 'What? Scared?'

'No, I . . .' I studied my shoes.

'What?'

'I always feel slightly foolish when we say we're private detectives.'

'I don't. I get like a sugar rush. Honey, you're the man, you're the brains, you're the solver, don't be embarrassed.'

I shrugged.

She held her hand out to me. 'Come on. And if we don't like the look of whoever answers, we can try Hallowe'en rhyming.'

'It's January.'

'Never too early.'

I joined her. She squeezed me. She rang the bell. It was an old-fashioned one and sounded laboured.

'We're not breaking in,' I said, 'no matter what.'

'Chicken.'

'You can't just say chicken.'

'I believe I just did.'

'I have a healthy respect for property, and privacy.'

'Chicken.'

Further debate was rendered irrelevant by a light coming on above us. I could now see that the paint on the door was ancient and cracked and peeling. There was a fair to middling chance of getting lead poisoning from it, although probably only if I licked it.

'See?' I said. 'Alive and kicking, scaremonger.'

'Chicken,' said Alison.

'Yes? Who is it?' A woman's voice, suspicious.

Alison nodded at me, I nodded back. She nodded at me, I nodded back.

Alison shook her head and said: 'We wanted to have a word with Michael?'

'He's not here.'

'When will he be back?'

'Who wants to know?'

Alison nodded at me. I nodded back. Alison sighed. 'We're private detectives.'

'Really?'

'Yes, really.'

'In Belfast?'

'Yes.'

'Private detectives?'

'Yes.'

'Stand in front of the peephole where I can see youse.'

Alison stood in front of the peephole. She glanced at me. I stood where I was. I don't like being observed, or judged. Alison grabbed my arm and dragged me into the picture. I winced. Haemophilia.

'Youse don't look like private detectives.'

'We're not supposed to,' said Alison.

'And what's up with Smiler?'

Alison looked at me, then hissed: 'What are you smiling for?'

'I don't know.'

'Well stop it.'

I did my best. Sometimes when I'm embarrassed I suffer from a kind of lockjaw.

'He's not smiling,' said Alison. 'He just has too many teeth.'

The woman was quiet for a while. Then: 'Is this a wind-up?'

'No, madam, I assure you . . .'

'Madam? Aye, right. Well I told you, he's not here.'

'Can we . . . come in and wait for him?'

She laughed. 'Good one.'

'Or is there somewhere else we can contact him?' That was me.

The woman said, 'He talks!' Then: 'Is this about that fucking dog?'

We exchanged glances.

'Yes,' I said.

'Now he won't shut up.' There was another, longer pause then, before a bolt was slid across. And a second one. Then a third and fourth. Then a key in a lock. And the beep of an alarm being deactivated. Finally the door swung open. A large woman, her hair tied back, a glass of white wine in her hand, a cigarette in her fleshy face, looked us up and down. 'I told him all these locks were a waste of time. If they're going to get you, they're going to get you. Youse might as well come in.'

She led us into the front room. Magazines were scattered across a sofa and on the floor. There was a grey-muzzled Labrador sleeping in one armchair, and an ashtray sitting on the arm of the other. I am allergic to dogs. And cigarette smoke.

'Park your bums there and tell us what this is about.'

Alison began. 'Well, it's quite boring really. It's not like *Columbo*.'

The woman tutted. 'Columbo wasn't a private eye. He was a cop. Rockford was a private eye. I could jump his bones, any day of the week. Maybe he's before your time.'

'James Garner,' I said.

The woman smiled.

'Anyway, we work for an insurance company. Your husband filed a claim and then—'

'My husband is dead.'

'Oh. I'm sorry. Was this just—'

'Five years gone. Michael is my son.'

'Okay. Right. Still sorry, but . . . pleased. Michael filed a claim, and then he quickly withdrew it and . . . Well, we're just doing a follow-up, on behalf of the company, to see if there was some reason, you know, if he was dissatisfied with his policy, or the service he got. They use a call centre in Scotland; sometimes the language barrier . . .'

'And they hire private detectives for that?'

'Yes they do,' said Alison.

'No they don't,' I said. 'Mrs Gordon . . .'

'Millie.'

'Millie. Let me be frank.'

'You've suddenly found your knackers.' Millie took a sip of her wine.

Alison was looking at me, pretending to be annoyed.

It was a variation of the old good cop/bad cop routine. We hadn't worked it out, it just came natural.

'Millie . . .'

'Are you here for him, that nutter who attacked him? Because if you are, you can just . . .'

'No, we're not.'

'Well you're not here for Michael. So maybe you're representing the fucking dog.'

She smiled, but it was a bitter kind of a one, with a hint of drunk thrown in.

'Millie.' This was Alison. 'We can't tell you about the case, but it really isn't about your son. It's a murder thing, and it's really complicated, and one of those complications involves the man I think we're both talking about, and the more we know about him the more it helps us to solve the case. We don't mean any harm to your son, honestly, we just want to know what happened with the dog.'

'Exactly,' I said.

'Do you have ID or anything, like a licence?'

'No, ma'am,' I said.

'Ma'am,' Millie repeated, smiling again.

'A licence, that's more of an American thing. We have business cards.'

Alison nodded at me. I rifled in my wallet and held one out.

'Sure any fucker could run off one of those,' said Millie, declining to take it. 'Not that it matters. He's not here anyway, he's gone off.'

'Gone off where?'

'England. Possibly.'

'For a holiday, or . . .'

'No, for fucking good. He was scared, wasn't he?'

Alison moved to the edge of the sofa. 'Of what?'

'Getting another hiding.'

It came out in dribs and drabs, and a few dribbles as well. She was liberal but careless with her consumption of the wine, though not so liberal or careless as to offer us any.

Michael Gordon worked in a bank, played football, had good friends, a steady girlfriend; just an ordinary bloke. His girlfriend lived in Comber with her parents. When he took her home at nights he usually drove through Hillsborough, then along the Comber Road. One summer evening, still bright, he was driving back down that road when a Jack Russell suddenly dashed out in front of his car. He braked, but too late. Michael, being a conscientious guy, jumped out of the car instead of driving on. The owner, having heard the skidding tyres and his dog's dying yelp, raced out of the house. Michael, having done nothing wrong, tried to explain what had happened, but the owner was in a blind fury: he punched Michael in the face, he bounced his head off the bonnet and he kicked him repeatedly in the stomach. The owner's wife came running out and dragged him off. Michael scrambled back into his car and drove home.

Millie poured herself another glass. It was sparkling wine, and bubbled up over on to the arm of her chair.

225

She massaged the spillage into the material before sucking her fingers. 'He'd done nothing wrong, yet that animal laid into him. You should have seen the state he was in when he got back here. I know he's twenty-seven, but he's still my boy. I put him in my car and took him to casualty. They couldn't do much about his nose, but they put a couple of stitches in above his eye.'

'You called the police, though?' Alison asked.

'Of course. Told us to come down and make a statement. Michael was miserable, God love him, but I made him go down and do it. I took photos of his battered face on my mobile. And the damage to the car and the blood over the bonnet.'

'Because . . . ?'

'Because you know what this place is like – I thought the bastard would try to sue my boy for killing his dog. And, you know, I thought we'd be entitled to a few quid ourselves.'

'So he informed his insurance company when, next day?'

'Nope, same night. Did that. Went to work as normal, he comes out and these two big fellas are waiting for him, bundle him into a car, take him up the Craigantlet Hills, put a gun to his head and say if he doesn't withdraw his statement, if he doesn't tear up his insurance claim, if he doesn't get out of the country real quick, then he's a dead man. Then they drag him out of the car and give him another kicking for good measure. He was outta the country without passing

Go.' Millie shook her head. Tears in her eyes. 'I thought all that shite had gone away, but I guess it hasn't. It's just been hiding.'

28

Alison had her arm looped through mine as we walked back down the Lisburn Road. The traffic had lightened; it was crisp and cold and the moon was out. We both felt sorry for the sad old woman, but not at all sorry that we had ruthlessly grilled her for information. She had refused to give us her son's phone number in England, but had promised to pass on our number to him before herself passing out in her chair. We let ourselves out of the house.

We no longer needed to speak to Michael Gordon directly. What had happened to him was unfortunate, despicable given that the man who had first attacked him was the most powerful police officer in the land. But people losc their tempers. The Chief Constable had apparently further abused his power by forcing Michael to flee his home. But what did it have to do with the missing Jack Russell or our case?

I said, 'This is about Jimbo and Ronny, it's not about Michael Gordon. And by the way, Michael Gordon not being dead means you owe me all the money in the world.'

'I didn't say he had to be dead, I said something must have happened to him to stop him answering his phone, and something did.'

'Ages ago. It's hardly the same.'

'*Anyway*. Does it help us?'

'Well it confirms that Wilson McCabe is prone to violence. That he's not above using a couple of heavies to get his way. So if Jimbo and Ronny did cross him, and they were killed shortly after, then there's a chance McCabe was either directly involved or ordered it.'

'Which gets Billy Randall off the hook . . .'

'No it doesn't. McCabe or someone is still setting him up for it. But at least it helps *us* to know that he's innocent. We can concentrate on who really is responsible. McCabe beat Michael up – but it's not just one man losing his temper; it's his job, his public image, he must have known that if it got out he'd be out on his ear, so he calls the heavy mob. But we're still only connecting him to a beating, not the murders. Then there's Greg and MI5. Why do they feel the need to hold Jeff and threaten us? Just to get their hands on a stuffed dog? Why are they involved at all? MI5 deals with national security and terrorism. It doesn't investigate murder. So, logically, the Jack Russell would have to have something to do with national security or terrorism, and it belonging to McCabe means that he must also have something to do with national security or terrorism, either investigating it, or involved in it, or he's a target.'

'You mean like the Jack Russell is a means of killing him? It's a bomb, or it's stuffed with anthrax?'

'Well there are enough former terrorists running around; maybe one with a grudge wants to remove the new head of the PSNI and start the Troubles up again. Or maybe MI5 themselves want to remove him.'

Alison stopped and looked at me. 'To a certain extent I'm okay with terrorism. There will always be misguided nutters. But if you think MI5 are trying to get rid of him, then that's . . . well that's . . .'

'A conspiracy that goes to the highest levels of power.'

'Bonkers,' said Alison.

We walked in subdued silence for a little while, me with one eye on the traffic in case it suddenly dived at us, Alison with her eyes down and her lips moving very slightly as she debated something with herself. We reached the bottom of Botanic Avenue and were just turning towards No Alibis when she removed her arm from mine and gave me a grave look.

'What?'

'We have to go back to Millie's house.'

'Why? She's out for the count.'

'Exactly. We left her asleep, with her ashtray on the arm of her chair, and a cigarette burning on the side of it. Do you remember the way she gave little jumps and starts in between snores?'

'Yes. So?'

'What if she knocks the ashtray over and doesn't wake up and the carpet catches fire? She doesn't have a smoke alarm, I checked. I always check. The smoke will kill her before she even wakes up.'

'She'll be fine, don't worry about her.'

'No, really, I think we should go check.'

I laughed. 'Would you ever wise up?'

I didn't mean anything particularly harsh by it, but Alison reacted as if I'd just slapped her across the face.

'What do you mean, *wise up*?'

'She's not going to catch fire. And even if she does, it's none of our business.'

'Of course it's our business! She got drunk because of us.'

'Bollocks, she was already steamboats when we arrived.'

'She was tipsy, but she wasn't plastered. It was talking about her son got her plastered. If she dies it'll be our fault.'

'Alison, for God's sake, she's a grown woman, she can look after herself. Anyway, the dog will start barking if there's a fire.'

'The dog was snoring louder than she was. I'm worried. We should go back.'

'Alison, you can't mother everyone.'

Her eyes nearly bulged out of her head.

'You think I should just concentrate on you, do you? Well I've news for you, buddy boy, you're going to have to start learning to stand on your own two feet, because when the little man comes along I won't have time to go running after you.'

'And what has that got to do with old Mother Hubbard?'

That was probably the wrong question to ask.

'You would just let her burn, wouldn't you? You selfish, arrogant dwarf.'

'Dwarf?'

'You're an emotional dwarf. You're stunted. You're . . .'

'Alison, it's your hormones . . .'

This, in retrospect, was also quite probably a mistake.

'Hormones? Hormones? And what the fuck would you know about hormones? Why don't you just fuck away off?!'

But, in fact, she was the one who spun on her heel and walked away.

I started after her. 'Alison, please . . .'

'Leave me alone!'

So I stopped.

This, also, in retrospect, was the wrong decision.

She yelled back: 'And you would, wouldn't you? You'd leave me out here in the middle of fucking nowhere! You'd have me go back to that fucking house, you'd have me break down the fucking door, you'd have me fight my way through the smoke and flames and you'd have me drape that fat old tart over my shoulders and carry her out of the house, and then you'd have me give her the kiss of life, and then you'd whine at me until I went back for the fucking dog as well, and all of it in my fucking condition, you fucking wanker!'

'Do you want me to come with you?'

'NO!'

There were a number of strategies I could have followed and perhaps should have followed. I could have walked some yards behind, like a bad dog. I could have thrown myself at her feet and begged forgiveness. I could have caught up with her in the Mystery Machine and given her a lift the rest of the way. I most certainly could have said, you wait here, I'll go and check if the old cow is still breathing.

But I just stood for about thirty seconds to see if she'd turn around, and when she didn't, I walked back to the shop. She was storming off in a huff when she knew full well that I only had about eighteen hours left before rogue MI5 agents carried out their non-specific threat. She was worried about an old smoker we hardly knew catching fire when we were up to our own necks in a conspiracy that threatened to threaten our national security. She was the selfish one. Sod her. She could rescue the old bag and then go back to her fricking jewellery and comics and leave liberty and justice and saving the British way of life to me.

I entered the shop via the back entrance. I turned the lights on and studied the books. I have an abiding interest in patterns. I particularly enjoy the strange patterns that are thrown up when a customer removes a book from one shelf and replaces it on another without me seeing. It's not about finding the book, it's about how it now relates to the books around it, and the sort of disruption and realignment caused by the space it leaves behind.

I did that for a while. It is quite relaxing. The patterns, the smell of the print, the little memories of reading each and every one of those books, the authors who wrote them, the originality or otherwise of the plots, the reviews, the sales, the attempted shoplift-ings. This was my shop. It was my story, my plot, my home. I was indeed feeling mellow, enough to even contemplate forgiving Alison if she first made a heart-felt and grovelling apology. The fact that I hated ninety per cent of human beings shouldn't reflect badly on her; if you liked people and had an interest in them, then being concerned about their well-being went with the territory. I suppose it *was* nice of her to care so much about a stranger. She had heart. She would be a good mother. When she returned I would take her to Starbucks. And she was bound to return. I was irresistible.

But still, no sign of her.

Killing time, I moved behind the counter to check my e-mails. It had only been a few hours since my appeal for information about Greg's car, but my customers, a collection of dullards, drunks and shoplifters, had rather unsurprisingly failed to rise to my challenge.

Nothing.

Bugger all.

I reposted the appeal, and this time added a note of urgency:

Please keep your eyes peeled. If I don't find this car by lunchtime tomorrow, I'm a dead man.

Less than thirty seconds later, which is about as long as it must have taken to type it, I got a response:

Drop you a line after lunch.

I didn't recognise his e-mail address. But no matter.

I despise this kind of smart-arsery. People who laugh at others' misfortunes. He needed to be taught a lesson, one he wouldn't forget in a hurry. I immediately barred him from the shop for two weeks and told him there was no point in even trying to join next year's No Alibis Christmas Club. I added that he might think he was being funny but he was in fact not.

I regretted it almost the moment I sent it. Times were hard and I couldn't afford to be losing even a single customer.

I e-mailed him again and explained that I was under a lot of stress, the case I was working on was rather dangerous and the store was experiencing financial difficulties due to the recession; he couldn't be expected to keep an eye out for a strange car, I'm sure he had a busy enough life, and I was more than happy to have him join the Christmas Club and looked forward to seeing him in the shop in the near future.

He e-mailed back:

Fuck off, you tit.

I immediately e-mailed back:

No, you fuck off. You're barred from the shop for good and I've checked your account and your taste in crime books is fucking shite. And Dorothy L. Sayers is read exclusively by old women and gay men. Which are you?

And he e-mailed back:

Fuck you and your progeny. Next time I'm past your tatty little shop, I'm going to put the windows in.

I e-mailed back:

I only have one window, you wanker.

He e-mailed back:

There's a window in your door, you fuckwit.

I e-mailed back:

Fair point. This is quite funny, isn't it?

He e-mailed back:

I'm going to fucking kill you.

People are *so* touchy. I signed out. I have enough troubles without wasting precious time on a nutter.

About a minute later the phone rang, and previous experience told me what to expect. It was important to get my attack in first.

'Don't you come near me,' I said. 'I've got friends in the police.'

But it wasn't him, it was Alison, breathless.

'She . . .'

'You shouldn't be running, not in your condition.'

'She wasn't there . . .'

I was about to launch in with 'See, you ridiculous idiot, I was right . . .' but thought better of it. I was a bigger man than that. I would be magnanimous. 'Well, it was good of you to go and check. She prob—'

'No, you don't understand . . . she wasn't there . . .'

'I get that, honey.'

'No, I mean . . . she hasn't been . . .'

'Catch your breath, there's nothing to—'

'LISTEN to me. I knocked on the door and she didn't come. I thought she was still asleep or overcome by fumes. I went around the back, the door was locked.'

'You did everything you could . . .'

'I was really worried about her. So I kicked it in.'

'You're always fucking kicking things!'

'Don't shout at me! Listen to me! I broke in . . .'

'And was there a fire?'

'Shut up! She wasn't there! She was gone, the dog was gone, all the fucking magazines were gone. I went through the house; all of the other rooms were empty, I mean completely empty. Do you understand what I'm saying?'

'Not really, no.'

'Then listen, you halfwit! I went next door. The woman there said Michael Gordon moved out last summer and the house has been empty ever since. Do you hear me? Nobody has been living there; his mother died years ago! We were set up, we were fucking set up!'

29

I have long mocked Jeff for his devotion to fantastical conspiracy theories – there is scarcely a moment in history he has not claimed as having been engineered by a Jewish conspiracy, Opus Dei, the Illuminati, aliens, the Magnificent Seven or a small group of junior clerks working for the Nationwide Building Society – while actually I have plenty of time for the more realistic conspiracy theories imagined by some of our finest novelists, many of whom are represented on the No Alibis shelves. There is Graham Greene's masterful 1943 novel *The Ministry of Fear*, Richard Condon's sublime *The Manchurian Candidate* from 1959, and even Umberto Eco's wordy 1988 effort *Foucault's Pendulum* has its moments. What I know from my many, many years of reading such thrillers is that characters who discover a secretive conspiracy are often unable to tell what is real and what is coincidence and are befuddled by the many conflicting facts, rumours, lies, propaganda and counterpropaganda they are faced with. They have to work hard, often at the risk of their lives or sanity, to unravel clandestine machinations and, er, win the girl. So I was certainly open to the *idea* of a conspiracy, and yet, I liked to think, not gullible. Jeff being kidnapped, me being threatened, the Jack Russell being the subject of a doghunt – they all felt bizarre, yet real enough. Although Alison's claim that someone had furnished an empty house with an old woman, an elderly Labrador and personal knick-knacks at what must have been very short notice, all in order to convince us that Michael Gordon had taken off for England when in fact something much more sinister had befallen him, felt like a step too far, I have to admit that having dealt in the past with murderous Nazis, I was no longer capable of being surprised at the lengths to which some people would go to befuddle me.

But I laugh in the face of befuddlement.

If anything, a lifetime immersed in the murky world of mystery fiction has perfectly equipped me for dealing with real-life shenanigans. There is scarcely a twist or turn even the most devious mind could conjure up that I have not already encountered between hard or soft covers. It would surprise me if 'they' had the wherewithal to truly surprise me.

I was just waiting for Alison to return from the house on the Lisburn Road, and was staring at the ceiling,

thinking through the case, when I was disturbed by a
sudden rattling on the security shutter; it certainly
caused me to jump, and to take a firm hold of the
meat cleaver beneath the counter. The rattling was
repeated, but this time with a drunken accompaniment: 'I know you're in there, I can see your lights
on, open up!'

I am used to drunks hurling abuse at me or the
store in general. In truth, the shutters are from the
cheap end of the market, and if you make a determined effort, particularly at the sides, you can just
about make out the lights on within. They are,
however, a considerable improvement on the early
days of No Alibis, before I invested in shutters. I learned
to my cost how vital they could be during the long
weekend of 13–15 June 1998, when a gang of drunks
laid siege to my premises for seventy-two hours,
changing shifts several times during that period to be
sure that there was always someone spectacularly
drunk enough to continue hurling abuse at me and
bang repeatedly on the windows. If I had merely given
them a friendly wave as I worked late then they would
probably have staggered on, but by suddenly switching
off the lights and hiding under the counter I piqued
their interest and hurt their feelings with one flick of
a switch, and as it coincided with a sudden upsurge
in our Troubles, and there were no police available to
deal with what they considered to be a minor matter
of public disorder, I was forced to survive for all of
that time on half a bottle of water and three Opal

Fruits. It was like the siege of the Alamo, but less dramatic.

This time, however, I had the relatively recent addition of the security cameras, with which I was able to zoom in on the drunk, who had continued his assault on the shutters. Even so, with the poor street lighting and the fact that he was wearing a poseur's wide-brimmed hat, it took several minutes for me to realise that I knew the man, and several more minutes of internal debate for me to decide it was wise to raise the shutters. It was out of fear for my own safety. Being bored to death is not the way I intend to go.

However, the fact that he was a Booker-nominated author, that he taught a weekly creative writing class in my shop, and had even penned two bestselling, critically acclaimed mystery novels, were some of the mitigating grounds that led me to press the button that raised the shutters and eventually admitted Brendan Coyle into the inner sanctum. One has to think of business.

My thanks were wrapped up in his opening remark: 'And about bloody time too.'

He had a half-drunk bottle of white wine in his hand. He took off his hat and skimmed it across the shop. It landed on the buy-one-and-get-another-at-exactly-the-same-price table.

'Brendan, have you been out on the town?'

'Yes, of course I have, Emil.'

He giggled. Brendan had taken to referring to me

as Emil in tribute to the boy hero of *Emil and the Detectives*, the 1929 children's novel by German writer Erich Kästner, which for a period in the 1960s had become required reading at primary schools across the country and which, he claimed, had inspired in him a lifelong fascination with crime fiction. It had not, however, inspired him enough to buy the copy of the first English-language printing of the novel, which I had acquired for a not inconsiderable sum off the internet on the presumption that a man of his means would leap at the opportunity to own such a perfect little reminder of his childhood. When I showed it to him, he actually almost physically turned his nose up at it, saying that he much preferred the less widely known 1933 sequel, *Emil and the Three Twins*, which he felt had been unjustly ignored because of the Nazis' concurrent rise to power. Since I was already several hundred smackers out of pocket, if he thought I was going to search that one out only to be fobbed off with another pathetic excuse, he could kiss my arse.

'I saw the light, and couldn't resist calling in to see my old buddy, proprietor of the finest literary establishment in town!'

Pissed again.

'What was the big occasion?' I asked.

'Oh, some little poet was publishing his first collection. I like to offer support where I can.' He suddenly patted his blazer pockets. 'Dash it, I appear to have left it in the bar. Oh well, no harm; better that the common man picks it up and perhaps learns something rather than an old soak like me. What're you doing here so late? Looking at your damned patterns again?'

'Who told you . . . ?'

Generally I keep my habits to myself. Not everyone understands.

'Oh, that little pal of yours who works here sometimes. What I understand you might refer to as a "slacker".'

'Jeff,' I said.

'That's the boy. Couple of pints soon loosens his tongue!'

Poor Jeff. I had always known he was weak with drink, a gossip and jealous of my success with a woman. But still. Poor Jeff, banged up by spooks; my fault, my fault, Alison had said. And she was not wrong. Without being wholly right. Which is my domain.

'Yeah well, I wouldn't be listening to him, the slabber.'

'A wise head on young shoulders. He knows things, about Chapple . . . Chapple . . .'

'Chappaquiddick.'

'That's the one. And not just Chapple . . . Chapple . . . you know what I mean. Other stuff. Closer to home.' Brendan gave me an outrageously theatrical wink.

'Yes, Brendan,' I said, 'it's all one big conspiracy. Even the Booker Prize . . .'

'Exactly! Those *bastards*!' He looked at his

bottle, then he looked at me. 'I say, old man, you wouldn't have a little old glass I could slosh this into, would you? One tries not to imbibe directly from the tap.'

I told him I would see what I could do. I went into the kitchen to pretend to look for one. I was long past the stage of regretting letting him in and was praying that Alison would very quickly arrive and shoo him out. She's better at that kind of thing. I don't like to confront if I can help it. I could stab you a million times in my own head, but I would have trouble saying no to you. Alison says I'm like silly putty in everyone's hands. I tried to tell her that silly putty was created by accident during research into potential rubber substitutes for use by the United States in World War II, and that it will dissolve when in contact with alcohol, which is exactly what happens to me, but she told me to *shut up*.

So I did.

'That, that Jeff one . . . when he got on to the moon landings, I just switched off!'

'Uhuh.'

'Nearly brought him with me, but he demurred!'

I stepped back into the kitchen doorway. 'You nearly brought him what?'

'I put it to the fella, let's break in and rearrange your shelves, that would fair put the wind up you, but give him his due, he wanted nothing to do with it! Blessed fool was trying to listen to the poetry . . .'

'He was . . . tonight? You're talking about tonight?'

'Yes, of course.'

'And Jeff was with you? My Jeff? With the hair and the combat jacket and the Amnesty International . . .'

'All the badges, your Jeff. He's so concerned, so . . . committed.'

'Where exactly was this?'

'Ah, down the road, where they do the poetry . . .'

'Brendan, listen to me. Tell me exactly where you saw Jeff.'

'Man, dear, you look like you've seen a ghost. The Holiday Inn, my dear chap; they do a lot of book launches, seeing as how nobody actually wants to holiday in this godforsaken place yet . . . What are you doing?'

'Take this.' I handed him one of my chipped Penguin Classics mugs. Agatha Christie's *The Murder at the Vicarage*. 'Now make yourself at home. There's more wine in the kitchen.'

'But . . .'

'Just do it!'

I had lowered the shutters again to stop any other drunks from wandering in, so took the back way out, locking Brendan in behind me. I hurried down the back lane. Just as I emerged on to Botanic Avenue, Alison came hurrying up, her face flushed with excitement and fear and exertion. Before she could say a word, I bellowed: 'Jeff's in the Holiday Inn! He's drunk and listening to poetry!'

She took only the briefest moment to compute that.

She had a wonderful facility for turning what I was thinking into a succinct and pithy observation.

'The fucker!' she cried.

30

At a No Alibis event, the launch of a new book or one of my theme evenings – *Victorian crime novels and why they're important NOW!* comes to mind; it was hugely popular if rather drab – you can be fairly certain that while there will always be a few amateur writers in the audience, most are there because they love reading and don't aspire to anything beyond that. Poetry events, on the other hand, are almost exclusively attended by other poets, who are, generally speaking, an extraordinarily wilful, selfish, egotistical, drunken, back-stabbing bunch of layabouts, and that's just the published ones. Those who have yet to see their names in bold type – and I discount the internet here, because any old shite can be published there – are all of those things, with added bitterness and jealousy and a propensity to sudden bouts of extreme violence. Entering the Holiday Inn Express at a little after ten o'clock on a Tuesday night was like venturing into a war zone. The smell of blood and innards and desperation was thick in the air, tobacco smoke clung to coats and beards, and puddles of vomit mixed with Guinness spillages to produce an odd moonwalking effect as we pushed through the crowds looking for Jeff, while being quietly aware that we were also there on the word of a drunk. But then, off in a corner, surrounded by girls, just lifting a pint to his mouth, my eyes met his, and he looked momentarily stunned. He set down his drink and quickly moved out from behind his table, stepping on toes, knocking over glasses, determined to get away.

'There goes the scabby little fucker now,' said Alison.

And there he went, and there we went, shouting after him, but our cries were drowned out by the hubbub and the righteous anguish of souls in torment, our progress hindered by poets refusing to give an inch. For a moment I thought we'd lost him before spotting him in the slightest gap between two bickering groups, bent almost double, squeezing through towards the toilets at the back of the room. I signalled Alison, who had been moving in a different direction, hoping to cut him off. She gave me the thumbs-up and we met at the entrance to the toilets. Once through the main door, the men's and ladies' were left and right, and we divided according to sex. The men's was empty save for a coot crying as he leaned over a urinal, his head resting on his arm against the wall.

Alison's voice echoed off the tiles: 'He's in here!'

I entered the ladies'. One woman was waxing her moustache in a mirror, another was assaulting the condom machine and repeatedly shouting, 'It ate my pound! It ate my pound!' Neither of them seemed to notice me. It was the story of my life.

Alison had literally cornered Jeff. 'Here he is. Here's the dirty stop-out.'

I wasn't quite sure yet why he was cowering the way he was. He was a young, fit man who worked out occasionally; he could have whipped me and Alison with one hand tied behind his back and one leg amputated at the knee, but his back was against the wall, and he looked truly terrified. I supposed we had the moral high ground, which has a strength all of its own.

'Hello, Jeff,' I said calmly. 'Fancy seeing you here.'

He held his hands up in a pacifying gesture. 'I can explain . . . I can explain . . . You . . . youse weren't followed here? Were you, were youse followed?'

'Followed, Jeff?'

'By *them*! They're watching, watching everything!'

'They're not watching in here, Jeff.'

I was in absolute control.

Alison was rather letting the situation get the better of her. She jabbed a finger at him and shouted: 'So spill the beans, you little shit!'

'I'm sorry . . . I'm sorry . . . They told me . . . they told me I didn't know what I was involved in, that if I knew what was good for me I'd stay away from youse, that I shouldn't go to work or call or even switch my phone on, just to lie low. He said youse were up to your necks in something and they kept asking me about a dog, a Jack Russell, where was it, where had we hidden it, they kept shouting at me, they kept yelling and saying give us the dog, where's the dog, give us the dog and I didn't know what they were talking about and they wouldn't believe me and I thought they were going to kill me . . .'

'Did they actually kill you, Jeff?' Alison asked.

'No . . . obviously . . .'

'Did they hurt you?'

'They shouted!'

'Where was this?' I asked. 'Were you in their HQ?'

'No . . . thank God . . . You go in there and you don't come out!'

'Then where?'

'They made me drive down the coast. A beach. I thought they were going to drown me.'

'Did they drown you, Jeff?' Alison asked.

'No, obviously . . .'

'Obviously.'

'They said if I co-operated, they could help me – help us . . .'

'Us?'

'Not us . . . us . . . Amnesty . . .'

'Oh *Amnesty*,' I said.

'Never mind *us*,' said Alison.

'And how were they going to help *Amnesty*?'

'They said they could arrange for Hugo Cadiz to stay in the country.'

'Who the fuck is Hugo Cadiz?' Alison snapped.

'He's a poet. A political activist. He's Chilean. They've been trying to send him home for months. Today his visa suddenly came through. They can do that!'

'So you sold us out for a visa?'

'I didn't sell you out! I didn't know anything!'

'So you think you somehow played them?'

'No! Yes! I don't know! All I know is that they said they'd help us out if I helped them out, but I didn't know anything.'

'So you made something up?'

'No!'

'You must have given them something?'

'No! Only stupid stuff . . .'

'Like what?'

'Just stuff about the shop, about you being preg—'

'You fucker!'

'They were shouting at me! They had me in a car, in the dark, by the sea. I thought they were going to kill me!'

'Fucker.'

'It's easy for you to say. You weren't there.'

'A man shouted at me, so I ratted out my friends.'

'Okay,' I said.

'Okay?' Alison spat.

'Yes, okay. Enough.'

'Oh, listen to the fucking voice of reason. Is this how you're going to stand up for your kid?'

'Alison.'

'Fuck off.'

She turned on her heel and strode to the door.

'Where are you . . . ?'

'I'm going to get a drink.'

'Do you think that's wise in your . . . ?'

'Oh fuck off!'

She stormed off. I looked at Jeff. He shrugged.

I said, 'Well, I'm glad you're not washed up on a beach.'

'So am I.'

'Because I'd much prefer Alison had the pleasure.'

'I'm sorry, but I really gave them . . . nothing.'

'Yeah.'

I turned and went after her.

As I reached the door, Jeff said: 'Do you think she's hormonal?'

I stopped, but only for a moment.

She was on a stool with a Bacardi Breezer. The length of the bar itself was packed with parched poets trying to attract the barman's attention, yet in those few seconds she'd managed to get herself served and create a space in which she could comfortably sit. She was giving off an aura of *don't mess with me*.

I came up behind her and said, 'Are you okay?'

She turned and smiled up at me. 'Course I am. Here.' She handed me an orange juice. 'He's just such a limp little . . .' She shook her head.

'Well, look on the bright side. It definitely proves that Greg's working to his own agenda, otherwise they'd have had him in their big shiny new building beating the shit out of him. Maybe we can afford to ignore his twenty-three hours or else?'

'Doesn't it just mean that he realised Jeff was a gutless idiot who would rat his mother out if you blew smoke in his face, so he let him go in order to concentrate on shafting us?'

'That's certainly another way of looking at it. But I thought I was the one whose glass was always half empty?'

She nodded. She gave me a long look, then said, 'Good point. Do you think then that they haven't been through your computer, or the shop?'

'Sounds like they haven't.'

'So they probably haven't bugged your house or installed secret cameras.'

'No.'

'Because your mother would have flayed them alive.'

'Definitely.'

'And if they haven't done yours, they haven't done mine, which means we're free to go back there right now?'

'Yes. But why? What are you planning?'

'You'll see.'

'Have you worked this all out? Do you know what's going on? Do you know where the Jack Russell is?'

She smiled. 'No.'

'Then?'

'I'm just feeling very, very horny, and we haven't done it in months.'

'Oh.'

'And I'm impressed with you. You took control of the situation. You restored order. And we ran all the way here, and you didn't complain once about your brittle bones, or your busted knee ligaments, or your blood pressure or your malfunctioning lung or any of your other bollocks.'

'It's the early-onset Alzheimer's. I forget—'

'Take me home now, before I change my mind.'

'Okay.'

We headed for the door. Jeff was standing there, talking to a girl. As Alison passed, she growled at him. As I passed, I nodded and mouthed: 'Hormonal.'

But I was grinning like an idiot.

31

Alison was snoring gently, and I was thinking about what would happen if I pinched her nose. And covered her mouth. The head is so full of holes, and the ear, nose and throat are *supposedly* connected; you would wonder why it isn't possible to breathe through your ears.

I was finding it difficult to sleep, which had been true since November 1976. No particular reason, besides Mother's cupboard. Now, in the semi-darkness – the curtains were half open, with a street light providing an orange glow – I lay back, trying to ignore the fact that I was being watched by hundreds of eyes. This was not my usual and justi-fied paranoia; it was the fact that every available inch of wall space was filled with Alison's artwork: characters bizarre and grotesque yet somehow sympathetic. I had been aware of the paintings before, but only from a distance, when I used to lurk in the undergrowth outside her window and watch her. Perhaps lurk is the wrong word. I would nestle in the bushes. I was standing guard. I had always been intrigued by her drawings, but this was my first opportunity to see them up close. She did good eyes. They say that the eyes are the windows of the soul, so it's a good job that my cataracts act like Venetian blinds.

I studied her. Beautiful. Younger than me. If I just used a pillow to smother her, then it probably wouldn't feel as bad as actually pinching her nose and clamping her mouth.

It seemed like the most natural thing in the world to do. Making love. With my various illnesses I had so little time left, so it would be good to go out on a high. I could finish her, then nip round to Mother's and enjoy putting her out of her misery. Then, God knows, I had enough medication stockpiled to take myself out and half the city if I chose to somehow get it into the water supply.

There was, of course, the problem of the baby.

She was the mother of my child.

I wouldn't want to kill a child; that would just be sick.

Presently I became aware that Alison's eyes were open.

'Hello,' I said.

'Hello,' she said. 'Are you thinking nice thoughts?'

'I was thinking about the Munich Olympics.'

Alison smiled blearily. 'I'm glad someone is,' she said softly, and her eyes closed again.

I never truly sleep, but I do enter a netherworld where I dream so frenetically that when I open my eyes I am more exhausted than before. There is also a lot of thrashing about. It was lucky that Alison was no longer in bed with me. I could hear her voice, and another woman's, coming from further down the hall, probably the kitchen, chatter and laughs. I had a sudden dread that it was her mother, or her sister. I had never been interested enough to ask if she had either, but the prospect of meeting them was enough to reduce me to a nervous wreck, a state of mind I don't usually embrace until after I've been verbally abused by *my* mother at breakfast. Alison I could just about cope with; being scrutinised by or having to make small talk with strangers without the prospect of commercial gain was just anathema to me. But I was fully awake now, rubbing at my skin, convinced that the bed bugs had been at me. One of the many reasons I find it difficult to sleep is that I stay awake to watch for them. They are generally active just before sunrise. They use two hollow tubes to pierce the skin. With one tube they inject their saliva, which contains anticoagulants and anaesthetics, while with the other they withdraw the blood of their host. It's a fucking wonder that *anyone* can sleep.

I got up. Alison's bra and pants were on the floor. I put them on.

Not necessarily in a perverted way.

I just wanted to know what it felt like to wear Alison's underwear.

I looked at myself in the mirror.

From along the hall Alison shouted, 'Are you awake? Do you fancy some eggs?'

'Just coming,' I called back.

I was fully dressed, in my own clothes. I shuffled into the kitchen, hands in pockets, but it was not Alison's mother or sister, unless of course it was some *huge* coincidence. It was Pat, the late Jimbo's intended and soon to be the mother of his child.

'Oh,' I said.

'She said you wouldn't mind.'

Alison was at the cooker, scrambling eggs. 'How would you like yours done?'

I wouldn't. I didn't. I shook my head and asked if she had a Twix. I had once known a child who was allergic to eggs, whose head had swollen to the size of a trombone. I like to minimise risk. I was not that child. Alison opened the fridge and gave me a Twix.

'I got them,' she said, 'just for you.'

'That's sweet, so it is,' said Pat. 'Jimbo used to do stuff like that for me, so he did.'

'Poor Jimbo,' said Alison. I was trying to make eye contact with her, but she was back to stirring her eggs. What was this woman even *doing here*? She was burying her man today, there were bound to be things to do. I sat down at the table. She was smoking and using a saucer as an ashtray. There were *no words*.

Pat smiled at me. Yellow teeth. 'Sorry,' she said, 'but we just got on like a house on fire, and she said to call if I wanted a shoulder to cry on, and I just had one of those nights where I couldn't sleep for thinking about him, and my family, they do their best, but they just don't know what I'm going through, and Ali does, so she does.'

Ali. *I* didn't even call her Ali.

'And you're more than welcome.'

Ali set down a plate for Pat, then returned with her own.

Pat said, 'These are gorgeous, so they are.' She nodded at me, and when she spoke I could see egg in her mouth. 'I should have guessed you weren't a cop. And Ali – we got on too well for you to be one, so we did. But private investigators, that's exciting.'

'It has its moments,' said *Alison*.

'Have youse gotten any further? The police tell me nothing.'

'Not really,' I said.

'Oh I wouldn't say that,' said Alison.

'We can't really talk about it,' I said.

'Oh balls,' said Alison. 'Her boyfriend was *murdered . . .*'

'I know he was.'

'. . . and she's having a baby. Imagine it if was our baby and you were murdered . . . I'd want to know. Wouldn't you want to know everything there was to know if I was murdered?'

Probably not, was the correct answer. I would just

move on. But I managed a nod and said, 'Well, there really isn't anything to report.'

'Apart from the Jack Russell,' said Alison. 'For some reason everyone's interested in the dog.'

'Why on earth?' asked Pat.

'If we knew that . . .' said Alison. 'I suppose it just stands out – why would anyone steal it? On the other hand, it could just as easily be a load of bollocks.'

'It's a mangy old thing, so it is.'

Pat nodded to herself for several moments, while Alison and I made eyes at each other. She was meaning for me to make more of an effort; I was meaning for her to show Pat the door.

'Youse wouldn't have a couple of Hedex, would you?'

'Of course, love.'

'We had a bit of a . . . well, do you call it a wake? It's more of a Fenian expression, isn't it?'

My eyes flicked up to Alison as she put down the tablets. She suppressed a smile. It was so totally un-PC, but probably not uncommon in Pat's neck of the woods.

'A party to celebrate his life,' Alison suggested.

'Aye, well, I don't like wake anyway, like he's gonna wake up.'

'That's not actually what it means,' I said. 'It means standing guard, or watching out for him.'

'Okay, Brainiac,' said Pat. 'Whatever. We had a few drinks too many, so we had, and I'm not half feeling it. Friends and neighbours, you know? It was nice, telling stories about him, so it was, but strange, him being there, in the middle of the room, in the box. Strange.'

'How did he look?' Alison gave me a look. I said, 'What?'

'It's not the sort of question you ask.'

'Why not?'

'It just *isn't* . . . I'm sorry, Pat, he has no sense of—'

I cut in with: 'My dad was a handsome man.' People stand on ceremony too much. 'But by the time the morticians got to work on him, he looked like Frankenstein's monster. Or maybe not him, but like he'd been beaten with a mallet and allowed to swell up. You couldn't see his eyes hardly at all. He looked like a pig. Piggy eyes. With make-up on. Like a Regency whore's make-up. Really heavy and pink. A piggy-faced whore.'

Alison nodded. 'Thanks for that,' she said.

'He did,' I said. 'Did Jimbo . . . ?'

'Christ,' said Alison.

But Pat was shaking her head. 'The coffin was closed. I didn't want to remember him dead, if you know what I mean? I wanted to remember him how he was.'

'Quite right,' said Alison.

'But now I'm all worried about the funeral,' said Pat. 'I'm worried about who'll be there. Don't they say that killers always turn up at the crime scene or at the funeral? What if he comes up and I shake his hand and I won't even recognise him. I won't be able to concentrate.' She smiled a little then. 'Didn't he always love a good bonfire? Sure, settin' fire to him today will be right up his street.'

She made it sound like it was some kind of Viking funeral, rather than a routine cremation at Roselawn. But she was right about the attendees – if reading countless thousands of mystery novels had taught me anything, it was that the murderer almost always showed up at the funeral. Most murders are committed by someone familiar to the victim and it would seem odd if they didn't attend the ceremony. Some gave Bible readings from the pulpit, others delivered tearful eulogies, all the while praying to God that the net was not slowly closing in on them. It was the nature of murder, and it brought me back to Pat, and who she knew who had known Jimbo and could possibly be responsible. I asked her again to go over his friends, his dealers, his customers, but she shook her head and took a drag on her fag and said, 'The detectives have been all over me, they took the names I knew, practically everyone I ever met, so it was, and I've heard nothing. I'm not going to suddenly remember someone . . .' She stopped then, and her mouth dropped open a little, and we both leaned a little closer, then she smiled and said, 'I mean, am I? You know what you know at the time and do your best. If they'd found someone, they'd have arrested them, they wouldn't let him come to the funeral, and if you knew who it was, you would have them arrested, so I'm thinking, so I am, that nobody knows anything and we're going to set fire to my Jimbo and it could be anyone there watching, so it could, maybe cheering because they know the evidence, something the cops haven't even thought of, is going up in flames.' Big tears began to roll down her cheeks. 'How am I going to get through today? How am I?' She ground her cigarette out into her ashtray saucer, then placed her hands palm down on the table. They were shaking. 'Why did my Jimbo have to die? Why him? What am I gonna tell my baby?'

She wanted a hug. But Alison had risen to rinse the scrambled egg pan. Instead she crumpled into me and sobbed, her whole body shaking. I don't like uncontrolled displays of emotion. I tried to eat the Twix and pat her back at the same time, but I couldn't get it quite right. She sensed my discomfort and let me go. She wiped at her tears.

'Sorry,' she said.

I sneezed.

'Sorry,' I said, and handed her some kitchen roll.

32

In the shop, after Pat had finally gone to prepare for the funeral, we were both pretty nervous. Although we had dismissed Greg's twenty-three-hour threat as just talk, the hands of the clock were still moving inexorably towards noon. Alison, taking her art more seriously and with her hours in the jewellery shop cut back, was there for me, both as my crime-fighting partner and for moral support, but she also seemed to feel the need to be very touchy-feely, which was awkward and embarrassing and would have been much more so if we had actually had a customer. I kept saying, 'Don't,' and she kept laughing and trying it again.

By 11.45 a.m. I had sought sanctuary in the kitchen. I was trying to restore some sort of order – Brendan Coyle had trashed the place looking for the wine I had lied to him about, so I guess that joke kind of backfired on me – when I heard the shop door open. I have a bell that sounds, and several buzzers and whistles. The kitchen door was closed to stop a puddle of Booker-nominated urine reaching the display area, so I couldn't be sure who it was, but with the chances of it being a customer rather remote, I had to presume that it was Greg, coming early, hoping to catch us off guard. I am *never* off my guard, but also I am never more than three seconds from running away – although running, in my case, obviously is not the same as running in, say, your case, unless you're in a wheelchair yourself or have splints or malformed muscles – so I already had the back door open and was preparing to make a calipered bolt for safety when Alison shouted back: 'Someone for you!'

It didn't sound like how she would announce Greg's arrival, so I hesitated, one foot already out.

'I'm busy. Who?'

'Come and see.'

She sounded cool, but not unduly distressed. So I moved back to the kitchen door and opened it just enough to let me see who it was. There, by the counter, looking sheepish, was Jeff. His hands were thrust into the pockets of his combat jacket and he was avoiding eye contact with Alison. He brightened, a little, when he saw me come properly into the shop.

'Hi,' he said.

'I was asking him if I could help him with a book, but he didn't seem interested.'

Alison was smiling, although in an American *have a nice day* way, devoid of emotion.

'Well,' he said, 'this is awkward.'

'Not for us,' said Alison.

Jeff gave me a hopeful look. 'I was wondering, you know, about my job, and if, like, I could have it back.' Alison snorted. 'Look, I'm sorry, I was just freaked out. And besides that I've been thinking about what happened, and now I know they had nothing to do with Hugo Cadiz getting his visa.'

Alison rolled her eyes and said, 'Hugo Cadiz.'

'How'd you work that out?' I asked.

'Well I went round to see him, and he showed me the document he needs to have him stay, and it was dated last week, and he showed me the envelope it arrived in, and it was posted two days ago, which would have been before they picked me up and took me down to the beach and shouted at me, so I guess they were basically bullshitting me.' He looked very briefly from me to Alison and back. 'I want back in. The shop. The investigation.'

'He's a double agent,' said Alison.

'I'm not, I swear to God.'

'He's a double-bluffing double agent.'

'I'm not, I'm really not. Give me a task and I'll prove it.'

'Well you could open those boxes of books and get them shelved,' I suggested.

'I mean some kind of mission.'

'Send him out for buns,' said Alison.

There was an impasse.

I wanted to support Alison. But, also, I needed Jeff.

He was cheap and strong and guilty of not really very much.

An impasse must always be filled.

Or perhaps it's a vacuum.

The shop door, almost creaking through overuse, opened for the second time in as many minutes, and I turned, fully expecting to find Greg, but instead found another familiar but for once more welcome face.

'Detective Inspector,' I said, 'an unexpected pleasure.'

DI Robinson's brow furrowed. 'Why? You left a message for me.'

At this point, Alison said she had to pop out to get some coffee from Starbucks. She averted her eyes from me as she passed. She opened the door, and just as we watched her, for she was eminently watchable, a BMW rolled slowly past the shop, right to left.

There was Greg, in the passenger seat, raising two fingers and a thumb, like a gun. Pointed up at first, but then moving slowly down to point at Alison. Except this wasn't sunny LA, and his window was up, and he bumped them on the glass, and then he fumbled for the button to lower the window, but too late, he was past.

It was funny.

But funny like a fire in an orphanage.

Because it was suddenly clear to me what the whole motif of the case was.

Ineptitude.

From the murders of Jimbo and Ronnycrabs, the

bed-shitting Jack Russell thieves and the non-kidnap of Jeff, from the police investigation to the rogue MI5 agent's threats, it all reeked of ineptitude; but there was no relief with this realisation, because ineptitude is not only what gets you caught, it's also what gets you killed.

33

Later she said she was worried what Greg might do to me. It was caring, but wrong. Greg didn't scare me in the way that, say, cows and other herbivores do; I had shown her before that I was prepared to stand up to him, and this lack of belief in me worried and annoyed me. Yes, obviously there were my health issues, the brittle bones, and the collapsed lung, and the blood pressure, and the Achilles tendon problem, and the arthritis, and the fibromyalgia, and the colour blindness, and the recurrent tinnitus, although instead of an incessant high-pitched squeal, what I actually heard was a brass band playing 'The Battle Hymn of the Republic' twenty-four-seven, but not too loud and quite hummable. I remained confident, though, that I could match wits with and outfox the likes of Greg the spy. Now I had been undermined by a dizzy blonde acting flaky and calling the cops. Later, she also said she was worried about Greg just shooting me, which, I had to admit, was a strategy I would probably have found difficult to outfox. But she knew she had done me wrong, which was why she had skedaddled, leaving me with DI Robinson and Jeff.

'Did I see what I thought I just saw?' Robinson asked.

I nodded.

'Weirdos,' he said. 'Anyway, what did you want to see me about?'

'A book came in, thought you might fancy it.' I turned to the shelf behind me where I keep the rarer volumes and customer orders. I pulled one out and showed it to him. 'It's a first edition of James Hadley Chase's *The Dead Stay Dumb* from 1939. Very rare. In America they called it *Kiss My Fist!*. Which is just . . . wrong.'

The DI studied me. Then the book. Then me. 'How much?'

'One twenty.'

'What do you think a DI gets paid?'

'Plus kickbacks.'

'Oh yeah.'

He continued to study me. He was pretty good at not blinking.

'I thought maybe you wanted something else,' he said. 'I thought maybe you were still on that little case of ours, and you'd found something, and you wanted to come clean, the way you did last time, and we both benefited from it.'

'You more than I.'

'You got your picture in the paper, you sold a few books, people come to you with their problems.'

'People annoy me.'

I was going to expand on that statement, then I thought, no, it pretty much said it all.

It was only at this point, being preoccupied by Greg's drive-by fingering, Alison's betrayal, and scrambling to construct a cock-and-bull story for the detective inspector, that I realised he was wearing a black tie, and why.

'You're going to the funerals?'

'Jimbo's. Ronny's is being delayed for about a week. Something about most of his family being in Canada. You going?'

'Maybe.'

'Thought you might. Thought as seeing I'm here I could offer you a lift, you know, reduce our carbon footprint. It's not for a couple of hours; maybe we could catch some lunch and we could talk about the meaning of life.'

To which the obvious response was: there is no meaning, and it's pointless. But perhaps that wasn't quite what he meant.

'Appreciate the offer, but I've things to do first.'

Robinson nodded at Jeff, who was on his knees unpacking books. 'What about the boy wonder? Maybe I should take him for lunch, see what he knows?'

Jeff swallowed. He looked up at me for support.

'Sure,' I said.

Robinson smiled. 'Let's cut to the chase. I'll give you a hundred for it, and nothing more.'

'One twenty.'

'Which part of nothing more do you not understand?'

'One twenty.'

'One ten.'

'One twenty.'

'One ten.'

'One twenty.'

'One fifteen, and not a penny more.'

'One eighteen.'

'I knew I could break you.'

'Plus VAT.'

'There is no VAT on books.'

'There is on rare books.'

'You're bullshitting.'

'One eighteen.'

'Deal.'

'Will you be wanting a receipt?'

His eyes narrowed.

He knew what I was saying. If the book really was for him, then there would be no need of a receipt, but if it was something he felt he had to buy, to keep up his cover story, then he would be claiming it back on expenses.

'You tell me,' he said.

'How would I know?'

'How *would* you know?'

'I wouldn't.'

'Wouldn't you?'

'Okay. No receipt then.'

'Okay.'

He counted out the cash.

I put the book in a No Alibis bag with *Murder Is Our Business* on the side, with the familiar chalk outline logo. I took his change out of the till and passed it and the bag across. He took the bag and nodded. I nodded back. He turned for the door. He exited the shop. He walked past the window, out of view. I looked at Jeff. He looked at me. The shop door opened again. I had expected a sheepish Alison, but it was DI Robinson again.

'Second thoughts,' he said, 'I will have that receipt.'

Alison tried to buy her way back into my affections with a dolce cinnamon frappuccino. But I couldn't be bought that easily, although obviously I took the beverage from her. I told her I had work to do, on the case, and I needed to focus. She looked a little hurt, and then nodded at Jeff.

'What about him?'

'He will man the barricades while I focus.'

'I could do that.'

'You would distract me.'

'And he wouldn't?'

'He's too busy grovelling.'

'You want me to grovel? Because you can kiss my arse.'

'No, I just want you to leave me in peace so I can get on with the case.'

'Okay. Fine. I'll just go and grow your baby.'

'Okay.'

'If it is yours.' She smiled. One of those cruel ones that pushes up the corners of the mouth. 'Catch you later.'

She went on out.

Jeff said, 'Told you she was a bitch.'

'So's your face,' I said.

I wasn't that upset with her, and she knew it. Jeff didn't really know how we got on. And that stuff about the baby. She was joking. Of course she was. If it were true, she wouldn't just have blurted it out like that, she would have held it in reserve until she could really do some damage with it.

I gave Jeff a series of pointless tasks to keep him busy while waiting between customers, then settled in behind the counter with my Starbucks to think some more about *The Case of the Cock-Headed Man*. With the Jack Russell and the threats from Greg, I'd allowed my attention to wander, but DI Robinson's reminder about the funeral had refocused it on Jimbo and Ronnycrabs and what could possibly have led to their murder.

With the co-operation of the banker who had come to me for help tracking down his Chinese girlfriend in *The Case of the Missing FA Cup*, I was fairly quickly able to gain access to both the business and private financial records of Jimbo and Ronnycrabs – a different bank, but they're all connected, and he *really* appreciated what I had done for him – and although some of the patterns of numbers deflected me from my purpose for a while, I relatively quickly ascertained that there was nothing startling there. But in a way, it was more about what wasn't there. Most tradesmen play fast and loose with the taxman, preferring cash rather than putting payments through the books. But if J & R had actually been employed by the new Chief Constable to decorate his house, that was one payment that would almost certainly have had to be made with a cheque or credit card. Someone in his position would keep everything above board. Admittedly, he had shown himself to be rather a rash individual by attacking the mysterious Michael Gordon, but that was surely a one-off. He would do everything else by the book. But there was no record of any payment. It didn't compute.

I looked at my watch.

There was still time before I, or we, depending on whether I deigned to take Alison with me, would have to leave for Jimbo's funeral. I needed to know more about what had gone on between the decorators and the police chief, and for all the wonders of the internet, some things still have to be done face to face by a brave man not afraid to look a potential killer in the eye and ask difficult questions.

I looked up from my computer.

'Jeff,' I said, 'I have a mission for you.'

34

All the way there, Jeff rumbled and grumbled, but he really had no choice. He owed me big style, and what I was asking of him wasn't that much of a gamble, although, it has to be admitted, enough of one for me to choose not to attempt it myself. All that was required of my young friend was that he kept a steady head and spoke confidently. He wouldn't even have to remember anything; I would be listening to it all via the open line on his mobile. The gambling bit of it was that I was relying on Chief Constable Wilson McCabe being out at work. Jeff would speak to his wife, Claire, and find out what there was to find out without making anyone unduly suspicious.

Finding the house on the Comber Road in Hillsborough wasn't a problem, it having featured so prominently in the *QIP* article I had downloaded from the internet. We cruised past once, saw the high wall, the sturdy-looking metal gates, the intercom, before turning the corner and parking in the shadow of its rear wall. We were now facing three other recently built large bungalows in what was still billed on a wind-battered poster board as an exciting and exclusive new development. McCabe's looked the pick of the bunch, apparently worth the extra risk to man and particularly beast that came with having it closer to the main road.

I went back over with Jeff what he needed to do. He nodded, but made no attempt to move.

I said, 'I know it's hard, but it's not easy for me either.'

'How exactly do you work that out?'

It should have been blindingly obvious. We were in the country, for God's sake. There were cows and goats and sheep and mice and rats and crows and geese and ducks *somewhere* in the vicinity. There were nettles and gorse and trees and dry-stone walls within *feet* of where we were parked. He knew about my allergies and fears, yet he was still deliberately putting off going up to the front door of the Chief Constable's house and claiming to be a member of the fictitious Northern Ireland Decorating Standards Council.

'Maybe if we went and got a bit of lunch first,' he whined. 'I'm useless on an empty stomach.'

'You're useless generally. Now get out of my car and do what you said you would do.'

'You're not very inspiring. If you think it's so easy, why don't you—'

'Just fucking go!'

'Okay, keep your hair on!'

It was a dig, but I let it go. I had used reverse psychology to fire him up, and now he had slammed the door and was marching back around the corner towards the Chief Constable's house. I raised my mobile. I could hear the swish-swish of Jeff's anorak as he walked. It was mine, obviously, somewhat small on him but preferable to his combat jacket. A suit would have been more appropriate, but there wasn't time. I wanted answers before I attended Jimbo's funeral, because I was quite certain that many of the major players in our little case would be there or represented there in less than two hours.

There was method in my, uhm, madness. This was, after all, the home of the Chief Constable. Sure, the Troubles were over, but it wasn't just going to be unprotected, so that any crim with a grievance could walk up and visit grim vengeance on his family. There would be sophisticated alarms, security cameras, possibly even a security team on standby somewhere close at hand. So all in all, it was much better that Jeff made the approach, and got immortalised on camera or jumped upon or interrogated. He was used to it. And at the first sign of trouble, I would, obviously, be out of there.

Jeff had evidently reached the front gates. I heard him push the button in the intercom. As he waited for a response, he whispered for my benefit: 'I'm not even insured.'

'Hello?'

'Yes, hi, hello. Is that Mrs McCabe?'

'Yes.'

Excellent. The first part of my gamble had paid off.

'Sorry to trouble you, Mrs McCabe, and for calling directly on you, but we don't seem to have a record of your home phone number. Tell you what it is. My name is Cain, James Cain, I'm the standards and procedures rep for the Northern Ireland Decorating Standards Council. You recently had some work done by two of our members, a Ronald Clegg and James Collins?'

'Yes, I . . .'

'Nothing to worry about, we do random follow-up checks to make sure the work comes up to the exacting standards the council demands of its members. I just have a couple of questions, won't take more than a few minutes of your time . . .'

'Excuse me . . . but aren't they . . . weren't they . . . are they not dead?'

'I'm sorry . . . ?'

'Jimbo and Ronnie, weren't they . . . murdered?'

'Murdered?'

'Just a few days ago . . .' There was a pause as she waited for Jeff to respond, but when it didn't come, she said: 'Hello?'

'I'm sorry . . . I just felt a little . . . weak at the knees . . . Jimbo and Ronnie, I was only talking to them the other week . . . I had absolutely no idea . . . Murdered?'

He sounded like he was fighting to catch his breath. There was another pause, and then a buzzer sounded.

'If you faint out there, someone will run over you. Come on up to the house.'

'Oh, thank you . . . if you're sure it's not too much trouble.'

The gate clanked open and Jeff crossed gravel. By the time he got to the end of the drive the front door must already have been open. I heard her say, 'Come on in. Would you like a cup of tea?'

'If . . . that would be . . . this is really a . . . dreadful shock.'

'I don't know how you missed it. It was all over the news.'

'I was . . . out of the country . . . over with my brother in Scotland . . . didn't really see much telly . . . and my work with the council . . . I'm kind of free-lance, they just send me a list of clients I need to visit, I'm barely ever in the office . . . Oh my goodness. Dead, you say? What happened?'

There were various kitcheny noises. Mrs McCabe went over what she knew of the murders while Jeff tutted. Eventually he said: 'This is very kind of you, Mrs McCabe. I know it sounds daft, but would you mind at all if I asked you a few questions about the work they did for you? It's just, I get paid according to the paperwork I submit . . . and technically . . .'

'That's fine, I understand. It was nothing very earth-shattering, really. This room, the front lounge, and one of the bedrooms upstairs. It's a new house, so it was in pretty good shape when we moved in, I just like to . . .'

'Make your mark.'

'Yes, I suppose.'

'And did they work well? Turn up on time? Furnish you with a quotation?'

'Yes, yes, and yes.'

'And did the final bill tally with the quotation?'

'Ahm, yes, it did.'

'And you settled that bill . . . satisfaction on both sides?'

'As far as I'm aware. My husband deals with all of that.'

'Is that him? He's in the police?'

'Yes. It's an old photo. You don't watch the news very much, do you?'

'It's *so* depressing. Ah . . . and a lovely wee Jack Russell. I'm very partial to Jack Russells, they're so intelligent.'

'I'm glad you think so. Bad-tempered, I say. Scampi, we called him. My husband doted on him.'

'He's . . .'

'He was knocked down in the summer.'

'Oh dear. I'm very sorry.'

Jeff was performing well, surprisingly well, yet he was learning nothing we hadn't already guessed. And with his mobile line already open, there was nothing

I could do but hope that he would actually realise himself that he was falling short.

'Well it's nice to have a reminder of him.'

'Yes. A photo is one thing. We also . . .'

It was, however, at this point that fate lent a hand. I heard a door open and shut, and then Mrs McCabe say, 'Honey, I wasn't expecting you till . . .'

The Chief Constable, home from protecting Ulster.

'Finished early. Who the hell are you?'

It didn't *sound* threatening, quite friendly really. But Jeff must have been spooked, because I could hear the confidence draining from his voice.

'I'm . . . Cain . . . James Cain from the . . . Painters Guild . . . I mean . . . it used to be the . . . now it's the Decorating . . . Council . . . We're just . . . survey . . . customer relations . . . You had some work done . . .'

'I trust you're carrying some kind of accreditation?'

'I . . . well, no, actually. Usually, but I left it in . . . the car . . .'

'I didn't see a car.'

'Bottom of the hill. I walked . . . wasn't sure which house . . . I think I've probably got everything I need . . .'

'Just hold your horses. Claire, how many times have I told you not to let anyone into the house without making sure who they are?'

'I know, I'm sorry, he was just upset.'

'Upset?'

'Our decorators . . .'

'Those thieving . . . ?'

'We don't know that, Wilson . . .'

'You think they stole . . . ?' Jeff asked. 'Mrs McCabe, you didn't mention . . .'

'I don't like to get anyone in trouble . . . or speak ill of the dead . . . and we really don't know . . .'

'Who else could it have been? Honey, this place is like Fort Knox, except of course when you leave the front gates open or let any eejit who presents himself through the front door. Where's your head office?'

'Botanic Avenue.'

Christ.

'Phone number?'

Jeff began to repeat my mobile number.

'That's a mobile.'

'It's a small organisation, it only has a part-time staff; that's the boss's number.'

'Well let's see . . .'

'Wilson, there's no need, the fella is only doing his job.'

'Claire, there's every need.'

I couldn't tell if he was dialling. But the line suddenly went dead. I could only guess or hope that Jeff had reached into his pocket to cut it. Within two seconds my phone began to ring. I stared at the *Unknown Caller* message knowing exactly who it was.

It was time to step up to the plate.

However, I was then distracted by a cow on the opposite side of the road, in a field. There was a fence that would stop her from attacking me. But our eyes met. She knew, and I knew she knew I knew she knew, that I was lactose intolerant.

The phone continued to ring.

It would be a tactical mistake to engage in conversation with someone who could turn out to be my nemesis. I wasn't prepared. I was in a car near a field with cows, far out of my comfort zone.

The phone rang on.

Until it stopped.

I stared at the screen until it faded to black.

Thirty seconds.

Sixty seconds.

Then I jumped as it sprang back into life.

He had left me a message.

No – a text.

But it wasn't from Chief Constable Wilson McCabe, or even the hapless Jeff.

It was from Alison.

It said simply:

HELP.

35

I am not the type of man who jumps to conclusions. I do not get on like a bull in a china shop. There was no reason to presume that Alison was really in danger, save for the fact that we were up to our necks in a murder case and that Greg had recently given her a drive-by fingering. She could just as easily have been texting, *HELP, I shouldn't be moving these heavy boxes in my condition*. There was a *reasonable* possibility. How much danger could she be in if she actually had time to text? If she *was* in trouble, it left me in something of a quandary. Jeff was *in there*, probably already exposed as a charlatan, but at least close at hand, whereas Alison was way back there, out of easy reach.

I could have answered the Chief Constable's call, but had chosen not to. There was method in my, uhm, madness. I now had his mobile phone number and could call and confront him at a time of my choosing, when I was sufficiently armed with evidence or vague innuendo. On *my* terms. Yes, it left Jeff exposed, but I felt that the gains outweighed the loss. He worked in the shop, for sure, and he was cheap, but even Mother knew more about mystery fiction than he did, and he had proved himself to be flaky. Under questioning he would give us up, again, but that was inevitable. However, if me, myself or I had spoken to the Chief in my condition, under surveillance by a cow, I would also have let something slip, and *that* would have turned an unfortunate situation into a desperate one, causing *both* of us to be hauled in for impersonating decorators. As it was, with Jeff now surely compromised, it was time to leave the scene before he gave up my location.

Before I pulled out, however, I sent a text to Alison: *What seems to be the problem?*

On the drive back into the city, I kept my eye on the mobile as often as I could without breaking any of the valuable and sensible instructions contained within the Highway Code. It was not in fact until I got stuck at the Boucher Road roundabout, and I was satisfied that the traffic around me was stationary and there was no immediate hope of progress, that I was able to check for the third time, and this time there was another, more specific message.

It said: *Meet me for coffee at the food court at Connswater Shopping Centre.*

That, my friends, was a very clearly a trap waiting to be walked into. The *very notion* that I would drink coffee in a *food court*, well, it beggared belief, and Alison knew it. She was sending me a warning. Don't come. Someone had her. Someone was trying to lure me in.

And yet what could I do?

It was Alison.

The love of my life.

The mother of my child.

A fantastic comic-book artist.

Who had also, clearly, *sold me out*. Just like Jeff. Why did people keep doing that? What was wrong with them? I don't have a backbone, but there's a medical explanation for that. These so-called lovers or friends were giving out my name like they were timeshare reps at the annual Gullible Convention. They just wilted when people asked them to do things. I would, very soon, have to consider the whole nature of my private detection business and the wisdom of employing partners or assistants. I was much better working alone, although I would still have to consider hiring someone to help with any heavy lifting work.

The traffic finally began to move. I was driving, but I still had to think on my poor bunioned feet. Disappointing as she was, I had to help Alison, although in such a way that any danger to my own well-being was rendered negligible. But I had just abandoned my regular gormless idiot to the Chief Constable, and my usually dependable and exploitable customers were not within easy reach. I needed somebody equally pliable and just as expendable, someone willing to make the ultimate sacrifice, even if they weren't quite aware of it.

'Mother – just sit there, and shut up, and listen.'

I had caught her at an ideal time. Not drunk enough to be paralytic and not so medicated as to be comatose. She had obviously screamed and sworn at me as I wheeled her into the back of the Mystery Machine and bolted her into place, but it was water off a duck's back. As I drove, she continued to vent her spleen, which was in better condition than mine, but I was experienced enough and patient enough to know that she would soon give me an opening.

'Are you listening?'

I met her eyes in the mirror. Her brain was half shut down and her motor functions ludicrously impaired, but the burning hate in her eyes continued to defy age and nature.

'Okay, you miserable old cow. I have looked after you my whole life. You have been a royal pain in the hole. You have been nasty, and vindictive, and evil for as long as I can remember, and I have asked nothing of you. But now Alison is in danger and you are going to help her. Do you understand?'

She glared back.

'We're going to have a baby.'

I kept looking for a reaction.

'Which technically makes you a grandmother.'

I waited, and waited.

Eventually she said, in her slugger's voice, 'Are you sure it's yours?'

But there was, I SWEAR TO GOD, a tear on her cheek.

We parked at Connswater. As I rolled her out of the side of the MM, I went over the technical details. She swore a bit and called me an imbecile, but essentially went along with it. I had a baseball cap that I pulled down low over my face.

'Lower,' said Mother, though with her twisted mouth it sounded like, 'Lover.'

It was only a slight variation of the move I'd pulled with Jeff. Mother would have an open line on her mobile phone so I could listen to what was being said, and an earpiece through which I could give her instructions and tell her what to say.

Once inside the centre, it was with some relief that I spotted a Shopmobility stand offering little electric vehicles to help the disabled manoeuvre themselves around. This meant that I wouldn't have to put myself in danger of being recognised by pushing Mother right up to the food court. She made a scene about transferring over and I snapped at her. The woman in charge took me to one side and said, 'Did you ever hear that song "No Charge"?', to which the obvious response was, 'Yes I did, Melba Montgomery sang it; she was born in 1938 and raised in Florence, Alabama; it was her only Billboard Pop Chart top forty hit. Now fuck off and mind your own business,' which I would have said if I hadn't been intent on my mission or afraid of her eyebrows.

I gave Mother her final instructions and a chilling warning about the home I would put her into if she didn't co-operate, then sent her on her way. I had my camera over my shoulder and an adrenalin buzz shooting through my system. I get that way when I put other people in danger. It's like reading a book – thrilling, but ultimately no personal sacrifice involved. I skirted the edge of the food court, which boasted a Burger King, a Streat café, a Subway and a Yangtze Chinese carryout in a semicircle around a large and busy seated area. But very quickly my eyes were drawn to a table right in the middle; it was Alison's white zip-up jacket, and her hair, and her ears, all from behind, but definitely her. And the two spides on either side of her, not much into their twenties for sure, with their skinned heads and white socks, and opposite, the big, big guy I immediately recognised as Girth Biggs, aka Smally Biggs, aka Samson Biggs, aka Willy Biggs, aka Aka because he had so many aka's. Whatever name you cared to call him by, Biggs was big in stature, and big into drugs and protection. He was also sometimes known as the Market Stall Don because he was like a defective Teflon Don, with charges only occasionally sticking. He had once sent two of his hoods into No Alibis demanding protection money – not just No Alibis, I might add, but every shop along

Botanic – but I had befuddled them by pretending to be deaf and they had ended up feeling so sorry for my pathetic state that they made a donation to the charity box I keep by the till and which I dutifully empty into my own pockets every Christmas because the deaf are pampered enough. The fact that Smally was sitting there with Alison, with a huge tray of Burger King fare before him, was both a relief and extremely worrying. On the plus side, he didn't know me from Adam Adamant, so at least I would be able to observe them unobserved, but equally, he wasn't Greg, or DI Robinson, or Billy Randall; he was a new player in our game and therefore an unknown quantity, and one with a history of violence to boot, literally.

I took a seat at a table on the other side of the food court, which gave me a good view of their position, but which also partially shielded me from them, so that I could duck in and out of their eyeline when required. I directed Mother to the table next to theirs. There were people just finishing their meal, but I instructed Mother to stare at them until they left. She didn't need much encouragement or to vary her usual look. They were up and away in seconds. Mother manoeuvred her electric car into a position facing Alison's table. It took my girl a second glance to recognise her. They had only met once previously. Although it was an experience neither of them would ever forget, Mother now looked significantly different, what with her lopsided face, thickly rouged cheeks and hair colouring, blue like bread going off.

It was the eyes that did it.

Every time.

Like the pits of hell.

Or Newtownards.

'Repeat after me, Mother.'

'Repeat after me, Mother.'

Smally Bigs looked up at her for a moment, then away.

'Don't mess with me, Mother. I swear to God.'

'Keep your hair on.'

Smally Biggs, whose hair was at the comb-over stage, glanced up again. Mother continued to study him. He lifted a burger.

'Okay, say this: Excuse me, young man.'

There was a long pause.

Then: 'Hey, fat chops.'

'Mother, for God's—'

'Give us a chip.'

'Mother!'

Smally looked incredulous. He nodded at one of his skinheads. 'Park the old bag somewhere else.' He said it with no more vigour than he might lend to saying, 'Pass the salt.'

One of the skinheads dutifully approached Mother.

She stared at him.

He hesitated.

Then she said, without prompting, but with more

clarity in her voice than I'd heard at any time since the stroke, 'Don't even think about it.'

The skinhead stopped, and his mouth really did drop open.

'Mother . . .'

'Now sit your arse down, and let me talk to the fat man.'

The skinhead looked back to his boss, who was himself lowering his burger.

'Who the hell *are* you?' he asked, at the same time indicating for the skin to retake his seat.

'Never you mind who I am, lard boy, you let yon little girl go, then we'll talk.'

Smally's eyes narrowed. 'So that's it. Where's the bookshop guy?'

'He's around.'

'Mother! For fuck—'

'He might be anyone. Him over there. Him by the bins. Him with the red face.'

'Mother! That *is* me!'

'They don't know that.'

'Who don't know what?' Smally asked.

'You mind your own business, podgy pig boy.'

'Mother!'

'You negotiate through me, or we don't negotiate at all.'

'Negotiate? Why would I want to negotiate. I got the girl.'

'Say this, say this: I got the Jack.'

'I got the Jack.'

'You got the Jack.'

'I got the Jack.'

'You haven't got the Jack.'

'I got the Jack.'

'You prove you got the Jack.'

'You prove you got the girl.'

'Mother . . .'

'The fuckin' girl is sitting here.'

'That proves nothing.'

'What?'

'Mother!'

'You let her go, we talk this through.'

'Well that would stop me saying, give me the Jack or the girl gets it. That would stop me having the upper hand. I don't know what fucking negotiating school you went to, but you suck at it.'

'Say: So we are negotiating.'

'So. We are negotiating, slaphead.'

'You think because you're an old bitch I won't smack you around?'

'You could try.'

'Mother . . .'

'I want the Jack.'

'I want the girl.'

As they stared each other down, something else caught my attention. A security guard in black puffa jacket and earpiece and cap was approaching. He stopped by Mother's vehicle.

'Madam, I'm afraid your car is blocking access to

the other tables. And to be here, you do actually have to purchase something. Company policy.'

'Young man . . .'

'Mother . . .'

'Madam, if you don't move the vehicle, you will be towed.'

'Mother, keep control, this is important. Be nice.'

'There's no need for that attitude.' It was Smally. 'She's not doing any harm.'

'Sir, with all due respect, this isn't the first time. Company policy dictates that—'

'Screw company policy.'

'Sir, to be frank, this is none of your business. We're very particular about making this a pleasant shopping experience for everyone; that means keeping all access routes free and clear, and it also requires a certain standard of behaviour from our customers, and that they show respect for all of the staff, which means watching your language.'

'Fuck that.'

'Do you know who he is?' one of the skinheads asked.

'That's not really my concern. I'm just asking that you refrain—'

'You get yourself out of here before I break your fucking legs, you fucking little Hitler.'

'Okay, sir, I'm afraid I'm going to have to ask you to leave.' The security guard raised a walkie-talkie. 'Can I have back-up to the food court, please. Sir, if you would just take your belongings, sir, and please exit the premises.'

'You're a fucking dead man.'

And he would be a dead man, I was sure, but for the moment there was probably a very good reason why Smally and his guys weren't putting up more of a fight. They didn't want to have to explain why they had Alison, or why they were armed, as I was sure they were.

Smally got up, the skinheads with him.

Alison sat where she was.

She had not spoken since Mother's arrival.

Smally loomed over her. 'Let's go.'

'I think I'll stay for a while.'

'That's not an option.'

'No, actually, I believe it is.'

Alison nodded around the food court. Smally followed her direction, and saw what I saw, other security guards approaching from three different directions.

'You come with me now, you little cu—'

'Sir . . . ?' The security guard turned slightly to his left and made a hand gesture indicating the closest set of exit doors. But in seeing him side on for the first time, rather than from behind, my heart stopped suddenly – which it is prone to do, given the leaky state of my aortic artery – as I realised that the security guard whose intervention I had been internally hailing as wonderfully fortunate was not in fact a security guard as God intended at all, but Greg, the rogue secret agent, and that the security guards he had himself summoned were just as likely to expose him as a fraud as escort Smally and his mates from the centre, and then Alison might be right back in danger again.

I had seconds to decide what to do.

The pattern on the floor tiles attracted my attention. A number had clearly been replaced at some stage, but the original pattern must no longer have been available; they were close, but not exact, and it was annoying. I've always been fascinated by floor tiles. The word is derived from the French word *tuile*, which is in turn from the Latin *tegula*. I keep abreast of the developments. Modern printing techniques and digital manipulation of art and photography have converged in custom tile printing. Dye sublimation and the application of ceramic-based toners now permits printing on a variety of tile types, yielding photographic-quality reproduction. High-temperature kilns are used to transfer images to the tile substrate.

'Hey, you.'

I looked up. Alison was standing by my table.

'You're a sight for sore eyes,' she said.

I know all about sore eyes.

Behind her, Smally and his two pals were hurrying off to the right. Greg was being surrounded by five security guards.

I stood. Alison threw her arms around me, and held me tight, which was unfortunate, given the state of my bones.

Moments later, Mother's Shopmobility vehicle crashed into the back of us. We would have been bound for casualty if it hadn't been equipped with bumpers to stop the mentally and physically disabled causing carnage.

'Sorry,' she said.

'Fucking watch where you're going,' I snapped.

'Don't speak to your mother like that,' said Alison.

'Thank you, dear,' said Mother.

36

It was only when Mother was safely bolted into the rear of the Mystery Machine that Alison turned on me.

'I was expecting my hero on a white charger.'

'I'm allergic to hors—'

'Instead your mother arrives in an electric cripple car.'

'Don't say cripple . . .'

'Don't start on me!'

'I thought you were glad to see me.'

'I was! But Jesus! Are there any lengths that you won't go to, to avoid confrontation?'

'Confrontation? That wasn't confrontation! Do you know who that was?'

'Some baldy bastard who wanted—'

'Smally Biggs!'

'I know who it was. I'm not stupid.'

'He didn't hurt you?'

'He pinched my arm.'

'If I'd known that . . .'

'What?'

'That's not the point. What did he say?'

'He wanted the dog; they all want the dog.'

'But why?'

'I don't know! It's like we're playing pass the parcel without the parcel.'

'Can we just get out of here?'

'Yes. *Okay*. I *suppose* you did come. But I don't understand, how did you organise your mum? And Greg? And where's Jeff? And are we still going to the funeral? And what did you find out? Is the cop a crook? Did Jimbo and Co. take Patch? Why are you just staring at me?'

But I wasn't staring at her. Some people think I'm staring at them because of my myopia and the slight cross in my eyes, but actually I was looking directly behind her, at Greg, hurrying towards us. He had lost the puffa and was now pulling on his familiar grey suit jacket.

There wasn't time to jump in the van. He was there, right in front of us, and looking concerned.

'Did he hurt you?' he asked Alison.

'Like you care.'

She put two joined fingers and a sticky-up thumb to her head, and raised her eyebrows.

'I do, and you don't want to be messing with him, and didn't I do my best to get you out of it?'

'Because you want the Jack Russell,' I said.

'No. Yes. Look, we've gotten off on the wrong foot . . .'

'Because you threatened us and kidnapped Jeff.'

'I made a mistake. Things were very confused. You were interfering in something very delicate, and for your own safety I had to try and scare you off. But you're in it now, and it's my duty to try and protect you, try and negotiate a way through this for you that won't end up with you being killed.'

'So you're not just covering your own back?'

'Yes, some of that too. Look, can we get out of here? Smally is probably still cruising about, and he won't feel so restrained out in the open. We'll go somewhere, talk it through, sort it out.'

'We can't,' said Alison. 'We have an appointment with death.'

'Please. A full and frank exchange of information.'

'We're on our way to Jimbo's funeral,' I clarified.

'So am I.'

'There isn't time.'

'It's important to talk before the funeral.'

'Why?'

'Because they'll all be there. Everyone. We need to know where we stand. *It makes sense*. And there's a Starbucks on the way.'

He had played his joker.

Alison thought my agreeing to meet Greg in the Starbucks on Boucher Crescent was just my way of getting rid of him. He'd go one way, we'd go the other.

But no, I made it clear to her that an exchange of information might be no bad thing.

'He's going to stitch us up.'

'He might turn out to be okay; it might be mutually beneficial.'

'In what way?'

I reached forward and turned the radio right up. Alison turned it back down. I repeated the action and gave her the eye. The penny dropped.

'You really . . . ?' she mouthed.

I nodded. How else would he have known about my obsession, or this one of them? Only through clandestine listening or observation. How had he known to arrive at Connswater? Because he was keyed in to my phone and reading my texts. For all I knew, he was already aware of my predilection for scratching cars with personalised number plates or my aversion to grapefruit. I needed him to stop delving. There were things I wanted nobody to know. Not Mother or Alison and certainly not MI5. It was vital that the holy bloodline was protected.

'Anyway,' I said, 'even the smell of that food court is bringing me out in hives. I feel the need for . . .'

'You always feed the need.'

'It's why you love me.'

'It's fairly low down the list.'

'There's a list?'

'Of good *and* bad.'

'And?'

'The jury's still out.'

From the back, Mother yelled: 'I need a Jimmy Riddle.'

'Hold on, we're nearly there.'

'Too late.'

Alison pushed Mother into the toilets at the Boucher Starbucks, promising to sort her out. I wasn't sure if that meant give her a hiding or tidy her up. In my day you had your nose rubbed in it and you learned not to do it again. As they disappeared and I took my corner seat, the front door opened and Greg came in. It was a small Starbucks, with a narrow column of tables running the length of the coffee bar, and then only slightly wider at the back. He couldn't have missed me. He nodded and went to the till. He ordered an Ethiopian Sidamo and brought it across. He sat down opposite me. He didn't ask where Alison or Mother had gone. I already had a Café Verona before me. He sat and said, 'So?'

'So what?'

'Tell me what you've been up to.'

'Tell me what *you've* been up to.'

He sighed. 'You know who I work for?'

'I know who you are employed by.'

'Meaning?'

'I know what your employers do, I'm not convinced that what you've been doing toes the party line.'

Greg nodded. Looking at him, up close, I could see now that he was younger than I'd previously calcu-lated. I had thought he was probably thirty-eight, or thirty-nine, or forty, or thirty-five, or thirty-six, or thirty-seven, that the thickness of his jawline was to do with advancing years and lack of fitness. But I decided that he was actually younger, maybe twenty-eight, or twenty-nine, or thirty, or thirty-one, or thirty-two. The extra weight was lingering puppy fat; the older appearance was worry and stress.

'Okay, yes, I am employed by MI5. We deal in national security.'

'Some of you do.'

'Look, I'm going to be absolutely truthful with you, on the understanding that none of it goes any further. If it comes to it, I'll deny it, and you'll just look ridiculous.'

'I'm a bookseller; looking ridiculous goes with the territory.'

He nodded slowly. 'Okay. Look. There's two parts to this. The first part is, I'll admit, entirely our fault. And when I say our fault, I mean my fault. I take full responsibility.'

'I got the impression you were trying to avoid taking responsibility.'

'No, I held my hand up, and they said, right, go and fix it without involving us.'

'So you're not a rogue spy; you're doing this with tacit approval.'

'Yes. No. I'm not really a spy at all . . .'

'But you work out of the big building where they keep the spies. Are you a chef?'

'No. Why?'

'No reason. Are you a gardener?'

'No. Right. Okay. I get your drift. I'm in the spying business, espionage, and I was in that business, hands on, right enough, but I'm no longer active. I'm a teacher. I teach spies.'

'Spyteacher.'

'That's it. You know we have a spanking-new tower block outside Holywood? It's real state-of-the-art. If something big goes down in London, Belfast takes control, okay? There's four hundred of us working there now, every discipline you'd care to think of.'

'Including chefs and gardeners.'

He stirred his coffee. I sipped and savoured. Alison and Mother were taking a long time. I glanced towards the toilets; so did Greg.

'What I'm saying is we're not just a branch office. We're the reserve hub if London gets hit.'

'Okay. I believe you.'

'But you don't just open your doors one morning and say you're recruiting spies. Actually, I take that back, that's exactly what we do; we do a milk round just like any other big company. We take on a bagful of graduates every year, but they have to be trained. Spies don't just grow on trees.'

'That would be Special Branch.'

'I heard your mouth gets you into trouble.'

'It's not me, it's the Tourette's.'

'It's not in your file.'

We locked eyes.

Kept it going as he raised his coffee and sipped.

But then he remembered we were in a rush, and glanced at his watch, and turned and looked towards the front door, then finally back to me.

'Problem is, this day and age, eighty, ninety per cent of them are whizz-kids, but everything they know they learned in front of a computer screen; they've no practical experience at all. They were in front of their Nintendos in the years when they should have been perfecting hide and seek. That's where I come in.'

'Hide and seek?'

'Practical experience. There is no substitute for actually *doing* something. You can send them into a mocked-up house, you can yell all you want at them over an obstacle course or a shooting range, but in-house training can only give you so much. They're always going to be aware it isn't real; they're never going to have so much adrenalin going they can't help shitting their pants.'

I smiled.

'What?'

I smiled some more. I couldn't help it. Everything was falling nicely into place.

'That's why you want the Jack.'

'Why do I want the Jack?'

'Because you gave your students a task, a practical, you sent them out on a spying mission. You weren't going to risk them abroad, you weren't going to send them into some foreign embassy here; you needed to find someone local, someone important enough and

312

inaccessible enough to give them a real sense of danger, yet someone who, if it came to it, and he found out, your superiors could probably sort it out. Except you didn't check, and it all went tits up.'

'Maybe.'

'You gave them a for instance. What if the Chief Constable was planning a military coup or was taking kickbacks or . . . whatever. How do we find out? And then you left them, literally as it turned out, to their own devices.'

He pulled his chair a little closer to the table. He cupped his hands around his coffee.

'Go on.'

'I don't know if they got into police HQ; maybe it's too hard, so they decide to focus on his nice new home. Except the Chief's no doughbag; he knows he has his enemies inside and out of the force, inside and out of the Government, so he has the place swept for bugs on a regular basis. Your guys have to figure out a way to get inside, and I'm guessing you put some restrictions on them, made them do it the old-fashioned way, surveillance, sure, electronics, but nothing they couldn't put together themselves in a lab.'

Greg was smiling now. 'You're good. You're really good.'

Of course I was.

And I wasn't finished. I pulled at my lip, thinking out loud.

'They couldn't crack it, could they? At least not until . . . somebody got careless. What was it, a change of shift? Someone's tired, doesn't want to take the long way home, so they drive directly past McCabe's house, and they get punished for it – the Jack Russell comes charging out, and your guy knocks him down, kills him. Then the Chief is there, but he doesn't lose his temper and beat your man up; he deals with it the way a cop should, because he's at fault, letting the dog run out, and because he knows that every single thing he does in life is going to be scrutinised. He offers his insurance details and asks for your guy's, and there's the panic, because once he has those, and finds out it's under a Government policy, then he knows he's being targeted by MI5.'

'So we had a crisis.'

'But that's just part of the training.'

'Trick is not to panic. We went looking for someone to stand in for our driver, pulled up Michael Gordon, Belfast native, but killed in a road accident in Birmingham seven months ago.'

'And the surveillance didn't stop?'

'No, of course not. It was part of the training, not being derailed by incidents, seeing it through.'

'Then, in following the Chief to the taxidermist, suddenly there was your opportunity, how to get inside his house. Bug the Jack.'

'It's called a Passive . . .'

'. . . Resonant Cavity Bug. It's the Great Seal!'

'It's the Great Seal.'

37

'What the fricking hell are you talking about seals for?' Alison demanded, appearing at our table after an eternity in the ladies' with Mother, who was now, very clearly, out for the count in her wheelchair. 'And by the way, never, ever inflict that on me again. I thought we might bond, but she tried to drown me in the toilet, there was a mad scuffle and we've broken the cistern. Anyway, are you not going to give a pregnant woman a seat?'

Greg, to his credit, got up and moved one across from a vacant table opposite. She then asked him to get her a coffee.

Greg, to his greater credit, held his temper, and went to fetch her one.

'We were just getting to the heart of the matter,' I said.

'You were discussing *seals*.' She clapped her hands

together like Flipper. 'Besides, it's important to show who's in charge.'

'You think *you're* in charge?'

'We. Us. And even *her*.' She nodded at the lolling, paralysed shell of my mother. 'You know she has a colostomy bag? I can understand old bats not plugging in their hearing aids, but not connecting up their . . .' She shook her head. 'Anyhoo – seals?'

'Seal, singular. And not that kind. The Great Seal . . .'

'Like the Great Aslan.'

'. . . of the United States of America.'

Greg arrived back with Alison's coffee and sat. 'The Great Seal, yes indeedy.'

'Of the United States? What has this got to do with . . . ?'

I told her. That in 1946 the Soviet Union presented a copy of the Great Seal of the United States to the American ambassador in Moscow – with a bug hidden inside it. It was a new type of device, called a Passive Resonant Cavity Bug, which was activated by sound waves from a conversation in a room. It hung prominently for years, at least part of the time in the ambassador's study, before a tiny microphone was eventually discovered. And that's what had happened here. Greg's students had taken it upon themselves to bug the Chief Constable's new house by planting the device in Patch . . .

'Purely as an exercise . . .'

'But it got stolen by Jimbo and Ronny . . . and it continued to be activated by sound waves . . . and we've moved on from the forties, so I'm presuming there are pictures as well as words?'

Greg nodded.

'And you think it was still working at Jimbo's when they got murdered?' That was Alison. We nodded. All of us. With the exception of Mother, who drooled. It almost seemed like we were all on the same side. Except, of course, we weren't. And we had to remember it.

Greg leaned back in his chair. He nodded appreciatively at me. 'You do know your stuff. Have you had any training?'

'Training?'

'In the services.'

Alison snorted.

'You seem to have a pretty good handle on this espionage business.'

'I've had a certain amount,' I said.

'Without leaving the comfort of his sofa,' said Alison.

'Ludlum, le Carré, Kipling, Childers, Horowitz, Hall, Diment, even Tom Clancy. They all know their onions.'

'Well, you've surprised me. And I've told you just about everything I can. The Jack is out there, and we want him back.'

He looked at me expectantly.

'So that you can hand him over to the police, because there's a double murder buried inside him.'

He clasped his hands. 'We don't know that. It may not have recorded anything; it all has to do with placement. He could just as easily have been stuffed in a cupboard and recorded nothing.'

'You mean you don't actually know? The pictures weren't being beamed somewhere?'

'It was a primitive device. The project was designed to test my pupils' initiative. It would have been too easy to give them high-end stuff so they could just sit on their arses. Whatever there is, it's in the dog.'

Alison was shaking her head, slowly. She stuck a finger out at Greg. 'You've no intention of handing the dog over to the police, you've no interest in solving the murders; you just want your tape back so that you don't get into hot water over bugging the Chief.'

He opened his mouth, and for a moment I thought he was going to launch into an elaborate justification of this, or a complete denial. But then he just said, 'Yes.'

'*Yes?*'

'That's what this is about, protecting my end.'

'But what about solving the murders?' Alison asked.

'That's not my concern.'

'Fuckin' hell,' said Alison, 'you're a callous son of a b, aren't you?'

He lifted his coffee. 'It tends to go with the territory.'

We pushed Mother back out to the Mystery Machine. I was debating if I would have time to take her home before we were due at Roselawn for the cremation, or whether I should take her with us and just leave the window open a fraction, as you would for a dog.

An open window might easily attract thieves.

It was a thought.

Greg walked with us, waiting, and then waiting some more for us to spill the beans about Patch. He had, as far as I could tell, played it straight. Now one of us had to tell him that we hadn't the foggiest notion where the Jack was.

'I'll just get Ironside fixed in the back,' I said, opening the side and lowering the ramp. 'Why don't you . . . ?'

I nodded at Greg, for Alison's benefit. It would be easier for her. She disliked and mistrusted him already.

Through the side of the van, as I was bolting the old witch in place, I heard her say, 'We appreciate your honesty. But it really wasn't anything we hadn't already worked out. Your man in there . . . he may look like an idiot, but there's not much that he misses.'

I was glowing and growling at the same time.

Greg wasn't happy. 'I'm putting myself on the line here; you said you'd help. I need the Jack.'

'And you'll get him.' I stood in the doorway. Alison smiled up, squinting against the low winter sun. 'But only if we're completely convinced that you're not going to turn round and stab us in the back.'

'Why on earth would I do that?'

'Because it tends to go with the territory.'

He sucked on his lower lip. He glanced at his watch. His eyes flicked up. 'What do you want?'

'Once I recover the Jack . . .'

'You mean you haven't yet?'

'I will. Today. As soon as we have it, we watch the

tape together, and you get me a copy of the scenes showing who killed Jimbo and Ronnycrabs. You do what you want with the rest of it.'

'Okay. That it?'

'Jeff may be in police custody as we speak. I want him released.'

'We have no control over—'

'I want him released.'

'Okay. Is *that* it?'

'No. An end to supermarkets offering huge discounts off the cover price of books. It's driving us out of business.'

'I can't just . . .' He stopped. He even smiled. 'So you'll get me the Jack? Today?'

'Sure I will. Or my name isn't—'

A thunderous banging from the inside of the van stopped me.

'Take me home!' Mother screamed. 'I need a shit!'

38

The dumper became the dumpee. With Mother safely tucked up in bed, with a tartan flask by her side and a remote control and a large television with the sound turned up to max, we were free to hurry along to Jimbo's funeral at Roselawn. She screamed after us about being left alone, about her mistreatment, about how she was going to tell the authorities, and then when Alison went back in to reassure her she screamed at her too, demanding to be left alone. Alison bustled back out, swearing under her breath.

Greg, reluctant to let us out of his sight, had tried to ride with us, but we resisted, and now he was trailing behind us in his BMW.

Alison had one eye on him in the side mirror. She said, 'I like a confident man, and it isn't usually you. *Do* you know where the Jack is?'

'Haven't the foggiest.'

'Then why did you . . . ?'

'I'm hoping it will become clear in the course of the afternoon.'

'Hoping?'

'Everyone will be there, and I will have the chance to study them, and their reactions, and their inter- actions if they have any.'

'Which will tell you exactly what?'

'I don't know yet. But getting everyone in one room, it generally works for Agatha.'

'Agatha, if it's the same Agatha we're talking about, has presented all the evidence and drawn her conclu- sions before she stands up to address the suspects.'

I nodded.

'You mean you have worked out who has the Jack?'

'No. But I know who murdered Jimbo and Ronnycrabs.'

'You do?'

'And I'm pretty close to making a cultured guess as to the location of the Jack.'

'But how? I've seen most everything you have, and I haven't the foggiest notion who killed who or what or whatever.'

'Well that's why you're the junior partner.'

'You say it with a smile, but you really mean it.'

'Because it's all there; it has to be. Look, I make my living out of detective fiction, and they all laugh at me because I put so much faith in it.'

'They . . . ?'

'They. Everyone.'

'Everyone doesn't . . .'

'Just listen. You see, we're all exactly the same. You think real police officers are somehow smarter than someone who designs hats? No, they just have better access to crime scenes, evidence, labs. But writers of detective fiction are every bit as smart, and quite often much, much smarter, because their experience is greater, they work in different fields; they can be astrophysicists, or turkey farmers or housewives, or jockeys or mountaineers or teachers or ventriloquists, and they bring all that experience to the table, whereas most cops are cops from the day they enter the academy, they haven't lived in the real world. Do you have any idea how many crime novels have been written over the past hundred years?'

'No, I—'

'Hundreds of thousands. And do you know what that means?'

'The market is over—'

'It means there's scarcely a crime that you can possibly imagine that hasn't already been imagined by a mystery writer, that hasn't been *solved* by a mystery writer. I'm not saying there are exact parallels with real life, but you take little things out of different cases, and you put them together, and you come up with a solution that is every bit as plausible as the one the cops have been working towards.'

Alison nodded for a little bit, then said: 'You really do live in your own wee world, don't you?'

I almost countered by asking her if she had ever heard of Ronald Knox, while knowing full well that she hadn't. He was a priest, a theologian and a crime writer, but he remained best known, at least in *our* community, for his Decalogue, ten commandments that every mystery story had to adhere to in order to not stretch the bounds of credulity. He had ruled that the criminal must be mentioned in the early part of the story, but must not be anyone whose thoughts the reader has been allowed to know. That supernatural elements must be ruled out as a matter of course. There must not be more than one secret room or passage. No hitherto undiscovered poisons may be used, nor any appliance which will need a long scientific explanation at the end. No Chinaman must figure in the story. No accident must ever help the detective, nor must he ever have an unaccountable intuition that proves to be right. The detective himself must not commit the crime. The detective is bound to declare any clue he discovers. The stupid friend of the detective, the Watson, must not conceal from the reader any thoughts that pass through his mind; his intelligence must be very slightly below that of the average reader. Twins, and doubles generally, must not appear unless we have been duly prepared for them.

These were, admittedly, written in 1929 and could benefit from some updating – e.g. instead of no Chinamen, no Russians. But they are still pretty relevant, not only to crime fiction, but to the real, actual

investigation of crime. They hauled me back to the
plausible when my inclination sometimes allowed
me to consider that aliens or Romanians may be
responsible.

'Aliens?'

'Did I say that out loud?'

She shook her head. She looked out at the traffic.
Then she asked if I'd remembered to take my medication. I had, because I'd recently been prescribed a pill
that helped me to remember to take my medication.

'When the baby's born, I'm going to help you get
off all that shit.'

She was so naïve. They would stop her. They wanted
me controlled. What with what I knew.

The cremation service for Jimbo was scheduled to
begin at three p.m. It was the last of the day. As we
drove through the gates, Alison pointed out a plaque
that said: *Cemetery of the Year*. The car park was not
packed. Fifteen seconds after we parked, Greg pulled
in behind us. He walked across behind us. The
Roselawn crematorium was housed in a red-brick
building with a large chimney. Outside the front doors
and a little to the right there was a small group of
men smoking and talking quietly to each other; they
looked uncomfortable in their suits and ties; two of
them had flecks of white paint in their hair. Just inside
there was a sign that said: *Internet access available*. It
was for relatives who couldn't attend and wished to
watch the service on-line.

The chairs were pinkish and so was the carpet. Pat was in the front row, being comforted by two women, who were probably her mother and sister. An elderly couple were not quite beside her, three chairs up. They looked nothing like her. Jimbo's parents. There were possibly a dozen other men and women, plus two children, whom I did not recognise. There was the Chief Constable, five rows back, flanked by three other officers, all there in their official capacity. He sat, back straight, shoulders back. Cap in hand. There was Smally, with his two skinhead sidekicks, in the same row as the Chief, but on the other side of the aisle. There was Greg, taking a seat in the back row so he could keep an eye on us. Two rows in front of him there were two soberly suited men who kept glancing back at him, and one woman, who, despite boasting a different hairstyle and smarter clothes, we immediately recognised as the woman who had pretended to be Michael Gordon's mother. DI Robinson was there, right at the back, leaning against a wall, repeatedly raising and lowering himself on the balls of his feet. To our right, once we had taken up our places to left of centre, and sitting rather awkwardly, were a dozen other spotted decorators in variations of funeral wear – black ties, knotted large, sports jackets with wide lapels, shoes that had been polished that morning, possibly for the first time since the last funeral. The doors opened again behind us, and Billy Randall came in, his remaining hair swept elegantly to one side, a black suit masking his portliness; his beefy minder

Charlie was with him, also in black, cheaper-looking but harder. Jimbo was already in place, on the dais, awaiting kind words and hymns before descending into the furnace to be burned up at nine hundred and eighty degrees centigrade. He would be reduced to his basic human elements through flame, heat and vaporisation. Not ash, but dried bone fragments that would then be pulverised into a fine sand-like texture that could easily be scattered.

The minister, the Revd Delargey, was elderly and emaciated. The bagginess of his jowls suggested that he had once been hugely overweight but had lost it in a hurry. His mouth turned down at the corners, his nose was long and pointy. He had bags under his eyes like abandoned tea bags. A hundred years ago he might have found gainful employment as a mute, paid to stand around with his sad, pathetic face, inspiring misery everywhere he looked. To give him a hand we could have done with another professional whose time has been and gone, a professional mourner, a woman who could shriek and wail and tear her clothes and claw her face to encourage others to weep, because this gathering was curiously emotionless. Half of us were there for the Jack or for other professional purposes, rather than to mourn the poor departed Jimbo. But even those who clearly knew and loved him also seemed short of a tear or two. Perhaps they were all cried out – certainly the senseless manner of his death, his relative youth, the fact that he was so soon to be a father, even the delay before his body was released by the police, each factor would or should have had them reaching for the tissues. But no, everyone was quiet, restrained, respectful, but certainly not overcome.

I remember my own father's funeral. The eulogies. How Mother would say under her breath, 'balls', 'bollocks', 'hypocrite' as each tribute was paid.

The Revd Delargey got the nod from a crematorium official, a linesman to his referee, and the proceedings got under way. He welcomed everyone. He talked about the difficult circumstances that brought us all together, but how we were not here to reflect on man's capacity for violence, but to celebrate the life of an individual, James Collins, a much-loved son and fiancé, and shortly to be a father.

'Jimbo,' he said, 'was a man of the people. He loved Pat, he loved his parents, and he loved his best mate Ronny, whose own life we will celebrate just a few days from now.'

I was wondering, seeing as how I was concentrating so hard on reading people, on weighing up the evidence, or deciding just how rash I was prepared to be at what was, after all, a funeral, if it would be impolite to open a Twix, as a kind of aide-memoire. It was in my pocket. I could be fairly subtle about it. I had also made a life-long study of the genesis of the Twix. It was invented in 1967. There have been more than thirty different variations across the world. In 2008 there was a limited edition Twix Cappuccino bar, which was only available in Poland. I have one. I bought it on eBay. When it arrived, the wrapping was split and there appeared to be a bite taken out of it. I wasn't sure if it was the vendor or the postman. I complained about both of them. To eBay and the post office. For a while my post was really late, but I never heard about the vendor. He wasn't even Polish. He was another Twix collector. From Nuneaton. Which I thought was a clue.

Alison said, 'Have you worked it out yet?'

I had to focus. We stood for a hymn. We sat. The Revd Delargey lectured us. He was some kind of a Presbyterian, and although he said it quite nicely, we were all apparently going to hell. Apart from Jimbo, obviously. He told us little bits about the deceased, things I hadn't known and which were all duly filed away in the trivia bank. They were going to have a baby girl and had already decided on Britney-Christina. Jimbo and Ronny played in the same darts team. Even though he grew up in a tough neighbourhood, Jimbo never got into any trouble with the police, which seemed to make him eligible for sainthood.

Then the reverend nodded down at Pat, and she came to the microphone with a crumpled sheet of paper in her hand and began to read from 'Desiderata'. Her voice was tremulous, her hands were shaking.

'Go placidly amid the noise and the haste, and remember what peace there may be in silence.'

I looked around the mourners, and I could see only two who were anywhere near crying. Alison, right beside me, and seeking my hand for comfort. And at the back, DI Robinson, still up on his heels, but glassy-eyed. All moved by tosh. It was a gross and manipulative poem. I had a musical version of it by Les Crane at home. I hated that as well. I had bought it to keep a run of serial numbers intact. Pat rattled on to the end.

'With all its sham, drudgery, and broken dreams, it is still a beautiful world. Be cheerful. Strive to be happy.'

A representative of the decorators came forward and paid his faltering, nervous tribute. He said that if Michelangelo was good enough to paint the ceiling of the Sistine Chapel, then Jimbo was good enough to do the walls and perhaps the guttering. He was famous for the speed and quality of his work. Jimbo, not Michelangelo, who was a notorious slacker. There were a few giggles. I glanced at the Chief Constable as he said it, but there was no reaction either way. The decorator had been reading from some notes he'd prepared, but then he shook his head and balled them up and said, 'That lad, he was just too young to go. When I looked down at his poor face, so peaceful, I could almost hear him saying, Billy, will you have a pint, 'cos that was the type of him.'

The other decorators nodded along, and when Billy stepped down, they patted him on the back as he moved along to his seat.

The minister stepped forward again. 'Now I think we have another eulogy. If Mr . . .' and he consulted his own notes for a moment, 'Mr Chandler would care to . . .'

For a moment there was no movement.

And then I stood up.

Alison hissed: 'What are you *doing*? This is a *funeral*.'

'No, this is a murder investigation.'

I stepped forward. It wasn't exactly Dead Man Walking, more Walking Near a Dead Man. I was aware of everyone gawping at me as I moved down the aisle, especially Pat, who was looking confused and examining her own order of service. I had called the minister from home, asking to be inserted, seeing as how I was the deceased's cousin, and he'd been most obliging, although he'd asked who was wailing in the background. Mother.

There was no reason for anyone to be upset. I was performing a public service. I was solving a crime.

I stood by Jimbo's coffin. I placed a hand on it. I studied it. I took a deep breath. I turned and walked to the lectern. I nodded around my audience of mourners and conspirators and murderers and I sneezed.

'Bless you,' said the minister.

I smiled.

It was the final nail in the coffin.

But not Jimbo's.

39

'Ladies and gentlemen,' I said, 'I come not to bury Jimbo Collins – or I mean, I do, I mean, not bury him, burn him up, I mean, not like a Viking, but you know what I mean, cremate him – but to expose who is responsible for his murder.'

There were gasps all around.

As you might expect.

At a funeral.

The Revd Delargey flapped towards me, distraught. 'This isn't . . . this isn't . . . ladies and gentle . . . I'm sorry, but . . .'

Jimbo's mother said, 'I don't understand.'

Pat shouted, 'What the hell are you playing at?'

Three of the decorators stood up. 'Sit down!' one shouted.

The Chief Constable sat immobile, body and face.

Greg leaned forward, resting his arms on the seat

in front of him. The fake mother of Michael Gordon glanced back at him for instruction, but he kept watching me.

Billy Randall wiped sweat off his brow; Charlie stood beside him, his head darting about as if an attack was imminent.

Alison covered her face with her hands.

The reverend put a spindly hand on my arm. If he hit me with all his strength, he wouldn't impact much, even with my brittle bones. In fact, I could probably have taken him. Elbowed him in the throat and dragged him down and kicked him.

But it was a funeral.

The decorators were definitely not happy.

'Get off the stage, you head-the-ball!'

They began to shuffle out of their seats and into the aisle, even though it clearly wasn't a stage, unless you considered all the world to be one.

'Let him talk.'

It was DI Robinson, from the back. He was ignored until he moved forward and said it again, louder, holding up his warrant card at the same time. I hadn't expected him to intervene. I had imagined that everyone would carry me shoulder high out of the doors into the car park.

Not everybody thinks the way I do.

For example, I was just noticing that the shoelaces in the Revd Delargey's black brogues did not match. One was thick and one was thin, although both were frayed.

But DI Robinson's voice was enough to return the crematorium to some semblance of calm. The decorators shuffled reluctantly back to their chairs. The minister wrung his hands and looked even more miserable.

DI Robinson said, 'This is still a murder investigation, and I'd like to hear the man speak. I appreciate these are unusual circumstances, but I think we'd all rather know who was responsible. This guy has a pretty good track record, and I'm thinking he must have a reason to stand up, here and now, in the middle of a service, upsetting everyone.'

'You would think that,' I said. 'You may not necessarily be correct.'

He glared at me. 'I better be.'

A frigid kind of calm had returned to the crematorium.

'Isn't it interesting,' I said, 'that a humble painter and decorator like Jimbo Collins should attract such an interesting cross-section of society to his funeral. Yes, of course, he was murdered, that was a tragedy, but even so – look who we have here. The Chief Constable, sir, representing the police, although I'm quite sure you don't go to the funeral of every murder victim. Several representatives of another Government agency – MI5, I believe. What possible interest could spooks and spies have in all this? And if poor Jimbo was so angelic, why would someone like Mr Biggs there feel the need to pay his respects? Even that other familiar face, Billy Randall. Here to check out that the cremation really does take place before he pays out on Jimbo's holiday insurance policy? Did he not have a miserable time on one of your cheapo breaks and make a big claim?'

'No,' said Billy Randall.

'Exactly,' I said. 'So why are you here?'

'Because someone is trying to frame me for these murders.' This had not become public knowledge, so there were immediate surprised whispers from the other mourners. 'I wanted to show everyone that I'm not running scared, that I'm completely innocent.'

'Hear hear,' said Charlie.

'Ah, Charlie. Your minder.'

'My security adviser.'

'With whom you paid a visit to Jimbo and Ronny just about the time they got murdered.'

'Yes. We had a legitimate reason.'

'Because they had made you the Cock-Headed Man.' There were more whispers and nods. Right enough, they were thinking, it's the Cock-Headed Man. 'But it was all quite amicable, you and your minder, who incidentally has convictions for all kinds of violence. You just went and had a little chat about the fact that they had made you a laughing stock all over the world.'

Billy Randall glanced at Charlie, who just gave a little shrug, before nodding around the mourners. 'I did nothing wrong. With all due respect to his family and loved ones here today, Jimbo was a little shit and Charlie could have wiped the grin from his face very easily. I chose not to.'

'But did you, during the course of your visit, notice their pet dog?'

'The stuffed dog?'

'That's the one.'

'Yes, I did.'

'Where was it?'

'In the living room where we were talking. Why? I don't understand the relevance of—'

'Because it's what this is all about. Jimbo and Ronny stole the stuffed dog from the home of the Chief Constable. Isn't that right, Chief?'

I don't know if anyone had ever addressed him simply as Chief before. He didn't look particularly happy with it, or maybe it was the fact that he was being questioned by a bookseller and part-time private detective in a crematorium full of mourners.

'The dog was stolen, I don't know who by.'

'But Jimbo and Ronny had recently completed work on your house?'

'They worked there. Whether it was completed or not is a matter of some dispute.'

'They stole your dog and you wanted it back, and there were no lengths you wouldn't go to to ensure its return, including murdering them. You have the expertise; you know how to cover your tracks. You killed them; stand up and admit it.'

'I did not and would not murder anyone. That is an outrageous slander, and when this is over I fully intend to make sure you—'

'Were you aware that the stuffed dog contained a recording device, placed in it by MI5?'

'That's ridiculous.'

'Placed in your Jack Russell by taxidermist William Gunn, at the request of MI5.'

'That's simply not . . . What would be the point? It only ever sat in my lounge.'

'Where you met with representatives of paramilitary organisations plotting to destabilise the country, foment civil war and ultimately seize power in order to proclaim a Protestant state, all of it captured by the bugged Jack Russell.'

'No.'

'Are you sure?'

'Absolutely.'

'Or do you do that kind of plotting at work?'

'I'm not even going to dignify that with a—'

'Which brings us to MI5, who bugged your dog, and your house, and threatened me and my staff. They've been running around like headless chickens looking for your dog because they've been caught out snooping. They claim it was a training exercise that went wrong, but frankly I'm not convinced. Greg, you're like every Little Englander who gets posted abroad; just because you have a gob full of marbles you seem to think that's enough to impress the natives. I think you got transferred to your nice new regional headquarters and blustered in thinking you were going to show the Paddies how it was done, except you screwed it up. Especially as according to the insurance report, it was your BMW that actually knocked down Patch, not the trainee you tried to blame.'

'That's simply not true.'

'Okay.'

'Can I ask where you're going with this? Because you're making a total prick of yourself.'

'Is it not rather enlightening to have everyone involved in one room? When's the last time you sat down with Girth Biggs, aka Smally Biggs, aka Samson Biggs, aka Willy Biggs, aka Aka for a chat?'

Greg merely shook his head, but Smally stood and gave a little bow, grinning.

'Surely, though,' I continued, 'Smally's an equally likely candidate for these murders. How old are you, Smally?'

'Forty-two, if it's any of your business.'

'And how many of those years have you spent inside for violent behaviour?'

'Sixteen.'

'And you control the drugs business in East Belfast?'

'I'm a community worker.'

'The same thing, is it not?'

Smally shrugged. 'What's your point?'

'My point is, Jimbo and Ronny were known drug-takers, they were fond of messing people about, and their bank accounts show they had very little money. With Jimbo having a baby due, they tried to scam you, and you had to teach not just them a lesson, but every punk in East Belfast who would even think about trying to rip you off. You slaughtered them to show everyone you were the boss, the kingpin, the Godfather, the Market Stall Don. It was you.'

'Sorry, mate, but you're way off the mark.'

'Uhuh, uhuh?'

'Jimbo is almost family. Pat there's my sister.'

'I knew that,' I said.

'And Jimbo was straight as they come, and we were all proud of him, and the reason I wanted that fucking dog was that word on the street knew it had something to do with the murders because all these suits were running around asking about it, but nobody knew what, so I tried to get my hands on it to help my sister the only way I knew how.'

'Exactly,' I said.

'So get off the pot or fucking shit in it.'

'Okay,' I said.

They were still outraged by my decision to stand up and confront them with my suspicions, but I had at least managed to suck them in. They wanted to know. Even the decorators were enthralled, like they were watching the Saturday afternoon matinée. I had always planned to throw accusations out willy-nilly to see what stuck or if any of the suspects cracked under public scrutiny, and the fact that none of them had was neither a condemnation of my approach nor the death knell for my ultimate objective, the unmasking of the killer. There is a joy in making people dance to my tune, even if they don't recognise that tune.

'Well,' I said, 'if you didn't do it, and you didn't do it, and you didn't do it, then who does that leave?'

I studied my audience. Several stared back defiantly. Others looked away. Even the decorators, innocent to a man, looked shifty under the intense spotlight of my two albino eyes. But finally my tractor beams settled where they were always going to settle. The show was over, the last dance performed, the bouncers moving in and shouting at everyone to clear out.

'Pat? It wasn't you, was it? Working class, you have paramilitary genes, and you're pregnantly hormonal; isn't that just the lethal combination? Ladies and gentlemen, I present to you nothing less than a crime of passion!' I pointed straight at her. *'J'accuse!'*

40

It took Pat a while to get all of the swearing out of her system. It took the decorators a while longer. They seemed to think it was a step too far, what with her being near enough a widow and definitely an expectant mother. Yet you cannot fail to expose a murderer just to spare her feelings, although you mightn't have thought that if you'd looked at Alison's face, and then her feet, moving down the aisle, prepared to lead me back to my seat or out of the building by the ear to save me from a lynching. She was stopped in her tracks by DI Robinson, beating her and the lynch mob to the front and shouting out, 'We've come this far, let him finish!'

He had authority, DI Robinson.

It was a good thing.

Although they were not kindly disposed to me, it did not alter the nature of the truth or my need to reveal it. Sometimes the truth is unpalatable. I do not sugar almonds.

Having quelled the crowd, Robinson glanced back at me. 'This had better be better than good, it better be better than good.'

I was confident.

'I believe . . .'

'You *believe*?'

'I believe I can *prove* that Pat murdered Jimbo.' I raised my voice again and addressed my audience. 'She killed him in a fit of temper brought on by his and Ronny's failure to be paid for the work on the Chief Constable's house and their subsequent theft of the Jack Russell.'

Pat was standing, her eyeliner all run, both hands on her pregnant stomach. 'Will . . . someone . . . get this . . . monster . . . out of here?!'

'Pat, I'm sorry, you told me that you wanted to remember Jimbo the way he was, so you had a closed coffin. Yet our decorator chum here has just told us that he looked down at Jimbo's face. Can you explain that?'

'Is that it?'

'It's part of it.'

'Jesus Christ!' she exploded. 'I did have the coffin closed because I didn't want to look at him. But I didn't have it nailed shut. Anyone who wanted to look could take a look and some of them did! Is that really fucking it?'

'No – no. It's only about forty per cent of it.'

Robinson, still with his back to me, glanced around. 'Are you kidding?'

'No, look, bear with me, this works, it fits, I've investigated dozens of crimes, I've read thousands of novels. I'm convinced. It all comes back to the dog.'

'This bloody dog.'

'Bear with me. Please. Everyone. Apart from the murderer, the dead dog is the only witness to these killings. It's also important as a surveillance plant from MI5. Right from the off they knew Jimbo and Ronny had it and were very quick to try and get it back, but for whatever reason – badness or money – they wouldn't hand it over; then when they were murdered, MI5 came to Pat, wanting to know where it was, even burgling her house trying to get it. She claims burglars stole it; maybe she confided in her brother there, Smally, and maybe he even sent the burglars to get it.'

'That's a fucking lie!' Smally yelled. 'You're a dead man!'

'You go near him, I'll kill *you*, you bastard!'

That was Alison.

'Please,' said the Revd Delargey, 'this is still a funeral. Could we not leave this until after the cremation?'

The decorators began to applaud.

'No,' I said. 'Absolutely not. This is my entire point. Pat claimed that the Jack Russell was stolen. Yet she was at my girlfriend's house this morning. That's her over there. Isn't she pretty? We're having a baby too. But anyway, Pat was over with us this morning, and she got upset and she gave me a hug, and I sneezed in her face, and the reason I sneezed in her face is that I'm allergic to dogs, even the lingering traces of dogs, even dogs in the same house. She had essence of Patch on her, his hairs, and they set me off.'

'Is *that* it?' DI Robinson asked.

'That's just mental!' Pat was shaking her head in disbelief. 'I petted the neighbour's dog on the way out this morning! Christ, if you're standing there because—'

'Because I also sneezed when I stood by Jimbo's coffin.'

'What are you talking about?' Pat demanded.

'What *are* you talking about?' DI Robinson seconded.

'I'm talking about Patch and the fact that Pat knew everyone was looking for him and she had to know why, so she opened him up and found electronics inside him.' She shook her head. I persevered. 'You might not have known exactly what it was, but I think you had a pretty good guess that it was something to do with surveillance, and you knew that if that's what it was, then it might have recorded you killing your boyfriend and then Ronny when he stumbled in on you. You're not stupid, you've seen enough movies, enough cop shows on the telly to know that if they can pinpoint a mobile phone or a heat source via helicopter or satellite, then there's a fair chance they could track down whatever you found in Patch, so you couldn't just get rid of it in the trash or throw it in a lake or bury it in the back garden; you had to make sure it was totally destroyed and Patch along with it. What's better than an industrial furnace capable of generating temperatures of nine hundred and eighty degrees centigrade?' I nodded at her, and then around my now mesmerised audience, before turning to look at Jimbo's coffin. 'What about putting Patch in the coffin along with your loved one, disintegrating the father of your child and the evidence that you killed him with one push of a button? Is that not what happened? Is it not? Eh? Eh?'

The 'Eh? Eh?' might have seemed over the top, but you must understand, I was trying to goad the suspect into an outburst that might condemn her further. I wasn't myself excited. I was calm. I have to be. Any excitement might unduly affect my blood pressure, which constantly hovers on the verge of stroke. My manner remains serene at all times. Some people mistake it for vacancy. They have learned, often to their cost, that I am anything but vacant.

Under these circumstances, however, it was rather difficult to remain completely serene. It was not only my accusation that seemed to upset everyone further; it was my demand that the coffin be immediately opened. It was, after all, the only way to prove or disprove my theory. They must have been able to see the logic in this, but humans are not often logical creatures; they are ruled by their hearts and their emotions, and they seemed to find it reprehensible that I wished to delay the final journey of their loved one even further. It is exactly these types of people who get hot under the collar when a train is delayed or traffic is in a jam, when really they need to relax and realise that in the grand scheme of things it doesn't matter if a bus, or a train, or a coffin, does not adhere to some ultimately meaningless timetable.

'What's the difference?' I demanded of DI Robinson as he pulled me off to one side of the crematorium. 'He's dead.'

'I know he's dead, you halfwit. And so will you be if you don't stop your yammering.'

'I'm only trying to—'

'I know what you're trying to do.'

'I'm not wrong.'

He took a deep breath and glanced back at Jimbo. Smally Biggs, several other relatives and most of the decorators had taken up defensive positions around the coffin. The Revd Delargey was saying a prayer over it. The crematorium manager, name of McManus, had arrived and was now bearing the brunt of a verbal assault from Pat. He did a lot of nodding, and then came over to us. He was a rotund man with an inappropriate number of laughter lines. He said, 'The cremation of a human body is a highly emotional occasion for those taking part. Our job here is to create and maintain an atmosphere of reverence and respect throughout the proceedings – and you, sir . . .' he nodded at me, 'have made a mockery of this day. You should be ashamed of yourself. And you . . .' he glared at DI Robinson, 'are scarcely any better.'

DI Robinson said, 'That may be, but this remains a murder investigation, and if there is even a remote possibility that evidence may have been—'

McManus cut in with, 'The Code of Cremation Practice forbids the opening of the coffin once it has arrived at the crematorium.'

'The law of the land is more important than—'

'Sir, this crematorium operates on a strict schedule. We are already long past the time when the last cremation of the day should have taken place. Unless you can produce a court order or a search warrant or something that gives you the authority to open that coffin, then I am going to give permission for the service to proceed.'

'I will get the paperwork, and if you even think about trying to start . . .'

'That won't be necessary.' I turned at the deep but restrained voice at my shoulder. It was the Chief Constable. 'Detective Inspector Robinson, if I could have a word?'

Robinson nodded immediately and moved off with the Chief Constable to the other side of the crematorium. McManus, not quite knowing what to say to me, but not wishing to endure another tongue-lashing from Pat either, moved away to stand by himself, hands clasped behind his back. Alison, seeing that I was now alone, hurried over.

'What's going on now? Honestly, I can't keep up.'

Robinson and the Chief were having an animated exchange, but a quiet one.

'I don't know,' I said. 'Robinson was in my corner, but the Chief is the Chief. So . . .'

'Are you absolutely sure about this? Because if they open it and there's nothing . . .'

My brow furrowed involuntarily. Surely she knew that I was always right?

Robinson came back towards us, but didn't stop. He stood at the front of the crematorium and called for silence and said that the Police Service of Northern Ireland wished to apologise unreservedly for the delay in proceedings, and that the service could now progress.

I just said, 'What?'

Mourners began to retake their seats. Pat glared across at me. The Revd Delargey, that professional misery, shuffled forward. The Chief moved to the back of the crematorium and stood by the door.

I said, louder, 'What are you doing?' DI Robinson raised his hands in a helpless gesture. 'You cannot let this happen. There is evidence in that coffin that this woman murdered two men. You cannot just let it all be burned up!'

'It's out of my hands,' said Robinson.

'Why don't you just get the fuck out of here?' Smally shouted.

'Gentlemen, please!' cried the Revd Delargey.

'Yeah, go on, piss off!' shouted one of the decorators.

'Come on,' said Alison, taking me by the arm.

'This is just madness! She killed them, and you're letting her get away with it!'

'Get out! Get out!' Smally's young henchman, the one who'd failed to properly confront Mother, joined in the yelling.

'Please, we need to begin!' shouted the Revd Delargey.

Alison began to push and prod me up the aisle. She is stronger than she looks.

'She's a murderer!' I shouted.

Pat remained in her chair, eyes front, focused on the coffin.

Halfway up, I pointed at the Chief. 'It's a conspiracy! It's a cover-up! They were bugging you, you halfwit; why would you let this happen if there was even a remote possibility of its being true?'

The Chief just shook his head.

Billy Randall averted his eyes.

Charlie wiped tears from his, but not sad ones, laughter.

As Alison propelled me towards the doors, insults and boos filled the air. I saw Greg.

'This just suits you fine, doesn't it?' I yelled at him. 'All the evidence going up in smoke!'

He winked.

'You're all in it together!'

I pushed back against Alison just once, just long enough to survey the entire congregation. 'Why is nobody listening to me? Have you all lost your minds?

The crematorium manager thrust the doors open

ahead of us. 'No, sir,' he said, 'but you appear to have lost yours.'

Alison pushed me out into a covered walkway and then along the path and into the car park, where she gave me a final little shove to release me.

'Fuck!' I shouted.

I immediately turned back towards the crematorium.

Alison put her hand out, palm up. 'Stop! There's no point.'

'You don't understand! They're going to—'

'I know what they're going to. And there's nothing you can do.'

'But I solved it! I worked out who the murderer was!'

'Settle, petal,' she said. 'You did everything you could.'

'She's going to get away with it! They're all wearing blinkers!'

'Yes they are. And you're right. I know you are. I'm absolutely mostly certain that you're right.'

'You don't believe me either!'

'I believe *in* you.'

'That's not the same.'

My attention then was averted by the music emanating from the crematorium. 'Angels' by Robbie Williams.

'They've started,' Alison said. Her hand sought mine. I withheld that pleasure. Failing to give one hundred per cent support was tantamount to betrayal.

'The fools,' I said. 'The bloody fools.'

A puff of white smoke rose lazily from the crematorium chimney. I cursed again.

'Come on,' said Alison. 'You solved it, that's the important thing.'

'No,' I said. 'No it's not.'

It was about justice.

And acclaim.

There was a low rumble from the crematorium, like someone had suddenly whacked a bass drum, then a much sharper one. Three of the outer windows cracked. The smoke emerging from the chimney turned black, and then flames began to lick out of the top of it. Within seconds the crematorium doors were flung open and the mourners began to stumble out, coughing and spluttering through clouds of smoke.

'Call the fire brigade!' someone yelled.

'There's a fire at the crematorium!' someone shouted into a mobile phone. And a moment later added: 'He fucking hung up on me!'

'Is it a bomb?' someone shouted.

'It just went off! Someone could have been killed!'

They all came rushing out into the gathering darkness, even the crematorium manager, looking lost and mumbling, 'What have you done, what have you done?'

Robinson and the Chief and his colleagues or minders went back and forth into the smoke, making sure everyone was out. The beautifully manicured lawn in front was dotted with mourners, some sitting on their coats, others standing stunned, while others still spilled over into the car park and sat on bonnets watching while the flames licked up into the roof of the crematorium and more windows cracked and smashed. In the distance a fire engine sounded. Then someone pointed, and there in the double doors stood Pat. She looked me straight in the eye. Alison would say later, no she did not, you imagined that, but I know it to be true. She looked at me, then stepped back into what was now becoming an inferno, and closed the doors after her. Overwrought with guilt, she meant to kill herself and her unborn baby.

But it was not to be.

Robinson and the Chief shouldered the doors open between them and dived back into the smoke. It seemed like for ever before they reappeared, dragging her out screaming and crying, saving two lives and a killer in one fell swoop.

I would have helped them.

But smoke gets in my eyes.

41

Back in 1947, Irving Shulman sold four million copies of *The Amboy Dukes*, but they are now rarer than hen's teeth and valuable enough in the right edition. This one was worth sixty pounds, but that didn't stop me firing his tale of juvenile delinquency on New York's East Side at the wall opposite my counter in No Alibis, breaking the book's spine and causing its yellowed, pulpy pages to float to the floor. *The Dukes* has aged quite badly, its drug references are incredibly tame by today's standards, but nevertheless, it is a classic of its type, pre-dating Evan Hunter's much better-known *The Blackboard Jungle* by seven years.

But I was *mad*.

I had gone into *The Case of the Cock-Headed Man* to prove that Billy Randall wasn't responsible for the deaths of Jimbo and Ronnycrabs, and now, though I knew who was responsible, it could never be proved.

The evidence had been destroyed in the explosion that had rocked Roselawn Crematorium. Jimbo's ashes were still up there, mixed in with brick and powdered glass and blackened wood. The papers said it had been caused by a malfunctioning furnace, but I knew better. I always know better. It was too convenient. Something had been planted in the coffin to absolutely make sure the evidence was destroyed if by chance the mighty temperatures of the furnace failed to break it down, or perhaps even set to go off if someone tried to open the box to look for said evidence. I would obviously not have opened it myself – I am allergic to dead people, and pine, and embalming fluid, and suits – but it could easily have been Alison, acting on my behalf, and she might now be dead, taking my baby with her. That, however, remained in the realms of *what if*, and was not something I dwelt a great deal upon. I was mad that Pat had gotten away with it, mad that everyone had conspired for their own reasons to get rid of the evidence, that I hadn't been able to remove the shadow of suspicion from Billy Randall.

I could not focus, could not settle.

I took it out on Mother. She said, 'Why don't you get a grip, you stupid little prick?'

As a result of this, and for the first time, I refused to give her a bath. She had to pull herself up out of her wheelchair and tumble into the tub, and only then run the water. She yelled, 'Stop looking at my tits and bring me the soap.'

I did neither.

Alison did her best with me, but it was a losing battle. If anything, I was getting worse. I had risked a lynching, then had my triumph ripped away from me by political and criminal shenanigans. She attempted to make love to me, but I put her in her place. It was not the time. It might never be the time again. It was as if aliens had waved at me, and me alone, and then gone home, leaving me convinced and the rest of the world either uninterested or disbelieving. She tried to tempt me with Twix and Starbucks, but the only appetite I had was for justice.

Jeff *especially* felt the wrath of my tongue. He had once again returned to my employ, but now armed with an official police caution. He seemed to think this put him on a par with some of the poor unfortunate big-mouths he championed through Amnesty International. I soon put him right on that. I used many swear words. He said very little in response. A couple of times I caught Alison and Jeff in close conversation, which they would then quickly drop. I knew they were talking about me, or plotting. The whole world was constantly plotting against me, including through fluoridation, but this was a little too close to home.

I raged on into February. It is one of the most forlorn months, together with June and September and April and March and October and November and December and January and May and August and July. Sales failed to pick up. I sacked Mother from the shop. She was verbally abusing the customers, accusing them of lingering, and stealing, and casting lustful glances at her. I knew of many other small bookstores across the country that had given up because of this miserable financial climate, and they didn't even have a mother to drive customers away. Cases for me to solve continued to trickle through the door, and I took several of them on, but I was barely interested. I either solved them quickly or passed them on to Alison. She was good, and happy in the solving of them.

She said one day, towards the end of the month, 'I'm becoming a big fat lump.'

'Yes, you are,' I said.

She burst into tears. She said, 'You are mean and spiteful.' She was wrong. I just do not sugar my almonds. 'I'm eating for two, you know,' she said.

I raised an eyebrow but said nothing.

She said, 'You know, you look like Mr Spock when you raise your eyebrow like that. In fact, you may actually be Mr Spock. That's exactly what you're like. Cold and logical and heartless.' I would not rise to the bait. She added, 'You know, some pregnant women eat coal.'

I would probably have snapped something at her if the door had not opened and a customer entered. I glared at her instead, and she glared back. If my dysfunctional tear ducts had not let me down again we could have been there for ever. I sighed and turned from her. The customer was already perusing the books opposite.

I said, 'Is there anything I can help you with?'

He turned.

It was the Chief Constable.

Plenty of people who come into No Alibis think they're pretty powerful – writers, sales folk, customers who seem to believe that membership of my Christmas Club automatically gives them rights; even the likes of Billy Randall, or Greg, the possibly rogue MI5 agent – but none of them have ever made me particularly nervous. Rather they inspired me to do great things. This Chief Constable was different; even standing by himself, in my little shop, he had an aura, a presence that made you feel guilty just by being in his orbit. I had a sudden tremor that he had come for my nail for the scratching of cars with personalised number plates, or had CCTV of me standing in bushes, watching. Alison also looked a bit weak at the knees, but it was nothing to do with her weight.

He was in plain clothes. At least, you tend to think of a policeman not in uniform as being in plain clothes, but I suppose he was just in clothes. They were not remarkable clothes, which made them normal rather than plain. They weren't dull. They were ordinary. Average. The meaning of average has changed over the years. No, not the meaning, the perceived meaning. The meaning of average has stayed the same, but people think it means less than it actually means. When you describe a kid's school report as average, you tend to think of it being not good enough. The Chief Constable was wearing an average, ordinary, plain black suit, with a not too garish red tie. He looked buff and his skin was smooth and his greying hair was cut short.

He said, 'Well I would like to buy a book, but mostly I'd like to have a little chat.'

'What sort of a book?' I asked.

'What would you recommend?'

'Something with a complicated plot and an un-satisfactory ending.'

He smiled. His teeth were photogenic, and hence not his own.

'Would you like a cup of tea?' Alison asked.

'That would be nice.'

Alison nodded at Jeff. 'Go make,' she said.

Jeff kept his eyes down and scuttled into the kitchen. The Chief Constable watched him go. 'Well,' he said, turning his attention back to me, 'you have been a busy little beaver, haven't you?'

I was still nervous, but also seething. This man, this top cop with the false smile, had perverted the course of justice and robbed me of my moment of triumph.

I said, 'You helped to destroy vital evidence. Because of you she's still—'

'If I could stop you there,' he said.

'You can't handle the truth,' I said.

It didn't sound that fearsome. Others have said it better. In fact, my voice sounded a little querulous.

I might have expected Alison to snort, but she remained focused. She moved to my side.

'Well,' he said, 'that's why I'm here. Detective Inspector Robinson has explained to me how helpful you have been in the past. He has asked me to clarify some details of this matter. He also said that if I didn't, not only would he leak them to the press, but also you would not leave us alone. You would annoy us until this case of yours was satisfactorily resolved.'

'That's my boy,' said Alison. 'Annoying till the end of time.'

But she placed a supportive hand on my behind. He couldn't see that. I liked it. I wished he could have seen it. It was proof that we were intimate.

'You're being blackmailed by your own officer?'

'I wouldn't say blackmailed.'

'I would.'

'My job,' he said, 'is a highly politicised one, I have to keep a lot of people happy, listen to many and varied opinions, pat a lot of heads. I also have to solve crimes, and ignore all of those people I'm supposed to keep happy. I have to be my own man, or I'm everyone's man. Do you understand?'

'No,' said Alison.

'There are a lot of people who would like to bring me down. I have to be constantly on my guard. I inherited a lot of problems, historical ones, and new ones, people fighting their own corners, defending their own interests. It's difficult to know who to trust and sometimes you end up trusting no one. Forgive me if I sound a little paranoid.'

'You're in good company,' said Alison. I would have said something, but she squeezed my cheek, which was therapeutic.

'I'm going to explain to you what really happened at the funeral, and why, on the understanding that it will go no further. Do I have your word?'

Word is a curious concept and not one that I have ever adhered to. However, I nodded. Alison too.

'My wife believes I'm quite obsessive-compulsive. I think I'm just aware of how the world works. I have always been obsessive about my own security and my own privacy. Particularly at home. I don't want anyone else listening to my private conversations. I don't want anyone else watching me make love to my wife. I don't want anyone standing in the bushes peering into my house.'

He didn't particularly look at me with this last comment. I could have argued with him. I think privacy is overrated. If you don't want someone to observe you, close the curtains, or build a bigger wall I can't slither over in the rain in the middle of the night.

'So when we moved in, I made a point of sweeping the house and grounds regularly for evidence of surveillance. I never found anything until—'

'The Jack Russell.'

He nodded. 'It was quite clever of them.'

'MI5.'

'Of course, although I didn't know that then. It could have been any one of our political parties, the Irish Government, gangsters looking for something to hold over me, big business, small business, anyone. I found it by a process of elimination, really – whatever was in the device, it was interfering with our television, flipping the channels. Once I had it, I brought some experts of my own in. It was quite a rudimentary device, really, used for recording only, not broadcasting. It meant that eventually someone was going to have to come for it. I had no interest in the messenger, as such, but in who he was reporting to. So, with the aid of my team, I merely replaced their own device with one of my own, almost identical, but much, much superior, one capable of broadcasting pictures and sound.'

'So Jimbo and Ronny were bribed by MI5 to retrieve it, but before they could hand it over they were murdered by Pat, and you have it recorded, so you do have the evidence, it's not gone . . .'

'Well, yes, up to a point.' He delved into his pocket and produced a memory stick. He held it up. 'Can you play this?'

I took it and plugged it into the PC. I sat in front of the screen, Alison at my shoulder. The Chief Constable did not attempt to join us, instead leaning on the counter. As I called the file up, he said: 'This is obviously an edited version.'

'Thought it might be.'

'I mean, there were hours and hours of me and my

wife sitting watching television, amongst other things. This segment shows purely what happened around the time of the murders.'

The images, when they appeared, were rather shocking in their clarity. We tend to think of surveillance pictures as being gritty and remote, but these were HD quality. The Jack Russell had been positioned a little to the right of the TV: it showed Jimbo and Ronny, sitting on their sofa, watching the screen and sharing a spliff. They were talking, about nothing much, but it was still a shock to see and hear them. Just the very fact of their being alive, and not knowing that death was approaching. They had solidly working-class Belfast accents and the sarcasm that goes hand in hand with living here. Then there was a doorbell and Jimbo got up. Voices could be heard in the background, but they were blurred by the television commentary. Ronny got up. Now we were looking at the empty sofa and listening to *Masterchef*. The voices continued, but louder. Then there were shouts, and screams, horrific-sounding and frustratingly off camera, as if the drama was taking place in the wings of a theatre.

And then silence.

I glanced back at the CC. He nodded at the screen again.

A new figure entered the frame.

He sat on the sofa, his white short-sleeved shirt splattered with blood. He leaned forward to a small coffee table and lifted the half-smoked spliff out of an ashtray. He took a drag. He shook his head and said, 'Fuck.'

It wasn't anyone I thought it would have been, and it certainly wasn't Pat.

'He's one of Smally Biggs' little helpers,' said Alison.

'His son,' said the Chief Constable.

42

Eventually, eventually, a rather sheepish Jeff returned with the tea. Later he admitted he'd gone outside for a cigarette before even putting the kettle on. The Chief Constable catching him in his house had clearly given him a bigger fright than he'd let on. Alison said, 'Will I be mother?' and then contorted her face as if she'd had a stroke as she poured. It was quite funny. There was even a plate of Jaffa Cakes. The image of Smally Biggs' son was frozen on my computer screen.

Alison said, 'He was a cheeky little shit. And he tried to feel me up.'

'Name of Darren. No record, but been raised in his father's image. We were aware of him doing some dealing, but this was a bit of a surprise. We enhanced the sound; they were arguing over an unpaid drugs bill. Jimbo and Ronny were trying to fob him off, and he lost his temper.'

'God,' said Alison, 'he looks so calm.'

'So Pat didn't . . . ?'

'We have footage of her coming in and discovering the bodies. Frankly, no one should see that. It would break your heart.'

I licked chocolate off my fingers and said, 'I don't understand. If you have this, why is Darren Biggs still out and about?'

'He's not. We picked him up this morning. We can't use any of this footage, obviously, but I'm pretty confident we'll be able to get a DNA match. Because he was under our radar he was never checked out, but from what little I know of him, even if we don't get the match he'll crack pretty soon.'

'But why didn't you pick him up immediately? Why put me, us, through this charade?'

'Because we had the Jack in place; we just thought we'd shake the tree and see how many apples fell. We could sit back and wait, pick out the rotten ones. There was no immediate panic.'

'You owe someone an apology,' said Alison.

I nodded along, at least until I realised she was talking to me. 'Who?'

Her eyes widened. 'Who do you bloody think? Standing up at her man's funeral and accusing her of murder? Wanting to rip the coffin open?'

'I wasn't that far out. It was her nephew, wasn't it? She was covering for him, she had to be.'

'We don't know that,' said the CC.

'You bloody tell her you got it wrong.'

'Right. I'm going to do that.'

'You'll do it. I'm telling you.'

'You're not the boss of me.'

The Chief was looking from me to her. 'Well,' he said. He put his hand out and clicked his fingers in the direction of the memory stick.

'Not so fast,' I said. 'It still doesn't explain what happened to the Jack. She said it was stolen out of her house.'

'It wasn't.'

'But her house was burgled?'

'Yes, by Darren, who'd heard rumours about the Jack through his dad, who knew MI5 were after it. He went looking for it, but didn't find it. Pat had hidden it well.'

'Why?' Alison asked.

'Because she heard the same rumours; she thought the Jack might have been stuffed full of drugs and wanted Jimbo to be remembered as a nice boy not as a dealer. So she decided to have it cremated with him. She asked the undertaker. It was an unusual request, being cremated with your favourite dog, but perfectly legal.'

'And you were quite happy to have your device cremated with Patch and Jimbo, because you already had your pictures. Except,' and I pointed an accusing finger at him, 'you made a mistake; you didn't realise your bug would explode in the heat and help cremate the crematorium. Isn't that right?'

'Well, no, actually. It wasn't our bug that caused the fire.'

'You would say that. Well I'm pretty sure it wasn't a malfunctioning furnace, like they said.'

'You're right. It was something more arbitrary than that. Nothing to do with this case at all, in fact.'

He nodded at me.

It was a challenge.

Although really, when I thought about it, none at all.

I should have thought about it much, much earlier.

Because I have one myself.

'He had a pacemaker.'

'He had a pacemaker. Since he was a teenager. Pat never knew.'

'I don't understand,' said Alison. 'How would that . . . ?'

'They're radioactive, they have a lithium battery, they explode under intense heat.' My brow furrowed then. 'But they would have found it at the autopsy and removed it.' The Chief raised an eyebrow. 'They did find it, but you had them leave it in. You wanted it to explode, you wanted to cause mayhem, you were . . .'

'Shaking the tree.'

Alison was aghast. 'You . . . at a funeral . . . you . . . caused that . . . You're supposed to be our Chief Constable, you're supposed to be . . .'

'. . . a lot of things. Listen to me. I'm sure you're perfectly decent people, in your little bookshop, and

your nice lives. Yes, you dabble in your private investigations, so maybe you've seen a few things, but you
don't understand what's really going on, you don't
see the bigger picture. People think the Troubles are
all over, but they're not, they're just different Troubles,
some of it historic, some of it imported, most of it we
just won't know about till it comes up and bites us
on the arse. But it's my job to keep watch, and it
doesn't help when people are constantly trying to
undermine me. So I have to flush them out, because
keeping an eye on the likes of MI5 there's a genuine
danger that the forces of evil will slip through. I,
we, cannot afford that, so sometimes I have to do
something that shows them who's boss. Do you understand me?'

I nodded. It was the first time I'd ever heard someone
say forces of evil outside of a comic book.

Alison said, 'You blew up a funeral.'

'For the greater good.'

Alison shook her head at him. And then at me.

'I should send the both of you round to apologise.
This isn't a bloody game.'

She was right, it wasn't.

Games have more rules.

The Chief Constable was leaving. He had his memory
stick. I suppose I should have been grateful that he had
come round to explain that Pat, who was perfectly nice,
but common, wasn't guilty, and that my client, Billy
Randall, was no longer a person of interest, and would

never have been if the CC had bothered to share downwards some of his underhand tactics. Darren Biggs would surely shortly be charged with the murder of Jimbo and Ronny. The role of MI5 in it all might never be publicly revealed, apart obviously from on the plethora of conspiracy theory websites Jeff would direct me to. I would never be sure if Greg really was just an agent trying to help out his dunderheaded pupils, or if he was from higher up, working to an agenda. I don't suppose it matters too much. The games would continue. Just like in the Olympics, a few deaths weren't going to derail them.

The CC paused with the door half open. He looked back. I think he was expecting our thanks.

Instead I said, 'You never got your book.'

'It's okay. I was only joking.'

'Joking?'

'I mean, it was just an *in*. I don't read fiction. God knows there's enough fact out there for me to be worrying about.'

'Well sometimes it's hard to tell the difference. Maybe you should give it a try.'

He laughed.

He actually laughed.

I felt sorry for him. He would never know the pleasures of Ellroy or Parker or Leonard, of Hammett or Chandler or Bentley or Spillane or Caine or Allingham or Goodis or Ambler or Greene or Sapper or Rohmer or Wallace or Conrad or Buchan or Childers or Thompson or Janson or Sayers or Doyle or Poe or Highsmith or Hall or Bagley or Simons or Tey. On the plus side, he would miss out on Brendan Coyle.

Nevertheless, as he moved through the doorway I said, 'Philistine.'

He glanced back, unsure of what he'd actually heard. He hesitated for just a moment and gave a short nod, before stepping out on to the footpath. As he passed across the front window, Alison gave him the international sign for wanking.

He kept walking. He may not have seen it. He definitely didn't see Jeff's Black Power salute.

Alison said, 'Good riddance to bad rubbish.'

'He's not that bad,' I said.

'I'm glad you think so. Now get on the phone to Interflora and send Pat some flowers.'

I smiled.

She did not.

'No way,' I said.

'Yes way. Or else you take them round yourself. I'm serious, you owe her. Just do it. Make me even prouder of you.'

She had a way of saying things. I sighed. She took that as affirmative.

'Good. I'm going to Starbucks. Where are you on the menu?'

I told her *precisely*. She said she'd be back in ten minutes, and she expected the flowers to have been ordered by then.

When she'd gone, Jeff said he was going to get a

burger from Springsteens next door and did I want anything. I shook my head. I had Vitolink. Besides, I was too busy watching Alison walk away. She was beautiful and she was carrying my baby, or at least someone's. But she was mine. And always would be.

Jeff went out, leaving me alone in No Alibis.

I love it here. It's where I feel most at home, with my books and their patterns. I will fight tooth and nail to keep it open. Books are important. Books are not beans. We stand against the tide, and pray.

I was happy, after a fashion. Although for the first time I had not correctly unmasked the killer, I had no doubt that I would have eventually. I had allowed myself to get hung up on one particular piece of evidence and its destruction, instead of taking it in my stride and approaching the case from a different angle. It was an important lesson to learn, and it would serve me well on future investigations, if I lived long enough.

I mixed up the Vitolink, opened a Twix, and sat behind my precious counter. When I felt suitably refreshed, I called Interflora and ordered a cheap bunch of flowers. I paid by credit card and gave them the address and the woman asked me if I had anything to say, and I said, 'Thank you?'

'I mean, on the card. With the flowers.'

'Oh, right. Ahm. Okay. Write: SORRY YOUR BOYFRIEND'S DEAD.'

I could already see Alison coming back, coffees in

hand. She wasn't really fat. I loved her. She was smiling to herself.

'Is that it?'

It is important to retain one's sense of humour at times of stress and sadness.

'No. Add: LOOKS LIKE YOU GOT AWAY WITH IT.'

The woman sighed. 'Is *that* it?'

'No, could you add one of those winky faces?'

So she did.

‿ͺ